KING PENGUIN

THE BOARDING-HOUSE

William Trevor was born in Mitchelstown, County Cork, in 1928, and spent his childhood in provincial Ireland. He attended a number of Irish schools and later Trinity College, Dublin. He is a member of the Irish Academy of Letters.

Among his books are *The Old Boys* (1964; Hawthornden Prize), *The Love Department* (1966), *The Day We Got Drunk on Cake* (1967), *Mrs Eckdorf in O'Neill's Hotel* (1969), *Miss Gomez and the Brethren* (1971), *The Ballroom of Romance* (1972), *Elizabeth Alone* (1973), *Angels at the Ritz* (1975; The Royal Society of Literature Award), *The Children of Dynmouth* (1976; Whitbread Award), *Lovers of their Time* (1978), *The Distant Past* (1979), *Other People's Worlds* (1980) and *Beyond the Pale and Other Stories* (1981). In 1976 Mr Trevor received the Allied Irish Banks' Prize and in 1977 was awarded the C.B.E. in recognition of his valuable services to literature. He has also written many plays for television, and for radio and the stage.

William Trevor lives in Devon, is married and has two sons.

WILLIAM TREVOR

The Boarding-House

A KING PENGUIN

Published by Penguin Books

Penguin Books Ltd, Harmondsworth, Middlesex, England
Penguin Books, 625 Madison Avenue, New York, New York 10022, U.S.A.
Penguin Books Australia Ltd, Ringwood, Victoria, Australia
Penguin Books Canada Ltd, 2801 John Street, Markham, Ontario, Canada L3R 1B4
Penguin Books (N.Z.) Ltd, 182–190 Wairau Road, Auckland 10, New Zealand

First published by The Bodley Head 1965
Published in Penguin Books 1968
Reprinted as a King Penguin 1983

Made and printed in Great Britain by
Hazell Watson & Viney Ltd, Aylesbury, Bucks
Set in Linotype Pilgrim

I

'I am dying,' said William Wagner Bird on the night of August 13th, turning his face towards the wall for privacy, sighing at the little bunches of forget-me-not on the wallpaper. He felt his body a burden in the bed, a thing he did not know. His feet seemed far away, and it came to him abruptly that he was aware of his feet in an intellectual way only. It passed through Mr Bird's mind then that physical communication with his nether half was forever gone.

'I am going out feet first,' said Mr Bird, a wit to the end. 'My legs have entered their eternal rest. Nurse Clock, I would have you record all this and pass it on to a daily newspaper. Nurse Clock, have you pen and paper?'

The nurse, seated some distance away, reading a magazine, read the message on the printed page: *Bingo and whist drives below stairs at Balmoral.* 'I am writing out your very word,' she said.

'Then listen to this,' said William Wagner Bird, and did not ever finish the sentence.

'Oh, God in heaven,' murmured Nurse Clock, feeling the presence of death and feeling thus that the invocation was proper. *Only at Balmoral do they share a room,* she read; and rose with that thought in her mind and covered the face of a man she had known for many a year and had disliked both in sickness and health.

The gloom gathered in the room as Nurse Clock set about her tasks and saw to it that certain decencies were observed. She did not glance again at the stretched figure on the bed, but worked briskly in her matter-of-fact way, packing away her personal belongings in her nurse's bag and tidying those of her late patient. The time was nine o'clock. 'I have been on the go,' said Nurse Clock aloud.

So it was that William Wagner Bird, a man of sixty-seven who had never married, died in the boarding-house on August 13th. Later his passing was recorded in a formal way only, by relevant authorities; for like others in the boarding-house, Mr Bird had had neither family nor personal ties. His parents had died five years back, in the same month, and had between them left him debts amounting to ninety pounds. He in his earlier lifetime had been in the travel business, a salesman of tickets to faraway places.

The boarding-house was an imposing building that suggested the reign of Victoria but which had been in fact erected at a later date. It stood at the corner of Jubilee Road, SW17, a turreted confection in red brick, with untended gardens at the front and rear.

When little Miss Clerricot had first stood upon the front steps, her gloved hand on the bell-pull, she had wondered as she waited for the sound of footsteps if she were not making a mistake. Nor did the figure that eventually appeared in the doorway reassure her. She entered the dimness of the hall and was left there alone. The silence of the house was like that of a convent, and in a moment she walked through the silence, following the person who had opened the door, into the presence of the proprietor. And immediately the person who had opened the door, a Dickensian ancient, had been severely upbraided for presenting so slovenly an appearance and was in fact, in Miss Clerricot's presence, dismissed from service. But Miss Clerricot herself had accepted the room she was offered, and came to like the boarding-house.

A brown wallpaper covered the wall by the staircase. The pattern it bore was one of large oval leaves that once had been depicted in a more subtle variety of shades: purples and dark greens, reds and russets. It was a late-night habit of Mr Studdy's to lift one of the three Watts reproductions and display for his personal pleasure the pristine glory of this wallpaper, and to make to himself the point about the effect of light on cheaply reproduced colour. 'A scandal,' opined Mr Studdy more than once, nodding sagely.

Throughout the house there were curtains and hangings and other wallpapers that matched the rich gravy shade of the paper on the stairway. Even the rubber plant in the hall had a tinge of it; and in the various areas of paintwork, the embossed borders that accompanied the paper up the stairs, the banisters and the painted portions of floors, it was ubiquitous. It appeared again, a colour wrought by time and wear, as a background shade in carpets and an overall tone in linoleum. In the three lavatories, one to each floor, it came into its own to such an extent that residents new to the boarding-house had been known to find it oppressive.

The brown of the boarding-house did not, however, universally command. Its effect was lightened by such touches as the three Watts reproductions, by several flights of china geese and by a series of silk embroideries worked in virulent colours that were spread over the backs of arm-chairs, ostensibly to catch the markings from the heads of Mr Studdy and others but really to cheer the rooms up. At Christmas, paper decorations were strung from picture rail to picture rail, imitation holly garnished the lantern-shaped light-fitting in the hall, and clumps of mistletoe were attached by drawing-pin to the centre of door-frames and were referred to often by Mr Studdy, especially in the presence of Miss Clerricot or Rose Cave. Mr Studdy had made an art of innuendo, just as Major Eele had made one of dumb insolence.

On the night of August 13th, Nurse Clock descended the stairs from the room where William Bird lay dead upon a bed. She carried in her hand her nurse's bag and beneath her arm, open at the relevant page, the magazine that contained the royal article. She was a woman of uniform proportions, stout about the legs and waist, though small in stature. She remembered as a child her mother claiming that she, Nurse Clock, had beautiful hair, and often, when much younger, she had examined the hair in a looking-glass and had discovered the quality her mother had been taken with: a foaming quality that was a kind of curliness. But nowadays Nurse Clock was more given over to other matters. Nowadays she rarely paused before a looking-glass to establish for herself the beauty of her hair.

'He is safe in the arms of Jesus,' said Nurse Clock. 'He has passed feet first to his eternal rest and has told me to record it. He felt himself dying, a process which began below and overcame his body.'

They turned to look at her, moving their gaze from the television screen, from the legal drama that had hitherto absorbed them. Miss Clerricot's face had whitened at the words; Rose Cave's displayed fear.

'Dead?' said Major Eele, and the others – Mr Scribbin and Venables and then Mr Obd – all said the word, too. 'Dead?' they said in unison, for often at night, grouped thus about the television set, they spoke in unison, giving an affirmative to an offer of cocoa or agreeing upon the time.

'Who is dead?' asked Major Eele. 'Not Mr Bird?'

'Mr Bird is dead. He died in circumstances that were not a little odd. I do not know what killed him.'

'Your honour, I object,' cried a voice from the television set, and someone rose, black Mr Obd from Nigeria, to quench the extraneous din.

'Mr Bird has died,' said Miss Clerricot, stating the fact, not seeking confirmation.

'Mr Bird has died,' said Rose Cave.

'He felt the hand of death upon him,' said Mr Scribbin. 'He told me so when last I saw him. "I will not last the summer," said Mr Bird; and naturally I am not surprised. I was expecting this,' said Mr Scribbin.

'Mr Bird has died,' said the plump Venables, employed in an office block to see that internal communications were kept on the move. 'Traffic controller' he called the position, and confused people, who imagined, naturally, traffic on the roads.

'Why is the television off?' asked Major Eele. 'Has no one noticed, we are sitting in this room staring at a blank screen?'

'Mr Obd turned off the television,' said Rose Cave. 'Did you not hear, Major Eele, what Nurse Clock said?'

'Nurse Clock said that Mr Bird was dead. So did you, Miss Cave. And then Miss Clerricot and then Venables. Scribbin only said that the man had felt the hand of death upon him. But before the repetition got going the African rose up and snapped off the telly. We have seen the writing on the wall: Mr Obd is a member of a tribe: Africa is a blood-bath.'

'You have got the order all wrong,' said Rose Cave. 'Miss Clerricot commented first, and then I. Then Mr Scribbin and finally Mr Venables. I think you owe Mr Obd an apology.' She smiled at Mr Obd, inclining her neat grey head.

'Oh yes, oh yes,' said Major Eele. 'Sorry, there.'

'Peacefully?' said Miss Clerricot, referring to the death, speaking across Major Eele and Rose Cave, addressing Nurse Clock.

Nurse Clock drew in a breath and blew it out again. She placed beside a chair her nurse's bag and the magazine, and sat down in the chair. It was the chair that Mr Obd had vacated in order to switch off the television set. He, seeing how things had turned out, eased himself on to a piano stool and hoped that Rose Cave would not notice. Rose Cave would say that colour prejudice was at work.

In the basement kitchen Gallelty and Mrs Slape sat by the range, sipping at two glasses of beer and talking of their lives.

'I am a wanderer, Mrs Slape,' said Gallelty. 'I pass by night through country towns. I pause in the sun by cathedral closes. I will take on any work. I will perform what the good God sends to my hand.'

Mrs Slape looked pensive, drawing away the glass from her mouth but allowing her mouth to remain ajar. In silence she offered Gallelty a cigarette from a package on her aproned lap.

'Are you fond of religion, then?' She was thinking of the reference to cathedrals and God, trying to place the younger woman in her mind. Gallelty had been her assistant in the boarding-house kitchen for only a fortnight. She had come mysteriously and had since worked quietly at the sinks and the range and the old gas stove.

'I will perform what the good God sends to my hand,' repeated Gallelty. 'Destiny sent me here, I am sure of that. 'Twas destiny, Mrs Slape, that guided me to the house of Mr Bird.'

''Twas something else, I thought,' cried Mrs Slape, laughing loudly, fat shaking on her body like weak jelly. 'The way you came, Gallelty, I'll never forget it.' For Gallelty, two weeks before, on a Friday morning, had pulled the bell of the boarding-house and had said with urgency: 'I am taken short, may I use your lavatory?' And in she had shot, a haversack upon her back, and had opened various doors at breakneck speed. Mrs Slape, alarmed, had called for Mr Bird, who listened to her story and waited in the hallway for Gallelty's egress. An hour later Mr Bird, on this the last day on his feet, had entered the kitchen and offered her Gallelty as a helper.

'My household is complete,' Mr Bird had said, and Gallelty had set to at the sink, peeling potatoes.

In the room upstairs the general conversation continued.

'Who should be informed?' asked Mr Scribbin, a man who was tall and almost shoulderless. He had shot up at seventeen and had retained his length ever since. 'Family?' pursued Scribbin, now fifty-five. 'Relatives?'

'Mr Bird was alone in the world,' said Nurse Clock.

'Where is Mr Studdy?' said Rose Cave. 'It is a pity he is not here at this time; he would know what next to do.'

'Do we not know what to do?' cried Nurse Clock tartly, smiling to take the edge off her tone. 'Why Studdy should be thought to know more I cannot see.'

'I only thought – Mr Studdy is a man of the world.'

'And what is that? Man of the world? I would have called the Major that.'

'You are sitting on a chair that was taken by Mr Obd. I do not call that kind, Nurse Clock.'

'Mr Obd is sitting, too,' returned the nurse, glancing at the Nigerian on the piano stool. 'Mr Obd, have I harmed you?'

'He is perched on a piano stool,' said Rose Cave.

'Mr Obd, are you happy?'

'That is not my duty,' explained Mr Obd. 'Let me tell you –'

'He could be working for the revolution,' said Major Eele, 'not sitting here turning off our television. There was a time, I may tell you, when houses like this were Europeans only.'

'Major Eele, come to our aid,' requested Nurse Clock. 'What is our next move? We know that Mr Bird has died alone. How do we act? Who is responsible?'

'The State,' suggested Venables, anxious to go on, smiling plumply. Nurse Clock snapped at him, a gesture of her face and teeth, soundless but effective. 'Major?' she prompted.

'I get around a bit,' said Gallelty in the kitchen. 'Holiday camps and that. I'm always on the go, but now I think that has come to an end. I shall settle down at last, Mrs Slape, here in the boarding-house, in Two Jubilee Road. "I've done all kinds of work," I said to Mr Bird, and he smiled at me and shook my hand, making the bargain over the wages. I'm sad to see him sick, Mrs Slape; a kindly man.'

'I'll never forget,' said Mrs Slape, and she laughed again, the jelly rippling all over her body.

'A box for Mr Bird,' said Major Eele. 'That is the very first consideration. The body to be laid out, with sundry applications of preservatives if it is to be placed on show. Is the body to be placed on show? In some town hall? Who was Mr Bird when all is said and done? Some say he was a local figure, known to shopkeepers, beloved by children. Did he in his time give heavily to charities, world famine and kindred things? Now, I suggest, Nurse Clock, that a collection be made, here in our boarding-house, and that we purchase black flags and bedeck the neighbourhood. May I say more? That we of Mr Bird's own house should black our faces as Mr Obd's is black and walk behind our master's coffin thus, to show our last respects. And now, in this hour of death, let us all here fall upon our knees and pray, since we may not have the television. *Our Father* –'

'Major, please. All that is in most poor taste. You have insulted a soul that is new in heaven, you have insulted Mr Obd, and you have caused our sensibilities to protest at so much ugliness in your speech.' Rose Cave it was who spoke, anger in her face, standing and looking down.

'My opinion was asked, my dear,' said Major Eele. 'I merely gave it. If my views are too extravagant for you, then seek the views of others. Death is in the house, good heavens;

you cannot expect conventions observed. People get carried away.'

'I am going to cry,' said Miss Clerricot, and she uttered the first moan, touching her face with a handkerchief.

'Mr Bird has died,' said Nurse Clock, entering the kitchen. 'He died a half-hour ago.'

'Dead?' said one and then the other.

'I do not know what killed him. No doubt the poor nurse will get the blame for negligence. He felt himself dying; it was a most extraordinary thing.'

'He caught a cold,' said Mrs Slape, 'through the soles of his feet. He walked with broken shoes out across the common. He should have known, him a cripple.'

Gallelty was staring, the twitch in her right eye working busily.

'Hardly a cripple,' corrected Nurse Clock. 'He dragged his foot a bit; it's not at all the same.'

'Oh,' cried Gallelty, shaking on her chair and sobbing.

'I could not save his life. He lay in my arms at the end and thanked me for my care. He kissed my hands, saying he had been sweetly nursed. Gallelty dear, control that now. Who was Mr Bird to you? You knew him only a fortnight.'

'Gallelty has the right,' said Mrs Slape, speaking sharply. 'No charge for tears, Nurse Clock. It's a private matter for Gallelty; we must look the other way.'

There was a silence then in the kitchen until the silence filled with the soft murmur of sorrow as Gallelty wept again. The women watched her, each with her thoughts, before looking the other way.

Later that night Studdy returned. He clicked on the light in the hall and stood there for a moment, listening for the sounds of the other residents. He looked up the dark stairs, narrowing his eyes. Then he extinguished the light and mounted the stairs in darkness. There were rules in the boarding-house: rules about noise after eleven o'clock, about the switching on and off of the communal lights, and punctuality in the dining-room. Studdy, a man who prided himself on his ability to keep on the right side of the law, trod softly, taking care to follow the line of the banister with the palm of his hand. He climbed to the top of the house, passing his own room on the second floor. There, in a spacious attic, lay William Wagner Bird, stiffening beneath the sheet.

Studdy lit a match, noted the sheet spread over the dead man's face and quickly made the sign of the cross.

'He has passed from us.' Studdy whispered the words, breathing hard, filling the room with the whiff of beer.

He lit another match, making certain, assuring himself that his brain had registered correctly. The moon, hidden all night till now, suddenly swept its light into the room. It fell upon the outlines of the figure on the bed, casting the shadow of the living Studdy over it. And when Studdy moved he frightened himself, because it seemed for a moment that the body beneath the sheet had shifted just a little.

Disliking the room and the eerie moonlight, Studdy left it. He descended the stairs and sat for a while on his bed, thinking about the death that had taken place above him. Eventually he rose and walked to his dressing-table, nodding as he made this brief journey. In a drawer he found a pad of lined writing-paper and half a packet of envelopes. In pencil he wrote as follows:

Dear Madam,

This is just to inform you that your friend, William Wagner Bird, died in this house during the night of August 13th. Before he did so he expressed the wish that you should be immediately informed on the occasion of his decease. He died in his sleep, holding in his hand a small bog-oak representation of a donkey. He had spoken previously of this ornament and was particularly anxious that you should have it as a token of ultimate esteem and gratitude.

Respectfully,

M. Moran.

PS. – The donkey may be collected any evening between six and seven at the above address.

Studdy reached for the telephone directories. In the L to R volume he discovered a name that pleased him: Mrs le Tor. He addressed the envelope, resolved that the cost of carrying it through the post was not his to bear, and propped it up on the table beside his bed.

'The midday mail,' said Studdy; and he eased off some of his clothes, humming a tune.

2

Concealed from the public eye, snug within his coffin, Mr Bird looked as he had looked in life. Despite his size and the flowing bulk of his flesh, he had borne always, since a child, the grey pallor of death; and he had a way of seeming as still as a statue. There was a new transparency about his skin, but it was as yet a slight thing, and the evidence of real decay was not apparent. Mr Bird had often thought about his funeral and visualized the scene. It was a pity he could not relish it now, for he more than anyone would have enjoyed this mourning that convention demanded. More even than Nurse Clock, who was enjoying it well enough but resented the drizzle that damped her face. More by far than the others of the boarding-house who stood by the graveside and made no pretence, who did not enjoy the thing at all.

They had come, all of them, for they felt attendance to be a duty. 'I am going to a funeral,' said Venables, the controller of office traffic, and his superiors – or a few of them, for there were many – had looked askance and sour and asked some questions about the deceased: who the deceased had been in life, and what the relationship had been with Venables. 'He took me in; he was like a father. I knew no father as a child.' So Venables took two hours off and promised to make them up. He had never before done such a thing, for he had never wished to nor had had occasion to. He felt himself a pioneer within himself as he stood by the graveside, but he did not care for all these trimmings that went with death and he reflected with pleasure that the ceremony could not last for ever.

The drizzle freshened the short grass of the graveyard and toned down the lime of new headstones. It was a suitable day for a funeral, though Major Eele had said that morning that he hoped for sun. 'I will stand about in sunshine till kingdom come,' he said. 'People have caught their deaths in chill churchyards.' The words had irritated others, who felt, in different ways, that the words were unseemly, implying, as they did, a lack of respect for death the universal thing.

Gallelty and Mrs Slape stood close together, behind the residents, humble in their stance, accepting the point that they were paid while others paid their way. 'I recognize the good in you,' Mr Bird had said that day to Gallelty, and she had said: 'I was taken short, I could not go on. I came to this house because it was at a corner.' 'Do not be sorry,' Mr Bird had replied, although she had not claimed that she was sorry and did not feel it. 'Do not be sorry that you came in an emergency to this house at a corner. Sooner or later we knew that this would happen, and happen it has. Where are you off to with that haversack?' And she had explained.

'What now?' said Gallelty to Mrs Slape, thinking of the death.

'What now?'

'Who shall pay us? What shall happen? I felt I had come home.'

Mrs Slape did not reply. She wore maroon, a fitted coat, and a hat that matched the colour. She was thinking of the kitchen and how pleasant it would be to be there at this moment, making the place cosy, ascertaining that there was something on hand to drink in the evening. 'God helps those,' was Mrs Slape's motto, carved out of a hard life.

'What shall happen?' repeated Gallelty, and Mrs Slape bade her be quiet.

They had agreed long since amidst their kitchen chores that neither of them had had the easiest of times. They talked of themselves as they worked by day and later as they sat in rest. They were, they said, well met; as good at listening as they were at giving forth. But now was not the time, thought Mrs Slape as she silenced Gallelty; now was not the time because words could not flow in a manner that was unrestrained. Now was a time that was given up to the committing of Mr Bird and one could not make it otherwise. One could not escape the significance of the hole that gaped in the ground, nor of Mr Bird encased in wood and deep within it.

'That servant girl is muttering,' said Major Eele. 'She mutters at an open grave, or else chews gum. Nothing is sacred.'

He looked across the distance at Mrs Slape in maroon and Gallelty murmuring in emotion. Gallelty's ferret face was all aquiver; he could see the twitch in her eye and her lips rising and falling.

'God is present,' called out Major Eele, cutting through the clergyman's words, staring hard at Gallelty. The others shuffled their feet, embarrassed by the Major saying so odd a thing and saying it so loudly.

Only the boarding-house people, with the clergyman, stood by the graveside. The clergyman, who had never known Mr Bird, nor even heard much of him until it was too late, wondered between moments of prayer what manner of man this one had been. Lodged in his mind was the information that the man had died at sixty-seven, that he had been of heavy build and with a foot deformity. Were these the family? wondered the clergyman, glancing round the semicircle they made and doubting that theory almost as soon as it was formed. 'God is present,' called out the man who might have been a brother, and the others, an African friend and maybe a daughter, sisters and servants, had rippled in a communal way, as a crowd ripples in church. And then, while all that was going on, the clergyman's glance fell on the face of Rose Cave and recognition trickled in his brain. He recalled her name; she often came and sat far back, and slipped away. Once he had shaken hands with her and learnt that she lived in a boarding-house some way away. He thought that odd, to live in a lodging-house nowadays, when so many people preferred bed-sitting-rooms, with cooking facilities that made them independent. All at once in the clergyman's mind the pieces linked: there was more information that he had known but forgotten until now: that the heavily-built man was himself the keeper of some boarding-house and had been, too, a singular man, a godly man, so the clergyman had heard, though not apparently a member of the Church of England, the church that now was called upon to hold this final service. So the man had been the landlord of the lady who was wont to slip away; and of all these others, thought the clergyman, inspired; and further thought that here was something just a little odd.

'Vouchsafe, we beseech Thee,' said the clergyman, 'to bless and hallow this grave, that it may be a peaceful resting place for the body of Thy servant ...'

The wet soil clattered upon the wood of Mr Bird's container. The clergyman closed his prayer-book and held it flat on his chest.

There were two wreaths, offered by the members of the boarding-house. Studdy had made the collection and had bought two rather than one, because two seemed the greater gesture; which was important since Studdy had wished to keep back some of the money. He had walked some way to find them, seeking – and discovering in the end – wreaths that had seen better days and were thus reduced in price. Studdy was thinking that he had made seven shillings in the purchasing of the wreaths, and thinking too that he had saved the sum of eight pounds eight, rent owed at the time of death. Money was important to him: he found it hard to come by. Watching the earth fall fast upon the casket, Studdy thought sadly that often before he had owed more in the way of rent, twenty guineas once and sixteen another time. He closed his eyes to drive away the thought, and opened them and saw the others strangely: as though the length of Mr Scribbin and the plumpness of Venables and the ferret face of Gallelty were new to him and were important and must be registered. He sought among the faces for an enemy and found one soon enough: Nurse Clock and he did not hit it off. He wondered if she knew about the eight pounds eight. It was not impossible, he imagined, that Mr Bird had released that information on his death-bed. She had looked at him oddly when he had displayed the wreaths, when he said that he had added an extra sixpence of his own. She had pitched up her head, snorting like a horse, blowing through her nostrils. You could not trust, thought Studdy, a woman who looked like that and who spoke so sharply. Whenever he saw her in her big blue skirt he wanted to stick a pin in her. He fingered the point of his lapel and felt the pin there, the pin he carried for that purpose: to stick, one day, into one or other of Nurse Clock's knees.

Sixty-seven years ago, to the very week, William Bird had been born. 'I fancy Wagner as a name,' his mother said in labour. 'I read it in a book.' Her husband, who was there at the time, agreed at once, thinking that this was not the time to argue. They were an inefficient couple and had left it late before calling in the midwife. 'What shall we do,' said the husband, 'if the woman does not come? Or does not come in time? Could I deliver the child myself?' He bit his nails and murmured further. 'You couldn't deliver a letter,' screeched the confined lady, laughing madly between bouts of pain. She was a person of forty-five, who claimed in after years that she had not known until the day before that she was about to bear a child. ' "You have got fat," he said to me, and then he said he liked me fat; he said he thought it right for a woman to be plump or at least a little plump. "It is all gas," I said; "I am blown out with gas from indigestion, I must see a doctor. Heavens above, what a thing to happen!" "Your time has come," the doctor said. Well, I didn't believe the man. "We never," I said; but he said yes, no doubt at all. "Here's a surprise," I said. "You've sired a child." "A child," he said, "at your age? Heavens above, what a thing to happen!" '

Late in life the child that was born to that feckless couple entered the business world, taking up a small position in a suburban branch of a travel agency. 'Nicer than a shop,' the mother said. 'Travel is the rage today.' For twenty-five years William Wagner Bird remained there, in the same branch of the travel agency. He sought love as the years went on, but concluded early that he might never be offered it; and at the age of forty-two, already a resident of the boarding-house, he found that he had been left the place in the will of the dead landlady. He seized the house and left the travel business. He blossomed like a bride on her wedding day, and he moved into middle age a different man.

After his death his silent laughter continued in the rooms and passages of the boarding-house; for the laughter was part of the place and part of its people. He in his time had sought these people out, selecting them and rejecting others. He sought them, he said, that they in each other might catch some telling reflection of themselves, and that he might see that happen and make what he wished of it. 'I rose from my desk, most downtrodden of men. I smote adversity to make myself a God to others.' There were people who had passed through the boarding-house who came to consider that Mr Bird was not entirely sane. 'Are you happy now, all of you, going and coming back? Are there complaints? The food and the rooms? A simple supper on Sundays: servants have souls. Servants have souls, they must have time off. Are there complaints about that, the simple supper we have on a Sunday? Anyone has only to say. I listen to all complaints. I sit at work in my little room if anyone wants me. Except for Sunday, my private day. Do you all see that, do you catch the significance? The Sabbath is a day of rest, food is simple, something cold.' He would stand at the door of some room in which they were gathered, his trousers warmly over his stomach; he would finish his speech and stand for a time in silence, while his laughter, not indicated on his face, oozed about the room, in and out among them.

He had known the suburb all his life, and for much of his life he had known the boarding-house. In the hall there was an elephant's foot, a container for sticks and umbrellas. In the drawer of the hallstand were two old tennis balls, dating back to 1912. Once, at the back of the house there had been a tennis court, but now it was a wilderness, rich in dandelions. Mr Bird used to look from the window of his room and smile to himself at the dandelions on the tennis lawn, thinking of his deformed foot.

'The British scene has lost a formidable figure,' said Major Eele, heading the procession away from the grave. Mr Bird it was who had brought the Major to his first strip-tease performance, who had recognized that that was what the Major required; he had introduced him to the Ti-Ti Club, signing him in for later visits.

'Ha, ha, ha,' cried Venables, imagining that Major Eele spoke in jest, taking the opportunity to release his nervous laughter.

Major Eele stopped at once in his tracks, so abruptly that all who followed behind him were obliged to stop also, even the clergyman, who had taken the opportunity to pick up his acquaintanceship with Rose Cave. Nurse Clock found her passage prevented by the suddenly stationary rump of Mr Scribbin; the clergyman in confusion dropped his prayer-book. Mr Obd was perplexed; he saw Major Eele turn to face them with a gesture; he saw that the man was angry and wondered if he might expect some verbal assault. Studdy, independent as always, had stayed for a moment longer by the grave and thus was unaffected. He only heard the Major shout and saw his right arm raised, as though addressing troops, as though inciting them to action.

Major Eele shouted some military monosyllable to arrest the attention of all present. Then he said in his tinny voice:

'Venables here has gone mad.'

A visitor to the graveyard, renewing wall-flowers in a jam-pot above a relative's remains, glanced up from her task and saw across the headstones and the crosses this little knot of assorted people, one very tall and one black, being harangued apparently by a small man. The lady hastened with the flowers, for she found it at once intriguing that such a scene should be enacted in a graveyard. She walked to the group with simulated casualness and heard the small man say:

'Venables sees this as an occasion when he should laugh and holler. Clearly, we should all have come intoxicated. Should we have come intoxicated, Venables? Remember, if you can, we are on hallowed ground. A man has passed to his rest. Sixty-odd years of living have slipped into eternity, and we in our weakness are saddened by our temporary loss. Yet here in the midst of all, the funeral words yet heavy on the air, another man sees fit to laugh and holler. Why not a tap-dance, Venables? Shall we all clap hands while Venables here breaks into further merriment, tap-dancing on the gravestones?'

Venables, his face as flushed as rhubarb, bent down his head and placed a hand across his eyes to hide his shame. The rest were silent, and the woman who had come to replace the wallflowers in the jam-pot heard the clergyman say that a misunderstanding had surely taken place.

'Misunderstanding?' demanded Major Eele. 'Tell us about that, sir. What misunderstanding has taken place? Step forward, we are all agog.'

The clergyman explained that he imagined Major Eele was mistaken, that Venables, he thought, had no wish to tap-dance in the graveyard.

'Has he not?' cried Major Eele. 'You do not know me, yet you elect to address me and ridiculously take sides with this freakish fellow. Let me assure you of this: I have today seen the glint in this man's eye; he spits upon the Church of England. I would wager money that left alone in this place he would tap-dance over the tombstones; aye, and gnaw bones –'

'No!' cried Nurse Clock, striding out. 'No, Major Eele, you have said enough. Major Eele is in drink,' she said to the clergyman, and the clergyman blinked, finding it difficult to respond with words.

Nurse Clock walked away, off on her own, her nurse's heels clicking on the hard path. She felt the eyes of all the others upon her, she who had ended the ugly scene, she who was today a special person, since she had nursed Mr Bird to his death.

The woman who had paused to watch all this saw the nurse move smartly off. She saw the clergyman hesitate and then move too; and saw the others follow, walking together because they walked towards a common goal. Last of all came the one remaining man, the one who had stayed at the grave. He came slowly, wagging his head and fingering the features of his face.

In such circumstances William Bird, called Wagner after a character in a book, born in 1897 to feckless parents, took his final leave. He was buried thus, to the words of the established Church, in the presence of his chosen people, on August 16th of that hot summer.

3

When Mr Scribbin had said that the death of Mr Bird was not an unexpected thing for him he was not telling the truth. Death came as a shock to the boarding-house, and as a personal shock, an ominous thing, to each one of its residents. Now that the funeral was over and the rough edge of that shock had lessened a little, there was an opportunity to survey the general situation. 'Well, that's the end of the boarding-house,' said Rose Cave, saying it aloud, although in fact she was alone in her room. She looked about her, noting the porcelain ornaments that she collected and the framed prints of Stratford-on-Avon, and the theatre programmes. She had made the bedspread herself, not caring much for the one supplied. She had gone to D. H. Evans in a sale and had run up the flowered fabric on Mrs Slape's old sewing machine. 'What pretty chintz; I do love blue.' Mrs Slape had watched her working at the kitchen table; while Rose Cave talked, telling about a one-time interest in Scottish dancing, and thinking how pleasant it was in the kitchen, thinking that she'd have more of the flowered material and make a pair of curtains as well. Afterwards she bought a half-pound box of Milk Tray chocolates and gave it to Mrs Slape, who said in her frank way that she never ate chocolates and had little use for this present offering. Upset, Rose Cave took back the little carton. 'Two bottles of light,' said Mrs Slape. 'D'you follow me, dear? Two bottles of light ale you could have got for that.' Rose Cave gave the chocolates to Mr Bird, who was well known for his sweet tooth. She had no idea how to go about the purchasing of light ale and so put off the making of the curtains.

'Just as well,' said Rose Cave now. The windows were large and of slightly odd proportions: curtains made for them might not easily be adapted for windows elsewhere. She had come to the boarding-house in 1954, when she was forty-two. 'I could not be alone,' she said to Mr Bird. 'All alone in a bed-sitting-room arrangement with hardly space to swing a cat. I do like people about me.' In fact, she had tried just such an arrangement. For two years she had returned in the evening and made herself eggs and toast and instant coffee, assuring herself that she needed no more, what with the Italian food, spaghetti and a meat sauce, that she took for lunch. Once a month she went to a theatre, to a seat in the gallery, and sometimes to the cinema.

They all thought as Rose Cave did; that the boarding-house must surely now come to an end. Mr Obd, tying his polka-dotted bow tie, thought it, and Mr Scribbin and Venables and Major Eele. Miss Clerricot drew off her black gloves and sat before her looking-glass, examining her face and visualizing her future. The boarding-house was convenient, and Mr Bird had been so kind. Mr Bird had looked at you with his *simpatico* gaze, like an uncle, a certain Uncle Beg whom she had known in her childhood, a jolly man who had taken her often on his knee and had nipped the back of her neck with his lips, like a playful horse. In the privacy of her mind, Miss Clerricot played a harmless game: identifying Mr Bird with Uncle Beg. Unlike Rose Cave, she had never lived alone in a bed-sitting-room. She claimed she could not boil an egg and had hinted at a gracious background.

In the kitchen that night, the night of the funeral, Gallelty voiced again her graveside cry: 'What shall become of us?' And Mrs Slape, occupied with meat, said that Gallelty had little need to act so broken-hearted. 'I have known this kitchen since the early days of Mr Bird, since first he came into power. You, on the other hand, have been here but a fortnight, and came in any case by accident.' But Gallelty, who bit her nails and had many fears, wept with the vigour of one whose luck had turned and then abruptly turned again.

In that August in SW17 no emotion existed to match the hatred between Studdy and Nurse Clock. It was almost a feat, like a piece of engineering: a great bridge, their only source of communication. In his later lifetime two things had been remarkable about Mr Bird's house: his own paternity and the venomous relationship of his two senior people. Senior they were and none questioned it; although in years they could not have thus aspired. Only Venables and Mr Bird had been longer in the boarding-house; and Mr Bird was outside such competition, and Venables somehow did not count.

What heightened the rivalry and the ugliness between the nurse and Studdy was a singular fact and one that had nothing at all to do with the house they lived in. Instead it involved a certain Mrs Maylam, an old woman of eighty-nine whom Studdy visited for purposes of his own and whom Nurse Clock had recently begun to visit too, in order to put injections into her legs. 'That's a dangerous man,' Nurse Clock had said to Mrs Maylam, after she had met Studdy leaving the old woman's flat. 'What's he doing here anyway? Smoking cigarettes, Mrs Maylam; it doesn't do you any good, you know.' But Mrs Maylam, tetchy and disliking the ignominy of having the stranger nurse lift up her clothes to put the needle in her leg, would hear no ill of Studdy and was clearly on his side – a fact that Studdy was aware of and played upon. Nurse Clock considered that he had stolen a patient from her and threatened to report him to some authority. She said there was a case against him, exercising influence over the elderly.

On the very morning that William Bird died Nurse Clock had visited Mrs Maylam. 'I'm having no more,' Mrs Maylam had said, meaning injections. 'No more jabs for me, madam.'

'Now, now,' said Nurse Clock.

'Bloody,' said Mrs Maylam. 'Can't you see I'm listening to my wireless?'

'Time for your little prick, dear.'

'You can put it up your jumper for all I care. I can look after my frigging self, you know.'

'Of course you can.'

'Mr Studdy's given me a potato. I'm trying the potato for a while now.'

Nurse Clock could see Studdy's coarse face grinning in

triumph. She could feel him near her, repeating the story to himself, reminding himself. As she cycled away from Mrs Maylam's place she prepared her attack on him, but when she arrived at the boarding-house there had been a message from Mr Bird to say he wished for her presence. His death put the incident temporarily from her mind.

'Now,' said Nurse Clock on the night of the funeral, 'we must think of a headstone. Should we have a few simple words? Or let the name and the dates speak for themselves? What does anyone think?'

'I would like the television on,' said Major Eele, making for the set and fiddling with the switches.

'A line from the scriptures,' suggested Rose Cave. 'He had a thoughtful ear for God.'

'No, no.' The matter was an important one: Miss Clerricot saw it as one on which she might openly disagree. 'Surely not the scriptures? Surely a line or two from Pope, his favourite poet? *A brave man struggling in the arms of fate* or *Oh, the pain, the bliss of dying!*'

'Good God!' said Major Eele, staring at everyone in turn. Had they gone out of their minds? he thought. 'He was not a Holy Roman,' he said aloud.

'You need not be,' said Rose Cave sharply, or sharply for her, 'you need not be a Roman Catholic to have words on your gravestone.'

Major Eele remembered the first day that Mr Bird had brought him to Green Street. A cold day, it had been, in early spring; on the tiny stage, on the left-hand side, there had been a single-bar electric fire. 'Some interesting stuff,' Mr Bird had promised, limping in front of him. 'I think you'll find it exciting, Major.' He followed Mr Bird down a narrow passage, across a yard, and then up uncarpeted stairs. In the room they entered men were sitting singly, staring hard. In a spotlight a woman of forty or so was taking off her brassière. Major Eele gave a little grunt. 'Sit down,' said Mr Bird. The woman was dark-skinned, an African or a West Indian. She moved her body about, swinging banana-shaped breasts. A man, an official, probably the proprietor of the place, flashed a powerful torch on her writhing torso. The woman smiled quite gaily, playing with the elastic of her knickers, the only garment she now wore. The curtains were pulled to. Mr Bird released his breath, signalling to Major Eele that something of greater worth was about to break. The curtains reopened: the woman had removed her knickers. She sat quite still upon a chair, looking vacantly into the middle distance, forgetting to smile. The man with the flashlight played the beam on her. He said something and she smiled. There was jazz music of a kind; Major Eele would have preferred something directly from Africa: the beat of tom-toms or the recorded sounds of jungle-birds and mosquitoes. The next performer was younger; white and slim. Major Eele kept thinking she must once have been a millgirl in the mill area of the North. The thought excited him for some reason, but he was disappointed because she was thin and white and didn't remind him of the tom-toms of Africa. They stayed for an hour and a quarter, seeing each performer many times. Afterwards, they didn't speak about it. They sat in silence in the bus that took them back to SW17, Major Eele with his thoughts, Mr Bird seeming bored, seeming not to think at all.

'He wasn't that kind of man,' said Major Eele. 'Not the sort to have slop on his gravestone. No, no, truly ...' His voice trailed away, leaving a pause that implied his greater knowledge of Mr Bird, and a manly relationship.

'Slop,' said Rose Cave. 'What on earth do you mean, Major Eele?'

'Slop. Gush. Like the inside of a summer fruit. You know as well as I do, madam.'

But Rose Cave shook her head, and Major Eele crept close to the television and turned up the volume. He was withdrawing himself from the conversation: he made that clear by turning his back and fixing his attention on the screen.

'I did not know,' said Rose Cave, 'that Pope was Mr Bird's favourite poet. I did not know that at all.'

'*The world forgetting, by the world forgot,*' murmured Miss Clerricot.

Nurse Clock drew her short nails against the fabric of her

skirt. She frowned to herself, keeping the frown in her mind, not showing it in her forehead.

'Surely we should simply say that Mr Bird has died and has in his time brought comfort and lived a pleasant life. Is that not all? I see no call for argument.' She spoke in this matter-of-fact way, a little loudly; like a matron who knew her way about. She had not informed the newspapers, as Mr Bird had wished, that he died in the manner he said: legs first, a creeping business from below. She believed that the newspapers might not be interested, that they had more to print than anecdotage of men dying in a particular manner. And now she believed that it did not matter much what went on the stone of Mr Bird's grave, except to state that it was he who lay below, that he was dead and had died in a certain year.

'*Go, good fellow!* I saw that once,' said Major Eele. 'Why not say that?' He turned from the television to speak, making it clear that he had listened to the others' conversation, and then regretted that he had allowed the disclosure.

Mr Scribbin suggested something: *A friend in need;* and Venables waved his arms in the air, agreeing or not agreeing.

'We are no nearer satisfaction,' said Nurse Clock.

'Or *Inordinate mastery of human affairs,*' suggested Mr Scribbin. 'Just that. Words like that. Simple and direct.'

Mr Scribbin, a shy man, as awkward in his manner as his gangling movements suggested, had never married. In later life he had sat in Mr Bird's room and reminisced, especially about his childhood, the time of life his tallness had affected him most. 'Small men are terrors,' had been the view of Mr Bird; 'given to outbursts of anger to prove their spirit. I never knew a small man I cared for, Mr Scribbin. Take heart from that. Imagine, He might have made you a dwarf instead.' But Mr Scribbin only said: 'A dwarf?' and mulled the image over in his mind, thinking of other dwarfs, female dwarfs whom he might have set up house with. 'Don't hold yourself so straight,' Mr Bird had said. 'Ease up, Mr Scribbin, you're like a ramrod.'

'I mean,' said Mr Scribbin, but no one listened. The television noise was loud. He left the sentence in the air.

'Miss Clerricot's quotations,' said Rose Cave. 'The lines from Pope. Too long, I'd have thought? Am I wrong? Perhaps I'm wrong.'

'D'you mean too expensive? Too much from the money point of view?' Miss Clerricot was leaning forward, her body folded like a boomerang, her chin jutting. 'I'll pay the extra,' said Miss Clerricot. 'How about the tombstone? Are we all going to chip in? How about the funeral?'

'Funeral?' said Mr Obd, not knowing he would have to chip in for anything.

'Who pays?' Miss Clerricot asked. 'Some funeral parlour'll send a bill. A couple of hundred I'd imagine.'

Mr Obd's lips moved, counting out his share. He licked the same lips; a nervous look developed in his eyes. 'We must pay?' asked Mr Obd. 'For the burial and the tombstone? Is that convention? I had not ever guessed.'

Miss Clerricot repeated: 'Does Miss Cave mean the Pope quotations would add considerably to the stonemason's bill? I'll give a little extra, I've got a bit put by: the dead come first.'

'I did not ever know,' said Mr Obd, and rose and left the room.

'You've upset him,' cried Nurse Clock. 'A shame, a shame, all this talk of money. Poor dear fellow –'

'Like misers,' said Major Eele. 'They save their pennies for the rebel armies.'

'Oblige us by turning down the sound,' said Nurse Clock. She turned to Venables and Mr Scribbin. 'What do the gentlemen say?'

'It is early to erect a tombstone,' said Venables. 'That is not done, I thought, until a year or so after the decease.'

'We need a decision,' snapped Nurse Clock. She did not think much of Venables: she thought of him as a fat fool and suspected him of laziness over washing.

'Ha,' said Venables. 'We have a whole year to make it in.'

'Nonsense,' said Nurse Clock, speaking with scorn. 'Who says we have a year? What is this new idea that we should spend a year discussing so morbid a subject? Yes, death is morbid, Mr Venables; you cannot escape that.'

Venables had a familiar pain in his stomach. He felt in the pocket of his flannel trousers for a pill. 'I wouldn't escape that,' he said, getting the pill surreptitiously into his mouth.

'Why shilly-shally, Mr Venables? We're here tonight; surely we can come to an agreement?'

'People like time, though –'

'Oh, stuff, stuff!'

Venables smoked incessantly. He would sit and smoke far into the night and when he rose he would find himself grey with ash. In a half-hearted way he would push it away with his hand, forcing it into the fabric of his clothes.

'In my kind of work,' Venables began, but Nurse Clock broke into his sentence with a fresh ejaculation. It was just a high noise that she made, but she suggested unmistakably that whatever it was that Venables was about to say it would not be pertinent and would, as well, be boring. Nurse Clock wished to have the subject of the gravestone dealt with then and there, because Studdy was absent, because Studdy in time would be presented with a *fait accompli*. Studdy had caught her napping and had taken it upon himself to organize the wreaths. She wished for no repetition of that.

On the television screen a man in a white coat was offering a packet of detergent to a downcast woman. The woman, feigning suspicion, took it cautiously. 'Very funny,' said Major Eele, and began to laugh.

'We should not come to any decision,' said Mr Scribbin. 'We are not all gathered together.' Studdy rarely came to watch the television in the evenings. Now and again he would come in later to see some boxing.

'That is unnecessary,' said Nurse Clock. 'What do you suggest, Mr Scribbin: that we should call a meeting? Are you putting us all on a tombstone committee, is that it?'

'Mr Studdy should be here. He was Mr Bird's right-hand man.'

'What nonsense! Studdy to be the right-hand man of anyone! You're making a big fat joke, Mr Scribbin!' She laughed. Good humour came on to her face. She laughed again, trying to turn the situation, trying to make it that Mr Scribbin had issued an excellent joke, that he was dryly witty.

'We know where Mr Studdy is,' Rose Cave said, laughing too, because being in a public house was something one laughed affectionately over, or laughed knowingly.

Miss Clerricot smiled and thought of an occasion when Studdy had come back to the house and had, in this same lounge, tripped over the feet of Mr Obd and fallen heavily to the ground. Remembering this and the amusement it had caused, Miss Clerricot laughed too.

All were laughing now except Mr Scribbin: Nurse Clock at the joke she wished to make it seem had been made, Major Eele at the downcast woman and the man in white giving her detergent, Rose Cave at the weakness of Studdy, and Miss Clerricot at the remembered image of Studdy falling. Venables was laughing because of nerves. Observing all this, Mr Scribbin was puzzled. 'Ha, ha, ha,' cried Nurse Clock, running a hand across her eyes to clear away imaginary tears. And Mr Scribbin assumed then that all were laughing at the joke she said he had made. He hunted among the words he had used for some unconscious pun but could find none there. He looked about at the others, and to show that he took no offence he joined in the fun. Nurse Clock watched him, the smile still stretched upon her face. She gave a final honk of merriment and saw him give one too, and knew that she had won.

'He's never here,' she said. 'He takes no interest. That's all I meant, Mr Scribbin. See?'

Mr Obd returned and said he thought expenses should be kept low. A lot was said about the gravestone, and further ideas were put forward as to the wording. Nurse Clock knew a man, a local stone-mason, who would do the whole job for a little less than the usual charge, being under some obligation to her. He was very good, she said: they were lucky to be able to place the matter in the hands of so good a man: he had won prizes for his gravestones. So the matter was left, with the boarding-house inmates who were present, all except Major Eele, feeling under some small obligation to Nurse Clock, as the stone-mason was to her. She had proved to be of sterling quality, knowledgeable about people who could do a good job and still charge less, eminently able to conduct a conversation and see it through to a happy conclusion.

In Rose Cave's mind there sat a pretty gravestone, a thing of elegance, slim and beautifully cut, bearing upon it the name of Mr Bird together with his two important dates and a single line from the wisdom of St Paul. Miss Clerricot saw a similar thing, a tombstone that was elegant too, though a little dumpier and which bore the comforting words of Pope: *Oh, the pain, the bliss of dying! Inordinate mastery of human affairs* the tombstone said for Mr Scribbin; and nothing, save name and dates, for Venables. By discreet nodding and winking, Nurse Clock had agreed with everyone in a private way, even with Mr Obd, who had thought it a good idea in the interests of economy to have simply a plain stone: a virgin surface, as he put it, without any words at all.

Late that same evening, at nine forty-two, the hall-door bell of the boarding-house rang and an intoxicated man entered the hall and was led by Gallelty to the television lounge. The man, a small and almost elderly person, merry on the surface but seeming depressed beneath it, gave his name and stated his business. He spoke generally, to the collected residents, for his business, he claimed, lay with them all. He was the solicitor with whom Mr Bird had deposited his will. He called so late, he said, because he wished to find them all together and to read out the news to the collected company. Later on, Studdy put out a story that the solicitor was not fully speaking the truth; that he came so late because he was a solicitor only by night and pursued some different trade by day. Certainly, the aspect of the man lent some credence to Studdy's claim: there was a seediness about his clothes and about his face; he had not led a dissipated life, one would have guessed, but somewhere in his life something had gone wrong. Studdy, who took against the man, although he had no call to, for the man insisted upon waiting for Studdy's return before making an announcement, put it about that in the daytime the man was employed as a postal official.

'Will you take cocoa, sir,' said Major Eele, 'while we wait for Mr Studdy?'

There was excitement in the television lounge; it ran around from face to face. It was there not because of personal expectations but because at least they would know what was to become of the boarding-house.

'Cocoa!' said the man. 'You're joking?'

'We have cocoa every evening,' explained Rose Cave, 'just about now.'

The man laughed, thinking this amusing, but in the end he had a cup of cocoa and a couple of biscuits, while they waited for Studdy's return.

4

Mr Bird had been a man of some bulk, tall and proportionally broad. His head was hairless except for a furrow of white fluff that grew at the back, from ear to ear. He wore, both inside and out and in all seasons, a panama hat, and he carried on his walks a silver-topped cane that he had found one day, twenty years before his death, in a public lavatory. On all these walks, and in fact all his lifetime, Mr Bird's left leg had not adequately performed its function: he moved unevenly, aided in his progress by the silver-topped cane.

Mr Bird's face had been, and still was for a short time, pale and round and not remarkable except for its paleness and its roundness and the fact that his eyes seemed colourless. In sixty-seven years no one had ever noted and remembered the colour of Mr Bird's eyes, not since the time when he had been in a cradle, when the noting of such details is common practice.

How greatly they delight me!

Mr Bird had written in his Notes on Residents.

How complete my suburban world is now that my house is full. In the evenings I rise from meditation on my bed as I hear the first key turn in the lock and I take up an idle stance on the upper landing. Far below me something that seems at first to be a pine tree mounts the stairs: it is the pointed head and lanky body of our Mr Scribbin, bearing beneath his arm a recording of the noises made by trains. He walks fast, panting a bit, his hair on end, his clothes loose on his body. 'Good evening, Mr Scribbin,' I whisper over the banisters, but Mr Scribbin does not hear, and I smile, understanding that Mr Scribbin has other matters on his mind. Rose Cave comes next. She walks in briskly, to disguise her weariness. She has a deep distaste for the work she does, but she is always so gentle, so determined to be fond of a world that has given her nothing. Then it is either Venables or Miss Clerricot. How I love to watch the blood run to the face of little Miss Clerricot, so pretty she seems to me, sitting in our television lounge wrapped in her own small shame. She is embarrassed to be alive and no one on earth can fully console her. Well, at least I have done a good thing – I have brought them all together; and though they are solitary spirits, they have seen in my boarding-house that there are others who have been plucked from the same bush. This, I maintain, lends them some trifling solace. Mr Obd and Major Eele, Nurse Clock and poor Studdy: they all need comfort, as do my servants. I have kindled some comfort in their hearts; I have created a great institution in the south-western suburbs of London. Such has been my work and my vocation as revealed by Our Heavenly Father. I am Thy servant, O Lord; in Thee do I exist. That I have taken comfort as I have supplied it to others, that I have drunk at the same stream, seems to me no sin. I have prayed and been given no sign that my actions or my thoughts are wrong. I adhere to the straight and narrow: I will fear no evil.

Several hours before the solicitor arrived at the boarding-house Studdy sat alone in his regular public house.

'One and eightpence,' said Studdy, laying the coins out on one of the little tables in what was called the bar-lounge. 'Now, boy, what can you serve me for one and eightpence?'

'A pint of beer,' said the barman quickly. 'Or a Guinness or a light ale.' He picked up an ashtray and emptied it on a tin tray.

'No spirits? Not a whisky?'

'Not a whisky, Mr Studdy. A whisky would be two shillings.'

'Now,' said Studdy, 'use your ingenuity. Measure me out a whisky that is a little less than the two-shilling measure. One and eightpence is eighty-three per cent of two shillings. Measure me out a whisky that is eighty-three per cent of the two-bob measure. Do that to oblige Mr Studdy, boy. Do that to oblige a customer.'

The barman shook his head. He knew that Studdy had further money hidden away on his person somewhere. It was a great ploy of Studdy's to try people's patience in this manner, hoping that in the end he'd get his drink at a cut price.

'That's against the law, Mr Studdy,' said the barman. 'What shall I bring you now?'

'Would I owe you the fourpence? I'm a regular passenger in here. It's not as though Mr Studdy is some fly-by-night you'll never set eyes on again. How about an IOU?' Studdy took his IOUs from his pocket and rapidly wrote 4d. on one. He added the landlord's name and signed the paper with a flourish. 'Here you are,' he said, dismissing the matter and picking up a newspaper left by someone else.

'I cannot accept that,' said the barman. 'Cash on the nail the rule is. You know that well, Mr Studdy.'

Studdy, behind the newspaper, took no notice. Then, at a further protest from the barman, he sighed and said:

'I have written the IOU, I have placed myself in your debt to the extent of four coppers. I cannot undo what already is done. If you are suggesting that we waste this IOU, why did you not prevent me writing it? Why change your mind at this point? I may have to see the landlord, boy.'

'I am returning your IOU, Mr Studdy. I cannot accept it. How could I prevent you writing it when you did so in a flash? Be reasonable now.'

'Reasonable? Who is being reasonable and who is not? Examine this matter between us and you will fast discover that reason is liberally on Mr Studdy's side. Declare to God, I've never known a man to be so difficult. Think of it, it is a question of four pennies.'

'You know the law, Mr Studdy; you know the rules of the house –'

'Be damned. Give over now. Serve me with a Scotch whisky and have done with it.'

'Two shillings, Mr Studdy.'

Studdy handed the man a ten-shilling note and groaned to deprecate the barman's folly. It angered him that there was more and more of this to-do as the years passed; nowadays whenever he asked anyone to oblige him there was all this fuss about nothing.

'Eight shillings change,' said the barman, passing over the glass.

Studdy had wished to keep the half note intact. He hated having to reduce a note to a jangle of coins.

'Where's my IOU?' he asked the barman.

'I gave it back to you, Mr Studdy.'

'Gave it back? Be damned, you did no such thing. Produce that IOU now and no further nonsense.'

'I haven't got it. You put the paper in your waistcoat pocket.'

'You know I never did that. I gave it to you and you cunningly took it off, charging me as well. That whisky has cost me two and fourpence.'

'I can't stand here, Mr Studdy. I have my work to do. I haven't got your IOU.'

'Then you must have placed it in the till. I shall have to see the landlord. Most certainly I haven't got it. Why should I? Why would I write an IOU and then place it in my waistcoat pocket? That would not make sense at all. You may examine me if you wish.'

'I have my work to do.'

'And I have my thoughts to think. I notice you do not suggest an examination of yourself. I am open to that; yet you are not. Now, to a neutral observer, where would the guilt lie?'

'You are off again, Mr Studdy.'

'I am not off anywhere. I warn you, you cannot get out of your unenviable predicament simply by saying I am off. There is a net of suspicion tightening in around you. Think carefully now before you speak. Do not give yourself away with some glib denial. I see it in your eyes: a host of assorted petty thefts and the guilt thereof. You're blushing like a schoolgirl; your hand is forever in that till.'

'Now, Mr Studdy, that's no kind of talk. You know I gave you back that IOU.'

'Boy, it has gone beyond the IOU by now. What is fourpence? A trifling sum that would buy you but an inferior chocolate bar. Yet you could not resist even that. You who have been helping yourself to the crackle of five-pound notes from that till could not resist the opportunity to rob a simple man by means of a trick. You could not pass it by. You could not see that a grain of seed may trap an eagle. You Irish are all alike.'

'It is you who are the Irish one, Mr Studdy. There's no Irish blood in me at all.'

'There is Irish blood everywhere, and if I were a hard type of man I would have the police in here and we would see Irish blood spurting like a fountain as they sought to capture you.'

The barman shrugged and went away. Studdy read the newspaper through; after glancing at the clock, he took his leave.

Studdy was a red-haired man of fifty-three. He was tall and heavy, and he wore, winter and summer alike, a thick, black, double-breasted overcoat with a large grip on its belt. Stuck into the left lapel was a small religious badge, the emblem of the Sacred Heart.

He walked slowly away from the public house. His big hands were deep in his pockets because he possessed no gloves. He was thinking about this now, his lack of gloves and the shame it induced, even in August; he was considering how he might without effort come by a pair. He mounted the stairs to Mrs Maylam's two-roomed flat, turning the problem over in his mind.

'Chilblains,' said Studdy to Mrs Maylam. 'In the winter of forty-six I was lucky to keep the right hand.'

'Green ointment for chilblains. I had a son had chilblains.'

'I've tried everything, Mrs Maylam. There isn't a cure known to modern science that hasn't been practised out on Mr Studdy's hands. Come February and I can do nothing with them. Isn't that the queer tale for a working man? Long splits from fingertip to wrist. I swear to God, it would turn your stomach.'

'I never knew that,' said Mrs Maylam, who had not heard him correctly. 'I thought you only had chilblains on feet and hands.'

'By dad, sir, they're everywhere. Could you loan me forty bob for a good pair of gloves?'

'Will I turn on the radio?' said Mrs Maylam. 'There's a music hall on the Light Programme.'

'Please yourself about that. I have to be on my way. I believe Mrs Fitz is giving a party on Saturday afternoon. She was wondering would I like to attend. Sure, it'd be something to do.'

'The bloody old hound. You'd never go, Mr Studdy?'

'Excuse me now, Mrs Maylam, while I just slip over and tell her to put out another cup and saucer. A party's not in my line at all, but I'd never like to disappoint old Mrs Fitz. I think she'd loan me the little sum for the gloves.'

'If ever there was evil in a woman's soul it's the case with Mrs Fitzgerald. She and that bloody strumpet who comes with the dinners. "Is your bed made?" she said to me. They have their noses everywhere.'

'D'you know that barman down at the Arms? I just had an altercation with that fellow. Oh, there's room for him in your gallery of rogues all right.'

'I might find you forty shillings for the gloves, Mr Studdy. It's the curse of us all, the climate we have to put up with.'

'Well, I'd be obliged, Mrs Maylam. Only I'm just that bit pressed. It's no time of year for the working man.'

Mrs Maylam rose slowly from her chair and found two pounds in a tin in the kitchen. While she was out of the room, Studdy put his hand into the back of her wireless and disconnected the wires.

'You're kindness itself, Mrs Maylam.' He pocketed the money, sniffing to clear his nose. 'Shall we put on the radio now?'

Mrs Maylam turned a knob but no light came on. 'The bloody thing's queer again. I'll have to get a new set one of these days.'

'Let's have a look,' said Studdy, standing up and peering into the back.

He poked about and said: 'I'm no hand with electrics. Shall I take it to the shop, Mrs Maylam?'

'I'm lost without it. Will they be able to do it tomorrow? Could you ever drop it in to me tomorrow night?'

'I'm wondering could I. I have a lot on tomorrow night. Well, we'll see what can be done. Don't let me forget it now when I go.'

'If I gave you six shillings would you buy a couple of chops and we'll have them for tea?'

'Definitely. Now, tell me about this woman and the dinners.'

Mrs Maylam, a big woman with a yard of grey hair wound round her skull, nodded. Her hands, with short, broad fingers, lay touching on the coloured pattern of her overall. She nodded again, and began to laugh with a screeching harshness. Then she ceased and said:

'What was that?'

'The woman who comes with the dinners.'

'Meals on Wheels. Sexy bloody bitch.'

'That's what I thought,' said Studdy.

The woman's name was Mrs Rush. Mrs Maylam said she never brought her ice cream. 'I fancy a slice of Walls. She knows it well, the young harlot. Kindness was never her way, Mr Studdy.'

They talked of other things. Studdy cooked a tin of tomato soup, mixing in a little milk. When he had eaten it he returned to the public house, with Mrs Maylam's wireless under his arm.

For some weeks he had been noticing the Meals on Wheels woman. 'You want to watch that food,' he had earlier warned Mrs Maylam. 'If I was you I'd drop it down the sink.'

The barman, dreading the process of again serving this customer, approached him.

'What'll you take, Mr Studdy?'

Studdy thought of the forty shillings. He eyed the barman sternly.

'Two Scotch whiskies is what I'll take,' he said.

'Two, Mr Studdy?'

'Two of Scotch. My friend Mr O'Brien will stop by later.'

No one had ever joined Studdy here in the evenings, but the barman, who was new, did not know this. 'I am up to your tricks,' said Studdy, looking at him carefully.

The man brought the whisky and was paid for it without argument. Studdy returned to his consideration of the Meals on Wheels woman. He drank one of the glasses of whisky and then called the barman.

'Bring me the telephone directory,' he ordered, but the man declined on the grounds that others might wish to consult it.

'L to R', said Studdy.

The barman persisted in his argument, saying the telephone directories were meant as a communal facility.

'You'll not last here,' Studdy told him, and rose and traversed the distance to the telephone. He copied out Mrs Rush's address and returned to his place. He sat over his whisky for a further hour, thinking matters over.

When it was time to go, Studdy approached the bar and asked for the landlord.

'An IOU has changed hands under unfortunate circumstances,' he explained. 'Your new barman had it out of me by means of a trick. I'd welcome it back, Mr Horney.'

'Have you asked the lad? What's this about a trick?'

'I was temporarily embarrassed, or thought I was, and passed him an IOU for fourpence at his suggestion. I then discovered a half note in my inside pocket and paid with that for my sustenance. *My IOU was not returned, Mr Horney.* You understand, sir, what I am saying? You take my meaning?'

'Indeed, Mr Studdy. Well, that is easily remedied.' Mr Horney took four pennies from the till and placed them on Studdy's palm.

'Thank you,' said Studdy. 'And one good turn deserves another, so may I warn you about that bar-lad of yours? His hand is never out of that till. I saw him lift a fiver.'

'You're mistaken, Mr Studdy? He's a good worker. He'll be here till midnight washing glasses.'

'Keep an eye on that till, Mr Horney. You wouldn't want the brewery crowd to hear about this now.'

'Thanks, Mr Studdy. I'll bear your advice in mind.'

'Would you ever mind sticking this radio in a corner for me? I'll pick it up tomorrow night.'

'Certainly, Mr Studdy. It's safe as a house in this bar.'

Studdy paused, rubbing his nose. 'I wouldn't ask if it wasn't for that bar-lad, but would you ever mind giving me a receipt? I'm embarrassed to say it, but if he'll lift a fiver he'll lift an old radio. Isn't that logic?'

'Oh come, Mr Studdy. I'll see the boy off the premises myself. No harm will come to your radio.'

'I'd rest happier, Mr Horney. It wouldn't take a second to

pencil out a little receipt. *Received from Mr Studdy, one radio.* I'll pick it up at six tomorrow.'

He handed Mr Horney a piece of paper on which he had already written the words. Mr Horney signed it in silence.

As Studdy walked back to the boarding-house his watery eyes were half closed against the smoke that rose from his cigarette. He pouted his lips, rolling down the lower one, revealing browned teeth set crookedly in their gums. 'I'm thinking,' he said to himself, the cigarette caught on his lower lip, bobbing up and down, 'that maybe I'll write a short note to Mrs Rush.' As he walked, he composed.

Dear Madam,

I put it to you that the organisation you are involved with, carrying dinners to the elderly and bedridden, is serving you as a cover for certain activities. I put it to you, madam, that you are using this charitable work as an excuse to take you out of the house, to account for mileage and petrol consumption on your husband's car, et cetera et cetera. I put it to you that your husband, Martin Henry Rush, would be interested in the comprehensive dossier that I and my assistants have compiled concerning your afternoon activities.

Respectfully,

A friend to decent morals.

PS. – If you wish to prevent this said dossier from falling into the hands of your husband please lift the bonnet of your car immediately upon stopping outside Mrs Maylam's place next Thursday. You will then receive further instructions.

Studdy entered the boarding-house at half past ten.

'There's a man in there to see you,' Gallelty said in the hall. She rose from a hard-backed chair with carving on it, smoothing the skirt of her uniform, setting the apron in place. Mr Bird had always insisted upon uniform: black for afternoons and evenings, a more casual pink for the morning.

'A man?' Studdy stood still, at once suspicious. 'What sort of a man, girl?'

Gallelty had been asleep. She blinked, thinking of her bed.

'Well, a man, Mr Studdy. A solicitor fellow, he wants to see us all. It's Mr Bird's will.'

So at ten thirty-one Studdy entered the television lounge

with Gallelty trailing behind him. He looked with displeasure at the expectant faces of the residents and then sat down.

'That is Mr Studdy. We are all here now,' said Rose Cave to the solicitor; and he, blowing his nose, drew from his bag papers on which nothing was written, and then found the will in the inside pocket of his jacket.

'Ha, ha,' cried Venables on learning that Mr Scribbin had inherited a pair of porcelain book-ends and a clock.

'To Major Eele,' said the solicitor, having paused, '*Astronomy Made Easy*. The title of a book,' he added, fearing they might imagine him to be talking gibberish.

And when he had finished, and had gathered up the blank pieces of paper, and had passed the will around for all to see, he rose and said he must go. He went, and Nurse Clock and Studdy did not look at one another, but sat, he with a scowl and she smiling, both of them with thoughts of their own, though thoughts that were inspired from the same direction. The boarding-house belonged to them jointly, to Studdy and Nurse Clock, provided they continued it as such, provided they made no change in its residents or its staff, unless death should dictate one, or unless, for their own reasons, staff or residents should wish to leave.

5

Of Rose Cave Mr Bird had written in *Notes on Residents*:

Miss Cave (52) was encountered by me in a cinema queue on April 22nd, 1954. The film was a re-issue of the famous musical entertainment of the 'thirties, *The Ziegfeld Follies*. Due to pressure of demand, neither Miss Cave nor I gained admittance and were eventually obliged to walk disconsolate away. It was at this point that I approached Miss Cave, simply by saying what a pity it was and how surprising too, for one did not nowadays expect to be driven away from a cinema. 'That is so,' said Miss Cave, a little suspicious I thought, a trifle stand-offish, but who is to blame her? 'I have seen you at St Joseph's Church,' I next remarked, which I fear was an untruth. I guessed that she was a resident of these parts and I guessed from her attire and from something in her manner (I had closely observed the lady for an hour in the queue) that she was of the church-going class. She might, of course, have been a Methodist or a Baptist or a Witness, and in that case she would no doubt have sent me off with a flea in my ear. However, I am not unsubtle in these matters, and I took my chance and plumped for the Church of England. 'I do not go regularly,' said Miss Cave. 'Nor I,' I replied, pleased to be able to speak the truth. 'Of late years I have taken to observing the Sabbath in a way of my own, quietly in my room. My leg' – at this point I struck the left limb – 'does not always allow me to act as I wish. It surprises me,' I added hastily, 'that tonight I was permitted to stand so long on this street.' 'Your leg?' said Miss Cave, and I explained at once that it was not normal, walking a few steps to make my point. 'Bird the name is. William Wagner Bird.' I essayed a small joke: 'Sir William as they used to call me in the far-off days when I was obliged to labour for my daily loaf.' The lady blossomed forth at this, and I thought at once that she was certainly a possibility. I pressed her to join me over a cup of coffee, remarking later, and very much in passing, that a vacancy had just occurred at the boarding-house.

Miss Rose Cave is troubled for reasons of her own. I have listened at her door and have heard her cry out in her sleep.

At half past eight on the morning of August 20th, a warm, bland morning, full of promise for the day ahead, Rose Cave walked down Jubilee Road, thinking about the visit of the solicitor and the tidings he had brought. She had grown used to the district, to the house itself and to the people it contained. She liked her room, the view from the window of trees and other houses, of the church spire in the far distance, of the rank garden nearer at hand. There were other boarding-houses, she imagined; and then she thought there might not be, not at least of the order that she required. Boarding-houses were becoming a thing of the past: bed-sitters and shared flats were the mid-century rage in London.

Already, in Rose Cave's time, SW17 had greatly changed. The big late-Victorian houses were being levelled, and rectangular buildings with many windows were going up in their place. The leases were running out in a clockwork way, street by street, avenue after avenue. But Jubilee Road and Peterloo Avenue, with Crimea Road and Mantle Lane and Lisbon Drive, formed a small pocket of resistance. They held out stubbornly, their leases still alive, like ancient soldiers of an imperial age. There were similar pockets all over SW17: the old order persisted, while paint peeled on window frames and doors, and garden gnomes, chipped and cracked, were varnished every spring.

At the junction of Jubilee Road and Peterloo Avenue Rose Cave passed St Dominic's, a Christian Brothers' house. One of the brothers, taking in milk, bade her good-morning. He offered a sympathetic word or two. 'We shall miss the familiar figure,' he added, and sadly shook his head.

That August in London there were protests in high places against dogs that were bred not to bark. A hairdresser confessed to a Sunday newspaper and wrote out his confessions for publication; huge posters carried this news at railway stations and on hoardings by the roadside. The Rainbow Men, in cars with caravans, were travelling all England bringing gifts to housewives. On the very day that Rose Cave walked to the bus-stop, thinking about the visit of the solicitor, a seventeen-year-old ginger tom-cat, kidnapped the previous Friday and held to ransom for a thousand pounds, was returned unharmed to its elderly owner. Waiting at the bus-stop, Rose Cave read in the *Daily Express* that marijuana had been discovered in the hollowed-out handles of tennis rackets. The weather that day was to be fine and warm.

Rose Cave, with short grey hair worn close to her head, had a face that had been once attractive in profile though a little sharp, full on. It belied her nature with its sharpness; it suggested somehow a grasping nature, even a certain ruthlessness and ambition. Rose Cave possessed no such qualities. She seemed sharp only when she recognized injustice, or thought she recognized it.

She boarded the bus and sat two seats from the front, beside a broad-shouldered man who did not give her sufficient room. She did not mind: the man could not help the width of his shoulders, she recognized that, and the alternative would be to stand, for there were no other empty seats. She read the front page of her newspaper, bought her ticket, and as she neared the stop where she daily left the bus she half closed her eyes and did what she did on that bus journey every day: thought about her mother's death.

'You are late,' said a man to Venables, a man with a moustache who always said such things to people, who was employed for that reason.

'Traffic has become so awful.' Venables smiled, and the man looked sour, noting that Venables had dandruff on the shoulders of the blue blazer he wore. He remarked on this also, causing Venables to flush and remove the blazer. 'Not here, old boy,' the man with the moustache said, speaking in a snarl.

Venables took his blazer to the men's washroom and brushed off the dandruff with his hand. It cut him to the quick that this personal remark should have been made so openly about his clothes, implying a condition in his hair. He began to shiver, and he felt tears mounting behind his eyes. With his blazer over his arm, he locked himself into one of the lavatory cubicles to calm himself.

'What should I do without you?' asked Mr Sellwood who once had won an OBE. 'Have you ever forgotten a thing in your life, Miss Clerricot?'

Miss Clerricot paused in the walk from Mr Sellwood's desk to the door that led to the alcove where she typed. Not before, as she remembered, had Mr Sellwood spoken to her in that way, praising her memory, raising the idea that she was indispensable. Often he had thanked her and said she had done good work, but that was to be expected, that was something that was a politeness in their relationship, a cliché that was used to keep her happy, to keep her pecker up when the work was onerous.

'Well, thank you,' said Miss Clerricot. 'Thank you, Mr Sellwood.'

Sellwood, thought Miss Clerricot, looking at the man; Sellwood once meant, she supposed, a man or a family responsible for the selling of timber, probably in small quantities. Probably, she thought, a man had once sold wood from a cart in a Midland town, wood bound into bundles, and had shouted his wares through the streets and had come to be given the title, having previously been something more simple, like Jack or Thomas. She examined Mr Sellwood's face, glancing rapidly, fearful of being rude. It was an odd reflection, connecting the small Home Counties moustache, the bifocal lens and the bald dome with a man astride a load of bound wood upon a cart. She blinked back the laugh that came quickly to her. She glanced again at the face of the man who would never now sit on a cartload of timber. The small moustache moved. The grey lips separated and met again. No teeth were seen. Mr Sellwood was speaking.

'No, no, Miss Clerricot, what I say is true. I do believe my affairs would be a thorough, awful mess – my desk would be a bear-garden without you!'

How odd to say a bear-garden, thought Miss Clerricot. Now, why had he said a bear-garden? Why liken a disorganized desk to that? It did not make much sense, yet she saw what was meant. She was used to him of course, that accounted for that; she understood the way his mind worked things out;

quite often, in the letters she typed, she altered certain of his expressions. He never seemed to notice. Or, if he did, it was to pause and compliment himself on the neatness of his phraseology.

'Don't go,' said Mr Sellwood.

She stood by the door, which she had reached while thinking it odd of him to use the word *bear-garden*. She looked back at Mr Sellwood, who looked at her from behind the ordered beauty of his desk, which in fact was due less to her efforts than to the small amount of labour that Mr Sellwood daily performed. It would have taken, reflected Miss Clerricot, many a long month to have turned Mr Sellwood's desk into anything like a bear-garden.

'Hmm,' said Mr Sellwood. He was a man of fifty-five who had lived for twenty-three years in Sevenoaks and came to London every day by train; a journey he enjoyed because he was a railway enthusiast. Mr Scribbin of the boarding-house was a railway enthusiast too, as Miss Clerricot knew to her cost, but not really one of the same ilk as Mr Sellwood. Mr Sellwood enthused about the British railway system in the same way as he enthused about the country's gas and electricity services. He waxed keen about the Pearl Assurance Company, and about several other, smaller, insurance companies. 'Banking,' Mr Sellwood proclaimed, 'is an interesting thing. Do you know how a bank works, Miss Clerricot?' Miss Clerricot, knowing fairly well, would only smile. 'A bank offers you what is called an overdraft. Now, an overdraft . . .' Mr Sellwood referred to trains, electricity, gas, insurance and banking as services to the community. He was interested in all of them.

Miss Clerricot was not a large person. She weighed seven stone and eight pounds on this August day, and the greater part of it lay about the lower area of her body, her hips and her thighs, although beneath her summer dress, grey with medallions on it, she did not seem unduly bulky in that region.

'I wonder,' began Mr Sellwood, looking at Miss Clerricot and seeing there a woman he had seen for several years: a black-haired woman with a face efficiently built around black-rimmed spectacles. He finished his sentence, inviting her to lunch with him.

Rose Cave thought about her mother's funeral until the bus drew in at her stop. All her life, until her mother died, she had lived with her, far out in Ewell, journeying to her work five days a week. She had never known her father, because, as her mother told her when she was fourteen, Rose had been born 'a child of love'. They had lived, mother and daughter, in a rented bungalow and had not often spoke of this father, though occasionally a look came into the elder Miss Cave's eye and Rose knew that she was thinking of him; thinking, she guessed, of a brief and violent courtship, for the man by all accounts had been a person employed by her mother's parents to hang wallpaper. 'Forgive us, my dear,' the elder Miss Cave had pleaded on her death-bed, and Rose had pressed her hand and held back the tears. Her mother had been her greatest friend. She died at sixty-two when Rose was forty-one.

The cremation had been so quick, casual almost, like some medical thing, some slight ailment that must be, and is, efficiently put right. Afterwards she wept in the rented bungalow, looking around it and not ever wishing to live there again. The wretchedness that her birth had brought to her mother, the snootiness it had caused in her mother's family, the difficulty it had placed her in, a single woman with a child to account for: all that had drawn them close together. She had felt she wished to share the wretchedness, at least in some way to alleviate it. Rose Cave lived a selfless life until her forty-first year, until the day her mother died. And then, when she moved closer in to London, closer to the work she did, she found it hard to feel that she was not alone. She joined clubs and societies to give herself something to do, but one night when she glanced around it seemed to her that she was just a little older than the other people present, and it seemed that the fact was noticeable.

'That cat's been returned, that kidnapped cat. An old-age pensioner gets a big reward. Fancy, Miss Cave.' The woman who brought round the cups of tea was smiling about the cat at her, in ecstasy on the stairs. Rose Cave smiled back; and just at that moment Miss Clerricot smiled too, saying yes to Mr Sellwood, saying she would like very much to have lunch with him.

Venables wept in the lavatory. He had tried to control his tears, but they came with a quick gush just when he thought that it was going to be all right. He sat down on the lavatory seat, holding his forehead in his left hand and his blazer in his right. He tried to think of something else, to banish away the face of the man who had been rude, but all that came into his mind was the scene in the television lounge the night before when the solicitor had said that the boarding-house was now the property of Studdy and Nurse Clock. Chagrined, he thought that neither he nor any of them had ever valued Mr Bird to the full. Mr Bird had been like a father to him; but why had he done that strange thing, leaving the boarding-house in that way? Venables could not see at all; he could not see why a man like Mr Bird, who had always seemed to be knowledgeable and sensible, had performed so foolish an act as to make out such a will. And why had Mr Bird left him a legacy of two pieces of cloth, antimacassars they might be, that were a sort of silk and had come originally from Australia? Venables could not understand.

'I can hear you, Venables. Venables, do you know what time it is?'

The man with the moustache, the punctuality man, was shaking the door of the lavatory.

'Coming now. Coming, coming.'

Venables waited for the sound of feet moving away, but did not hear it. He remembered his father banging on the lavatory door when he was a child and shouting through it, just as the punctuality man had. Venables sighed, wiping the marks of his tears with a piece from the paper roll. Would he ever, he wondered, escape from people who banged on the doors he locked to demand his egress? His father's big brooding face, with a moustache eight times as large as the punctuality man's, flashed into his mind. He could hear his voice: 'What are you up to, you scut? Come quick now or feel the razor strop.' And, as Venables remembered, he felt the razor strop whether he came out at once or not. He felt it almost every day of his childhood, for sins like picking his nose or standing on the outside edges of his feet or spending too long in the lavatory. His father, who had lately become a Seventh Day Adventist, was now in Wales somewhere.

'He came here in 1940,' Mr Bird had written,

> and remained during the war years and indeed ever since. Thomas Orpen Venables (49), psychologically unfit to play a part in the hostilities, is a man given over to loneliness and tears. I do not recall the precise manner of his entry here, but I rather imagine he was recommended by a resident who has long since taken leave of the boarding-house and the greater world. He it was who gave me the idea of collecting my solitary spirits together, and for that I have always had a kind thought for him. Venables goes in fear of his life, escaping a Mr and Mrs Flatrup, a couple of no doubt foreign extraction, whose daughter he put in the family way and did not bear the consequences. He suffers, perhaps as a result of his terror, from a stomach ailment. Venables, I believe, is dying.

He could hear the punctuality man washing his hands. He pulled the chain and replaced his blazer.

'You should see to that before you leave the house in the mornings,' remarked the punctuality man. 'You're meant to set an example, old boy.'

Nurse Clock's bicycle, fitted with an engine to aid her on her many journeys, coughed temperamentally on Athens Hill.

'It doesn't like an incline,' said Nurse Clock to Mrs Maylam. 'It doesn't like an incline and that's the truth of it!'

She smiled blithely and deposited her small black bag on the table beside Mrs Maylam's chair. She took off her coat, revealing a crisply starched apron and the blue dress of her uniform.

Mrs Maylam asked: 'What doesn't like an incline? I don't understand you.'

'Well, of course you don't! Now, now, we mustn't worry

about not understanding. It's only my little bicycle that doesn't like an incline.'

'You didn't say that. We're not bloody mind-readers, you know.'

'Of course we're not!' cried Nurse Clock. 'And we cannot be expected to associate the splutter of Nurse Clock's cycle with the first words she utters. It is nothing to worry about. Even in the prime of life we might not be so nippy in our thoughts.'

Once upon a time, many years ago now, Nurse Clock had come across a small type-set advertisement in *Nursing World*; it caught her eye with the headline *What Would You Do if the Queen Called?* The advertisement went on to speak of a pair, a Sir James and Lady Lord-Blood, who organized a charm course with guaranteed results and were at present enrolling for the summer months. Nurse Clock, who did not entirely believe that the Queen would call, nevertheless thought that the course might be useful to her in her work. She paid out some money and reported at the church hall where, mornings only, the charm course took place.

Lady Lord-Blood spoke of fat and flushing and beauty through personality. She expatiated on vowel sounds, but the opinion of Nurse Clock, shared by some of her fellows, was that Lady Lord-Blood's own vowel sounds were not entirely above suspicion. Sir James, a lean man, scarcely broke silence at all, limiting his activities to the collecting of fees and the composing of further advertisements. One of the other students, a woman called Mrs Cheek who claimed she had never in her life forgotten a face, spread a rumour that Lady Lord-Blood had more than once, ten or so years ago, lit her to a seat in a Hammersmith cinema. Mrs Cheek said that, strictly speaking, the Lord-Bloods' name was Haines.

All fees and all extras, such as the use of the hips apparatus, were payable in advance. It was therefore regarded as a serious breach of contract when, on the Thursday of the second week, the Lord-Bloods failed to put in an appearance at the church hall. This lapse and the lack of any message to explain it so incensed Nurse Clock and Mrs Cheek, who were among the keener spirits, that they repaired at once to the home address of the Lord-Bloods, a grim barracks of a house some two miles to the east. They hammered loudly on the door and were eventually rewarded by the advent from within of a partly-clad male Indian. Their request for Sir James and Lady Lord-Blood plainly foxed this man. 'Try Haines,' said Mrs Cheek. 'Haines,' said Nurse Clock. 'Haines,' repeated the Indian. 'Haines, certainly. I beg your pardon, ladies. I believed you to say some different name.' They were allowed into the hall and directed down a flight of steps to a basement. When they knocked on the prescribed door Lady Lord-Blood's voice called out in a peremptory manner, bidding them to enter. They did so and paused. There were the Lord-Bloods, Sir James unkempt and in his night attire, his wife, if such indeed were the relationship, in an old-fashioned blue kimono, with a part of a fried egg on the way to her mouth.

'Yes?' said Lady Lord-Blood suspiciously, laying down egg and fork. 'Yes?'

'We have come for an explanation,' shrilled Mrs Cheek. 'We are not at all satisfied.'

Sir James in his pyjamas was buttering a piece of bread. 'Now, ladies,' said he in a voice that Mrs Cheek afterwards described as 'that of a labourer'.

'Eh?' said Lady Lord-Blood.

'There was no college at all,' Mrs Cheek went on, 'only a church hall. We paid you money. You said in the ad you had a college. Nurse Clock and I would have our money back.'

'They want their money back,' repeated Lady Lord-Blood.

'Then want must be their master,' suggested Sir James, laughing and eating his bread. 'Go away,' he added. 'You have no right here.'

Mrs Cheek commenced to shout abuse, banging about the room. Nurse Clock stood still, anger affecting her in a different manner. 'Go back to your cinema,' shrieked Mrs Cheek. 'You lit me to my seat in the cinema at Hammersmith.' She pointed her forefinger at Lady Lord-Blood. 'Your name is Haines.'

'I came in good faith,' said Nurse Clock quietly, 'yet you

taught me nothing. You absconded before the lessons had run their course. Mrs Cheek and I are naturally grieved.'

'We are unwell today,' explained Sir James. 'We are unable to go out. As to not teaching you anything – well, Mrs Clock, there was very little we could do.' He sighed. His verdict, seeming sincere, hurt her the more for that reason. She was thinking deeply about it when Mrs Cheek, without much warning, picked up a pot of jam and flung it with force at the wall. Chaos followed and was in a moment added to by the arrival of the Indian, complaining that the noise interfered with his studies. He turned to Nurse Clock and said that he was in training to become an accountant and would return soon to Dacca in Eastern Bengal. 'Where the muslins come from,' said the Indian.

'Give Nurse Clock her money back,' demanded Mrs Cheek. 'If she is beyond reclaim, do the decent thing by her. Nurses do not earn much.'

'Alas,' said Sir James, and said no more.

'Charm must be there to draw out,' said Lady Lord-Blood. 'If Nurse Clock has no charm it is not our fault. She did not say so when she wrote. We are the put-upon ones.'

'Nothing can be done about Nurse Clock,' said Sir James, and smiled to soften the blow.

'At least her vowel sounds are nicer,' his wife put in.

'Yes, yes,' said Sir James, brightening and smiling more.

The whole episode of the charm course had a profound effect on Nurse Clock. She was thirty-eight at the time, and she resolved, there and then, in the presence of the erring Lord-Bloods and the Indian and Mrs Cheek, that she was made as God had designed her. She became, then, fully herself, accepting herself and seeing the role she must play. 'I am E. A. Clock, State Registered Nurse, born beneath the sign of Gemini.' These words ran through her mind as she stood in awkwardness before the Lord-Bloods and Mrs Cheek, in the presence of a dark-skinned man from the town of Dacca in Eastern Bengal.

In a moment she turned away and departed from the house. She walked through the lifeless suburban roads, meditating on herself. There, in the quiet peace of an English summer morning, she accepted again the judgement of Sir James and Lady Lord-Blood, ill-qualified though they were to issue it. From that day forth she put behind her certain desires and ambitions. Out of absurdity came truth for Nurse Clock in her thirty-eighth year.

'A prick,' said she to Mrs Maylam. 'You shall feel only a little prick.'

She held the hypodermic up to the light.

'I'll feel nothing,' cried Mrs Maylam. 'Get the hell out of here with your little pricks.'

Nurse Clock sighed. Slowly she packed away the articles of her trade. She said:

'Have your bowels moved, dear?'

Mrs Maylam met her gaze in silence. Behind the lens of metal-rimmed spectacles Nurse Clock's eyes were strangely without intensity; milk-blue, hazy.

'Bugger off,' said Mrs Maylam.

Later that day, in the afternoon, Major Eele left the boarding-house and set off briskly towards the centre of the city. He would, as was his wont on these occasions, walk for a mile and a half and then mount a bus. He was going to see a film called *Island of Purified Women*, a work with an all-female, all-African cast.

Island of Purified Women (in which Major Eele was greatly disappointed and afterwards said so at the box office) should, on the face of it, have appealed more rightly to Mr Obd. But Mr Obd did not care for such productions. He had often, in fact, spoken against the exploitation of the black woman by big business interests, especially the employment of his countrywomen in the strip-tease clubs that Mr Bird had given the Major a taste for. In his youth, as a student of law, Mr Obd had protested more against such things. Nowadays, although far from accepting them as part of society, he raised his voice only when he felt it vital to do so, which was rare.

On the evening of that day in August, at a time when Major Eele was finding *Island of Purified Women* wanting and was planning his subsequent attack on the box office personnel, Mr Obd, his day's work done, was standing in a flower shop. He was well known in the shop, for he went there often: in winter for michaelmas daisies and veronica, in summer for roses and carnations, for dahlias and asters in season. He himself was particularly fond of the aster and would have preferably bought nothing else, but Miss Annabel Tonks did not much care for the flower, and had often said so. Nevertheless, he did occasionally offer a bunch of asters, interspersed with a few late roses.

'Two dozen pink carnations,' ordered Mr Obd.

'What weather!' said the assistant, glad that someone at last was buying up the wilting carnations. 'They're at their best, you've caught them at their very prime.'

'I am very fond of pink carnations,' said Mr Obd. 'These are indeed beautiful.'

'It's pleasing to see them leave the shop in their prime. There's a month of life there yet. One pound sixteen. Eighteen pence the bloom.'

Mr Obd paid, and the assistant closed the shop, pocketing twelve shillings because the carnations were strictly speaking a shilling each. Mr Obd marched off, holding the flowers in the air, clenched tightly, on a level with his shoulder. Passers-by noticed them and several thought what a colourful sight it was, the pink carnations carried so formally by a man from Africa.

Mr Obd rang Annabel's doorbell four times. He thought he could hear some noise inside, a suppressed noise, like very low voices. He thought, too, that when first he had come to the door he had heard the sound of a wireless and then the abrupt cessation of such a sound. But he could not be sure. Annabel shared her flat with another girl: it was possible that the other girl was expecting someone she did not wish to see. Mr Obd had become used to such things in England. 'It is I,' he called out, and rang the bell again. 'It is I, Tome Obd.' But the door remained closed.

It had happened before that Annabel had not been there when he called. He had therefore formed the habit of writing her beforehand a longish letter which, in the event of her absence, he would leave with the flowers on the doorstep. Once or twice he had even had his chat with her and given her a letter as well.

He placed the flowers on the doorstep and wrote on the envelope of the letter he had prepared: 'Well, dear Annabel, I see you are not at home so I have written you this little letter. Stay cheerful, and may we one of these days shortly again visit the cinema. Your own Tome.'

Feeling gloomy, he walked down three flights of stone stairs and made his way back to the boarding-house.

6

Studdy had gone down to the kitchen to see that all was running smoothly, and to issue a single instruction. He wore an old pair of carpet slippers that he had that morning come across in one of Mr Bird's cupboards. It was late in the afternoon, the quietest time of day there.

He called for Mrs Slape and then for Gallelty. The latter came after a minute or two and informed him that Mrs Slape was resting. 'Rouse her, girl,' he commanded, his cigarette moving about, precariously stuck to his lip.

'A good clean kitchen,' Studdy said when Mrs Slape presented herself. 'I like to see a clean kitchen, a decent kind of place: let us keep our standards up. Mrs Slape, I'd like to see more fish served in this house. I'll say no more, only that. I'd never interfere. But more fish, and oblige Mr Studdy.'

'It isn't everyone that likes fish, Mr Studdy. I know that from past experience.'

'Oh, I love it,' cried Gallelty. 'Cod steaks and whiting. And salmon trout. Have you ever had salmon trout, sir?'

'Certainly,' said Studdy. 'Certainly I've had salmon trout. Any amount of it.'

'The price is prohibitive.' Mrs Slape spoke firmly, as one who knew the ins and outs of economic catering.

'Not of all fish.' Studdy was at once on his guard, judging whether or not Mrs Slape was defying him, whether she was being obstructive or helpful. 'Fish is one of the cheapest goods there is. As witness the fish-and-chip shop trade.'

'I was referring to salmon trout. I know the price of fish, Mr Studdy. I was referring to the delicacy, salmon trout, a cross-bred fish –'

'Heavens alive, Mrs Slape, now, I am never suggesting we

have salmon trout. Not even on Sundays. Salmon trout is a fancy of the girl's here, and if she wants it she must buy it in a café on her night out. That's understood now, Gallelty? There'll be no salmon trout in this house, that I can assure you.'

'The girl must learn to hold her tongue, Mr Studdy. You caused that confusion, Gallelty, with your interruption about salmon trout. Mr Studdy was speaking to me.'

Gallelty apologized. She did not know what to make of Studdy. She had asked Mrs Slape what it would be like with him and the nurse in charge, and Mrs Slape gave it as her opinion that things would scarcely be affected at all in the kitchen. But Gallelty could not forget Mr Bird, nor the conversation he had held with her on that first morning, when she had arrived with a haversack on her back, ringing the bell and saying she had been taken short.

'Come up to my little room,' Mr Bird had said, and added on the way: 'My name is William Bird, I own this house.' In turn she told him who she was, first of all her name, and then a little of her history. 'I'm off to Plymouth now,' she said, 'to find some suitable work. I'm a Manx girl really. England doesn't suit me.' 'Plymouth's no place,' interjected Mr Bird. 'A sailor's town. No place for a maid at all.' 'I've been in trouble; I've knocked about a bit. Notice the way I walk? I was under training for a policewoman. You'd never believe it?' 'My dear, I'd believe everything. Let me tell you, this house you are in is a boarding-house; it is a place of my own invention. Every one of them here is a solitary spirit. Alone. Every man jack. D'you follow me, m'dear?' 'I am alone,' cried Gallelty. 'I am alone, my belongings in this haversack, brought up by nuns, en route to Plymouth.' 'You must stay here,' said Mr Bird. 'You must stay here, you will like it. In this old boarding-house no one has told the unvarnished truth for the last fifteen years. Mind you, I've had my failures: men and women with the appearance of being one thing but in fact being frauds. D'you understand me now? D'you see?' Mr Bird had led her to the kitchen, mentioning wages on the way, and then had taken to his bed with a temperature and had faced death with a full house.

'I'd like to see more fish served,' Studdy repeated and tramped off, wondering where Nurse Clock was and planning in his mind how he could foil her or be rid of her entirely.

Later that evening, when Studdy was out, Mrs le Tor called.

'I am Mrs le Tor,' she said in the television lounge, having been led there and left there by Gallelty. 'I have had a letter from someone called Moran of this address, concerning the late Mr Bird of this address also. Does any of that ring a bell?'

Mrs le Tor's introduction of herself was greeted by a silence.

'I can read you the letter,' said Mrs le Tor, taking it from her handbag and doing so.

'He did not die with any donkey in his hand,' said Nurse Clock sharply. 'I would not allow a wooden donkey in the bed of a patient.'

'There is no Moran in this house,' said Major Eele. 'Nor ever has been in my time. Venables, has there ever been a Moran? Venables here is our oldest resident.'

Venables shook his head. 'I do not think so. I cannot remember a Moran. We had a Miss Beatrice Bowen once, just after the war. She had to go; Mr Bird did not take to her ways.'

'Mr Bird, you understand, was a strict man.' Major Eele wondered about this woman who had mysteriously found her way into the television lounge, her painted finger-nails and her fat body. Why was she here? What was she after? Clearly she had written the letter herself as a pretext to gain admittance. Some sort of prostitute was she? They got up to all sorts of things now that the police had driven the business underground.

'Mrs le Tor you said your name was? Well, sit down, Mrs le Tor, and we'll see about discussing this further. Mr Obd, give Mrs le Tor a chair. That man there will give you a chair, madam. I find this most interesting, a letter of that nature. Eele the name is. Major Eele, actually.'

Mr Obd vacated his chair and sat on the piano stool.

'I do not think,' Rose Cave began and checked herself, remembering the presence of the stranger and thinking she could not say that Mr Obd should not offer her his chair.

Miss Clerricot sat still, puzzled, but not by Mrs le Tor. Never before had Mr Sellwood invited her to lunch; never before, in all her days of seeing to his office needs, had he talked to her so freely or so much. 'Martin's is an interesting bank,' he had said. 'I have an historical interest in Martin's Bank, I do not know why, except for some reason I find it an interesting bank. Founded as it was in 1563.'

'You could have knocked me down with a feather,' said Mrs le Tor, 'getting a letter like that. I simply didn't know what to do.'

'Is this your work, Venables?' Major Eele inquired severely.

'I'm sorry?'

'Well, that's that,' said Major Eele. 'Venables has been pulling your leg, Mrs le Tor. Why I do not know, but at least the man apologizes. You will scarce believe it, dear lady, but at the funeral of this same Bird this man here saw fit to dance and holler in the graveyard –'

'I do not understand. In what way have I been pulling Mrs le Tor's leg? I have never before laid eyes on her.'

'You wrote her this letter. You said so: you said you were sorry.'

'No, no, I did not say I was sorry. I wrote no letter. I do not know Mrs le Tor –'

'You see how it is, madam? This could go on all night. One moment we have an apology and the next a denial. Truth to tell, I do not know what to make of modern England.'

Nurse Clock said: 'Mr Venables did not write the letter to Mrs le Tor. He said sorry meaning pardon.'

Major Eele looked amused and then began to laugh.

'Venables has a very intellectual way of talking, Mrs le Tor. You can't understand half of what he says. He's got a gramophone in his bedroom –'

'Mrs le Tor does not want to know what is in Mr Venables' bedroom,' said Nurse Clock.

'Well, you never know.'

'Mrs le Tor, would you care for a cup of cocoa at all? We generally have something of an evening, with biscuits.'

'We all sit round,' said Major Eele, 'nibbling biscuits and watching the telly. We like one another here.'

'I don't understand at all,' said Venables, red in the face. 'I have no gramophone in my bedroom –'

'Apologies, there,' cried Major Eele. 'I owe this bloke an apology, Mrs le Tor. It is this other man, our Mr Scribbin here, who has the gramophone. He plays recordings of railway trains in motion.'

Mr Scribbin seemed about to speak, perhaps to interest Mrs le Tor in the recordings referred to. He said, however, nothing.

'Take no notice whatsoever,' said Nurse Clock. 'What about a cup of tea?'

Mrs le Tor refused this offer and asked again if anyone could think of an explanation for the letter she had received.

'It is a pity Mr Studdy is not here,' said Rose Cave. 'He might know about such matters.'

Miss Clerricot rose and slipped away. She felt the business of a letter written to Mrs le Tor was not at all her affair. She wished to be alone to try once again to puzzle out what had come to pass that day. Three o'clock it had been when they returned from lunch, she and Mr Sellwood; and she had felt her face flushed from the wine he had given her.

Of Miss Clerricot, Mr Bird had written in *Notes on Residents*:

Little Miss Clerricot (39), known to me, I fear, by no other name, came to this boarding-house in 1956. How she had heard of the place or why she sought it out remains a mystery. There was no room vacant at the time, but I turned out a man called Fortune who had been getting above himself and seemed a bit of a fraud. From the very first I found Miss Clerricot adorable. I repeat a few lines from the poet Pope when I encounter her throughout the house; it is more interesting than remarking on the weather and so much more rewarding. Miss Clerricot blushes most charmingly and raises a hand to cover a portion of her countenance. It is a shame, this ill-feeling that exists between Miss Clerricot and her face.

She drew the curtains in her room and put on the light. She looked at herself in her dressing-table mirror and saw the face referred to by Mr Bird, the same face that Mr Sellwood had taken out to lunch, and she saw once again that it was plain, too red about the cheeks, too hopelessly unmanageable. It was her mouth, she supposed, shifting her lips about, twisting them and making them go sideways, pouting them, and finally placing the tips of two fingers over the corners where the two lips met. Her mouth was too wide: her mouth cut right up into her face, chopping the whole thing in half. Miss Clerricot sighed before the mirror, watching herself sigh and reminding herself that she must not do that too often in public. They had come to her when she was eight years old and placed a pair of spectacles on that face, which of course had finished off the joke that God, forgetting mercy, had begun. At eight years of age she was just becoming conscious of the face, just beginning to realize that whatever else lay there it was not her fortune. Her spectacles had drawn greater attention to it, picking it out in the classroom, marking it down as an object for closer examination. An obsession developed within her about her face. As an adolescent girl she could not bear to see it in a mirror or in the glass of a shop window. Thinking of it sitting there, a few inches down and forward from her mind, made her depressed and often affected her physically, causing her to shiver. Walking in the street, she looked at other faces, quite nice, simple, straightforward faces, faces perhaps with slight flaws, noses a bit crooked, eyes too small, too slanted, too close together. She saw faces with pinched nostrils and hair on the upper lip, faces with narrow foreheads, or foreheads that were particularly broad or particularly deep, or hair that grew low into the forehead, a widow's peak outside the bounds of its domain. She noted faces without eyebrows or without eyelashes, with peaked chins or double chins or chins that were lost, chins that you couldn't see at all, that had probably never been formed. After such excursions through the streets, looking about her in this way, she would return with lifted spirits to her mirror, deciding it was all nonsense not to look at herself too, and would sit down with her eyes closed and then, preparing herself, open them very suddenly. But it never worked: her own dejected eyes stared back at her, defying her.

Yet for two and a half hours Mr Sellwood, married no doubt to a woman with a perfectly presentable countenance, had sat opposite her most dreaded possession and had taken it apparently in his stride. Of course, he was well used to it, he had seen it many times before, he had had ample opportunity to examine it and think about it, to work out improvements in his mind, to wonder what had gone wrong, to feel sorry that she should have to bear this cross. Yet because of her sensitivity she was aware that today had been the first time that Mr Sellwood had had the opportunity to eye her constantly and repeatedly for so lengthy a period.

'Where's she gone to?' Major Eele asked in the television lounge. 'I call that suspicious, slipping out like that when we're just about to investigate this mystery.'

Mrs le Tor seemed alarmed to hear this complexion attached to what she had imagined was a simple misunderstanding of some sort. First it seemed that the man in the blue blazer had been under suspicion and now the woman who had just left the room.

'I did not at all mean to suggest that there has been any– '

'Hanky-panky?' suggested Major Eele. 'You are being too polite, Mrs le Tor. What you mean is, you imagine there has been some hanky-panky and are too good to say so right out. How do you feel, Nurse Clock, Miss Cave, Venables, Scribbin? Has there been hanky-panky? Is this a case of mystery and detection? Is one of us to be murdered? Obd here? The gentleman on the piano stool, Mrs le Tor, hails from the dark continent and is known as Obd. He works for the rebel forces: the letter you have received may well be a coded instruction fallen by error into your hands –'

Mr Obd said: 'I do not understand you, Major Eele. I am surely a man of most liberal views. I have many things to think of –'

'Quite, quite. Do not fret, there. Listen, Mrs le Tor, allow me to introduce my fellow guests. This lady in uniform is Nurse Clock, often seen on our suburban roads astride a mechanized bicycle, carrying comfort and medicaments to the ailing. Next we have Venables, whom I have already indicated as our oldest inhabitant as it were, and then Scribbin who has the gramophone, and then Miss Cave, Miss Rose Cave, a delightful name I always think, though I fear the lady does not greatly care for an old profligate like myself. Well now, how about this letter thing?'

Rose Cave said: 'To me it is the work of some demented person who had heard of Mr Bird's death; someone outside, a stranger unknown to us.'

Major Eele pursed his lips. 'Well, certainly that's a theory. Someone by the name of Moran, you think, my dear? Well, yes, certainly –'

'There is no demented person of that name in the neighbourhood,' said Nurse Clock. 'I am in touch with these things in my work. There is no demented person called Moran anywhere near here.'

'The nearest demented Moran,' said the Major, 'would probably be in Hampstead, would it?'

'Ha, ha,' said Venables, and Major Eele turned on him, glaring.

'What the hell are you laughing at? You're not laughing at Nurse Clock, are you? She'll have you out on your ear. He's forgotten you're in charge now, Nurse.'

Venables protested and Mrs le Tor said she had better go.

Rose Cave said: 'I am so sorry, Mrs le Tor, that all this has happened. It is a most unfortunate thing, and there seems to be no explanation. I think we would all offer you apologies, as Mr Bird himself most certainly would have done. It seems a shame that there is not even an ornament to collect, as your letter implies.'

Mrs le Tor rose and drew on white gloves. Major Eele said:

'Would you like an ornament, Mrs le Tor? There are plenty here, some of them left to individual residents by the dead man, others the property of the boarding-house. You can have a volume on astronomy that I got. Would that interest you in the least? I have little use for astronomy in my daily round.'

But Mrs le Tor said no, and thanked the boarding-house residents individually, and then took her leave.

'Clear as crystal,' said Major Eele. 'She wrote that letter to get herself into the house. She had her eye on Scribbin here.'

Nobody replied. Nurse Clock read a magazine and was later

called out on a case. Rose Cave read a library book. The others watched a play about love on the television.

At a quarter to eleven, when Studdy returned, Major Eele was alone in the television lounge.

'Come in here, Mr Studdy. Can you spare a minute?'

Studdy entered the television lounge and sat down. Major Eele turned the sound down on the television.

'A Mrs le Tor called round. A big white woman, obviously a prostitute. I didn't say anything in front of the ladies, but I wondered if you'd perhaps heard of this kind of thing before in the locality? Women calling round, offering their services in a straightforward way? I wondered if we should do anything about it.'

'A Mrs le Tor? What did she say she wanted?'

'Oh, a cock-and-bull story; the usual thing. She had a letter signed with the name of Moran, saying that Bird left her a donkey in his will. Clearest case of how's your father I've ever seen.'

'A donkey? Mr Bird had no donkey. Your friend's a horsewoman?'

'Not my friend at all; don't malign me, sir. I don't know anything about being a horsewoman. We didn't discuss horses. She was led into the room by the maid and then stood here and handed round this letter. Interesting thing was that the little Clerricot woman fled at once. D'you see what I'm getting at? The Clerricot's face was like a sunset. It's my contention they're in it together.'

'Heavens alive, Major, you're not saying to me Miss Clerricot is on the streets?'

'There's no one on the streets, Studdy. Didn't you know the police had fixed all that? All the organizations are driven underground. Hyde Park is cleared. Everything is underhand, slipping pound notes into fellas' hands. It's my contention the whole thriving business is in the hands of our coloured friends.'

'I'm interested in Miss Clerricot going like that,' said Studdy. 'I wonder why she did that. Was she embarrassed at all? You say she was red in the face, but sure she's always red in the face.'

Studdy stretched out his legs and opened a button at the top of his trousers. There were beads of sweat on his forehead and his nose. His hands clapped gently together, an aid to his concentration.

Major Eele said: 'Definitely embarrassed. Beside herself. I watched her closely. The way she crossed the room there was no doubt about it that she wished to get out as fast as her little legs would carry her.'

'By dad,' said Studdy, and Major Eele said 'Yes?' thinking that the man had said 'My dad' and was about to embark on some anecdote or opinion of Studdy senior. Silence reigned for a minute or two. Both men were puzzled, Major Eele by Studdy's reluctance to finish his sentence, and Studdy by the reported behaviour of Miss Clerricot. Why, he wondered, should she react at all to the presence of a woman who was certain to have been a stranger to her, since he himself had picked her name out of a telephone directory at random?

'I wouldn't know what to make of it,' Studdy opined at last. 'Tell me, Major, was the nursing woman here? What's her name, Clock?'

'Nurse Clock was present throughout the proceedings.'

Major Eele observed Studdy clumsily thinking. He saw an opportunity to create a pleasant mischief and did so immediately.

'Nurse Clock, in fact, took charge, saying she was the boss of the house now, explaining to the pro that Bird had left her the goodwill and the property. She didn't mention you. "What about Mr Studdy?" I said, but Clock said not a word. She passed the remark by. The way she was going on, you might have been dead. To tell the truth, I felt a bit ashamed.'

'Ashamed, Major?'

'Talk like that in front of the woman, and in front of me who knew it was all a pack of lies.'

'Weren't the others there? Mr Scribbin, Mr Venables –'

'Not when the nurse passed that remark. We three were alone. Perhaps we were standing on the doorstep. I'm not sure.'

Studdy sighed deeply. 'It's a big responsibility, a going

concern like this, with the whole thing tied up to a queer type of nurse.'

Major Eele shook his head, to denote sympathy. He did not feel sympathetic. He did not feel anything. He was on neither Studdy's nor Nurse Clock's side, and was aware only of a slight though angry disappointment that Mr Bird in his wisdom had not seen fit to leave him a part at least in the boarding-house and its running. He was an older man than Studdy; he had always, he thought, got on very well with Mr Bird.

'There'll be changes?' suggested Major Eele. 'Changes in routine and personnel, I've no doubt?'

'Ay?' said Studdy, who was thinking of ways in which he might get rid of Nurse Clock.

'You'll introduce changes, I dare say?'

'As it stands, change is disallowed by the late proprietor. I have a legal brain looking into the matter now.'

The Major laughed and rose from his arm-chair. He knew that Studdy was telling lies, talking about a legal brain. It had been a good evening, what with the visit of the professional woman and the opening of the breach between Studdy and Nurse Clock. Greatly pleased, he made his way to bed.

Mr Obd was unable to sleep. Annabel Tonks' face haunted him, smiling at him, full of sympathy and generosity. He remembered the games of ping-pong they used to play. He closed his eyes and heard, perfectly, her quiet laugh and the sharp crack of the table-tennis ball. He tried to drive himself to sleep by thinking of the colour blue, a big blue expanse, an unnatural thing, like a desert with blue sand. He began to count.

He counted all the Christmases he had spent in London; he looked back over a series of annual holidays; he tried to count all the times he had sat down in the past, in restaurants and cafés, with Annabel Tonks. He saw people bringing them coffee, cappuchino coffee, three-quarters foam; he saw Annabel smile her crooked smile and lean back, snuggling into her chair, smoking, listening to him. He wondered what had gone wrong; and he remembered with pain the time when she had stopped playing ping-pong and then had stopped, apparently, drinking coffee. That was twelve years ago. He got up and put on the light. Mechanically, he wrote to Annabel Tonks.

Studdy wrote to Mrs le Tor. He used on this occasion a sloping backhand with curly capital letters.

Dear Mrs le Tor,

I put it to you that certain parties would be more than interested in your present activities. I put it to you that you are fast becoming a gossip subject in this neighbourhood, calling in on houses full of men and carrying on in a flagrant manner. My assistants and I have a comprehensive dossier, compiled from nothing but the facts. I put it to you that certain witnesses may be induced to come forward and that I am in a good position to help you in this affair, as I do not wish to see a good name tarnished. I suggest you put a postcard in Dewar's the tobacconist's advertising for a basement flat. I will take this as a sign of goodwill, and negotiations can then easily be begun. I have your interests at heart. I knew le Tor in his lifetime.

Respectfully,

A friend to decent morals.

Rose Cave dreamed of the bungalow in Ewell. She was sitting on a chair in the middle of the small hall reading a novel by Francis Brett Young.

'Why are you there?' cried her mother, her voice high and querulous. She could not see her mother. The voice came from behind her.

'I am only reading,' said Rose Cave, although she may have not used those words exactly: she was aware of the meaning she intended rather than the precise way she had expressed herself.

'Why are you sitting in the hall?' asked Rose Cave's mother; and she in turn asked why she should not, demanding a reason against sitting in the hall with a book, and added:

'Why are you not dead, Mother? I made sure you were dead, the way you looked. All the arrangements are made, a place booked in the crematorium. I have visited an undertaker's premises for the first time in my life.'

'I am alive,' said the elder Miss Cave, and floated past her daughter, making no sound.

'I am alive,' she repeated, this time in the bed-sittingroom that Rose Cave had taken after moving from Ewell. 'Poor, poor Rose, to have life pass her by because her mama was naughty with the wallpaper man. The sins of the fathers ... My dear, shall I tell you? How it happened? At four o'clock in the afternoon?'

'No, no, no,' cried Rose, pressing the palms of her hands to her ears. She made a groaning noise in her throat, trying to wake herself before her mother could explain the details.

Mr Scribbin, wearing green pyjamas, left his bed. He crossed the floor of his room in his bare feet, which were long and narrow as he was. With great care he placed a record on the turn-table of his gramophone. Class A4 Pacific 60014 hissed its way out of Grantham station, increasing its steam for the ascent to Stoke summit.

Nurse Clock slept. On the chair at the bottom of her bed lay her uniform, and beneath it, modestly, her underclothes. Her black workaday shoes, polished before retirement, stood nearby. Beside her bed a pair of fluffy slippers awaited Nurse Clock's feet when she awoke. The room was a tidy one, reflecting the brisk nature of Nurse Clock's mind. She dusted it daily herself, not quite trusting the dusting of Gallelty or of the charwomen who came every week to do a few days' work at the boarding-house. On the mantelshelf, displayed beneath glass, was a little piece of the Garden of Gethsemane, brought to Nurse Clock's mother by a soldier returning from a war, and a coloured portrait of the Queen, and a toby jug, a gift to Nurse Clock from a grateful patient. The patient had died two days after making this gift, somewhat unexpectedly, because the jug had changed hands in an atmosphere of recovery and joy at survival. It often caused Nurse Clock some little sadness when in passing she observed the toby jug and meditated upon the facts of life and illness and death. Still, she was not one for morbidity and could quickly pull herself up. One of Nurse Clock's theories was that a nurse should be a tonic to others. 'Why not to oneself too?' she asked herself, and forgot about the toby jug and the circumstances in which it had come to find a place in her room.

Never in her life had Nurse Clock dreamed at night. She lay

now, on the night of August 22nd, smiling in her sleep, unaware of anything. Polishing her black shoes before making for her bed, she had thought about the evening's events: the visit of Mrs le Tor, the letter that purported to have come from the boarding-house. Nurse Clock had not yet formed a plan in her mind; she had not yet adopted, as it were, a course of action in regard to her joint inheritance of the boarding-house. 'I am struck all of a heap,' she had confessed to a patient of hers, a Mrs Corry, to whom that morning she had presented the whole march of events. 'No need for nursing now,' Mrs Corry had pointed out, but Nurse Clock had quickly explained that she could not live without her trade. And then it had occurred to her that there was a room to let at the boarding-house, since Mr Bird was dead and out of his. 'A pleasant enough room,' she said to Mrs Corry, 'though not large. Why not come now? You have said more than once you are not suited.' 'I have had a tough life,' said Mrs Corry, as though requesting Nurse Clock not to force her, as though indicating that she could stand up to little more. 'The boarding-house is as pleasant an establishment as you'll find in the area,' replied Nurse Clock, thinking that a room might as well be earning rent. 'Nice people there are there, a mixture of sexes, most excellent food.' So eventually Mrs Corry, an admiral's widow down on her luck, had consented to make the move, but later Nurse Clock had returned to Mrs Corry and said she had decided against filling the room at the moment, and had seen Mrs Corry look sad.

In her sleep Nurse Clock snored, though only slightly. She woke herself and turned on her side. Below her Studdy snored loudly and did not wake; and across the landing from Studdy Miss Clerricot dreamed of another lunch with Mr Sellwood. 'Married?' Mr Sellwood was crying out, beaming with a smile. 'Who said I was married, my dear?' He spoke of banks again. Barclay's and Lloyd's and the National Provincial, and beneath the table his foot, by accident, lay lightly on the foot of Miss Clerricot dreaming.

Mr Obd had dropped into a light sleep from which every hour he recovered and rose to add a piece to his letter. Venables dreamed that the Queen had asked him to take Prince Charles to a cinema matinée. It was a pleasant dream, for usually he dreamed about the Flatrups, the mother and the father and the skinny body of the daughter which, twenty years ago now, he had been offered and had taken. The Flatrups led some scattered life, wandering from hotel to hotel where they were employed as a trio of kitchen staff. Old Mr Flatrup had written to Venables from many addresses, demanding fifty pounds for Miss Flatrup's abortion. In his dreams they descended on him with sharp instruments, shouting at him, swearing and blaspheming.

Rose Cave dreamed on about her mother. 'Your dad was a Mr Bird,' said her mother. 'That Mr Bird who died, whose funeral you went to, my dear, to whose wreaths you contributed two shillings. Didn't I ever tell you, he came to paper an upstairs room and laid me down instead?'

Major Eccles felt the linoleum cold beneath his feet and padded across it, forgetting about his slippers, to make the journey to the lavatory. He flushed it loudly and on the way back banged with force on Mr Scribbin's door. The roar of the doubled-chimneyed *Lord Faringdon* ceased abruptly, bringing to a halt an evening express en route from Peterborough North to King's Cross.

At three o'clock that morning Mr Obd, rising for the fifth time to add more to his letter, imagined he heard a sound and cocked his ear to catch it better. He thought he heard the dragging noise that Mr Bird used in his lifetime to make with his deformed foot: a soft noise it was, as the foot moved from step to step on the stairs. He listened again and imagined he heard it anew, and thought, as well, that he heard a kind of laugh, a suppressed thing, like the guilty snigger of a child in a classroom. Then he shook his head and went about his task, for he knew full well that Mr Bird, foot and all, was dead and buried and could hardly be dragging his way about the house or sniggering peculiarly in the middle of the night.

7

'Well,' said Nurse Clock, 'arrangements must be made, you know.'

If I had a pin, thought Studdy, I would sink it into your knee. He thought rhetorically: he knew that the pin was still in the point of his left lapel.

'So much to do,' went on Nurse Clock. 'What do you think, then?'

Studdy could feel his feet moving in his shoes. He located a hole in one of his socks and made a note to cut his toenails later that day. He said: 'I do not know what to think.'

Nurse Clock was conscious of a short spasm of irritation. She smiled agreeably. 'We need to have a chat,' she said. 'So much to discuss.'

Studdy did not reply. Nurse Clock had caught him on the way out. He was anxious to be on the move, to take up his stance opposite Mrs Maylam's flat and await the arrival of Mrs Rush.

'To tell the truth, I'm in a desperate hurry, missus.' Studdy spoke cheekily, knowing she wouldn't care to be addressed in this way. Realizing all that, she smiled again.

'We had better make an appointment in that case,' she said. 'We can't let the residents down, you know. A house like this takes running.'

'What?' asked Studdy.

'We must pull together, Mr Studdy, and sink our past differences. What do you say to that? Mr Bird made us into a team.'

Studdy winced. Deliberately obtuse, he said: 'Mr Bird is dead.'

'Indeed he is. And buried too. "You have nursed me sweetly," he remarked, and set out to join his Maker. I say "set out", for he paused en route to call back. "Lay your cool hand on my forehead," said Mr Bird in a failing voice; and off he went, carrying the mark of my palm to the kingdom beyond. It was the most touching moment in my life, Mr Studdy, though I have seen the hand of death stretched out a thousand times.'

'I am sure you have, missus.'

'Mr Studdy, I wish you not to call me missus. I am not married, as you full well know, nor ever have been.'

'Pardon, Nurse Clock. I thought you had married a man in the nineteen-thirties.' Studdy watched her face. He was given to saying most things that came into his mind to see if they caused a reaction. 'I thought I heard that said in the neighbourhood.'

'You never heard that said in the neighbourhood. You know that well.'

'A case of mistaken identity in that case. I am thinking of some other nurse.'

'You are forgiven, Mr Studdy.' She spoke merrily, playing a cheerful part, baring her teeth again. '"See they wash my body," said Mr Bird, "and shave my poor old cheeks. It is terrible to see a dirty man in a coffin." Well, of course I had his wishes met with. Naturally I am more used than most to last-minute requests. You know old Bishop Hode has passed along ?'

'Outside ? Gone walking, do you mean ?'

'Mr Studdy, you're a scream! We're going to get on like a house on fire, you and I. Bishop Hode gave up the ghost at eleven o'clock last night. I was called out for the occasion.'

'I never knew the Bishop.'

'Nor ever will! When they're beyond their ninetieth year there's not much point to anything. Bishop Hode used to spend the major part of his day in the airing cupboard.'

Studdy knew that. He knew that old Bishop Hode, who had lived alone with only a charwoman to tend him, had developed in later life the odd habit of locking himself up in his airing cupboard. It was something that had interested Studdy very much; he had often thought of writing to him.

'I heard tell of the Bishop. I heard tell a funny thing or two.'

'Funny?'

Studdy wagged his head, indicating that what he had heard was extraordinary, even sinister. 'The rumour had it that the old lad climbed into the cupboard to escape the woman who came with a syringe for his legs.'

He examined her face closely. He imagined he could detect a flush. Have I caught her on a raw spot? he wondered; and pen and paper immediately took form in his mind.

'The Bishop had to have his injections,' said Nurse Clock. 'He was under the doctor, with the strictest instructions about leg injections. He'd be alive now – oh, Mr Studdy, I'd been meaning to have a word with you: I understand you gave Mrs Maylam a potato.'

'I often do a message for the old lady.'

'You gave her a potato to wear on a string round her waist. As some kind of protection against rheumatism.'

'God, is that the time? Well, cheerio now, missus –'

'Mr Studdy, I asked you a question.'

'Sure, what harm does it do the old soul? What harm could a simple spud –'

'I have my duty, Mr Studdy. You are leading the old woman on with superstitious nonsense. It is a matter I intend to take up with Doctor.'

Studdy said nothing. He buttoned the bottom button of his overcoat and passed a hand over his face, feeling its features with thumb and forefinger.

'I shall be seeing Doctor this very morning.'

Studdy held his nose by the tip and drew his breath hard through his nostrils. This was quite noisy. Nurse Clock shivered; she had seen and heard him up to that kind of thing before.

'I shall be seeing him,' she repeated, 'and I feel it my bounden duty to pass on the information –'

'Doctor's a great fellow,' said Studdy, wagging his head in admiration. He did not know which doctor she was referring to, and he knew that she knew he did not know, and he knew that his casual reference to an anonymous medical man would irritate her beyond measure.

'He will not stand for interference with his patients,' Nurse Clock warned sharply. 'There is no doubt in my mind that he will have that potato in the dustbin in a trice. Mrs Maylam could lose her life with this kind of carry-on. If she's to continue to be mobile she must take those injections. You know that, Mr Studdy.'

'Sure, the poor soul –'

'She was smoking a cigarette the other day. I'm to understand you gave her that too. D'you want to slaughter her?'

'You're very hard on that old lady. Sure, what harm does a gasper do her? The woman's in pain, Nurse.'

'That is the precise point. Cigarettes and potatoes will hardly cure the pain, now will they? Whereas medical attention –'

'Mrs Maylam doesn't eat the potato, you know. Did you think she ate the raw potato? It's threaded on to a string and must be kept against the flesh. A very well known cure for rheumatics. I'm surprised you hadn't heard of it.'

'There's not much you don't hear of in my profession, Mr Studdy. Potatoes on string, badger's oil, rhubarb – there's not a quack cure I haven't heard of.'

Nurse Clock talked on, about the cures that people performed or failed to perform on themselves and on others, and Studdy did not listen. He was aware of the woman less than two feet away from him, her voice droning, rising and falling to denote amazement and incredulity at the folly of her fellows. He could have reached out now and sunk the pin into the thick fat of her knee where it glowed palely within the black stocking. He could have caressed the knee and taken even greater liberties. It seemed to Studdy that whichever action he might choose to perform in terms of the nurse's knee she would not in this particular moment notice it. And as she talked on, he too became engrossed in his own way. They sat opposite one another in the television lounge, two presences sharply opposed and yet for the moment oblivious of that opposition, oblivious of almost everything except what separately occupied their minds. Nurse Clock spoke of an onion cure for deafness and of an old man who had poured this boiling broth into his wife's ears and had later come up for manslaughter. Studdy thought about what Major Eele had said the night before concerning Miss Clerricot and her reactions to Mrs le Tor. He had observed Miss Clerricot that morning at breakfast and he thought he had detected a certain uneasiness in her manner. He thought she had seemed on edge, moving about on her chair rather a lot. As she rose to go she had upset something and had not noticed. If it hadn't been for his prior engagement with Mrs Rush, he would have followed Miss Clerricot to her place of work and kept an eye on her movements at lunchtime and at five-thirty. Studdy sighed. It was all very difficult: sometimes it seemed to him that none of it was worth it, writing endless letters, tramping along the streets and hanging about in doorways. Only once in a lifetime did one really do well, like the time a man in South Wimbledon had given him a present of sixteen pounds. But that was that, and Studdy knew better than to tap the same source again: people got hysterical when you went too far. He had even heard of people who had gone to the police.

'I knew a man who ate tar,' Nurse Clock was saying, and something that she had said a moment ago sprang to life in Studdy's ear. 'There's not much you don't hear of in my profession, Mr Studdy.' Studdy leaned back, his fingers probing at the orifices on his face, touching his teeth and gums, moving up towards the nostrils. He thought: Nurses get into people's houses. Nurses sit at bedsides and hear things said in delirium. Nurses make tea in the kitchens of the crippled and the elderly. They poke about in drawers and in tin boxes full of string and letters. Nurses are often confidantes; they hear family secrets; they bend their ears low for the final words of dying men and dying women. They are in at childbirth if they wish to be. They hear a mother's guilt as she moans in labour, and between the bouts they collect a little meat, a fact or two of interest. Nurses attend to people in a weakened condition. Nurses can sell little services, can stop clocks and weather glasses and offer to have them speedily repaired. Nurses can say that new sponges are essential in the bathroom, that a little electric fire would cheer a bedroom. Nurses can tot up a bill for such errands at the end of a long month and hand it sweetly over, deploring the rise in prices. Studdy raised his eyes to Nurse Clock's face. Teeth were showing, an eye winked to emphasize a point. Nurse Clock was talking to the air, chatting away about cases she had known.

He could see her doing it well, handing out a bill and gossiping on, her gaze fixed on a corner of the room, a smile deployed over the lower area of her face. Excitement seized Studdy. He felt a breath of heat form on the back of his neck and then increase, spreading into his scalp. He felt warmth in his stomach, and then a trembling there. There was sweat on the palms of his hands.

'By dad, Nurse, you've convinced me,' he said. 'Will I tell you where I'm going to this instant minute ?'

Nurse Clock, considerably surprised by this *volte-face* on the part of her partner and adversary, requested that she might be told.

'I'm going down to Mrs Maylam's to release her of that potato. D'you know what it is, she might lie on that thing in her sleep and do herself no good at all.'

Studdy departed, and Nurse Clock sat alone for a moment. Mr Bird's will had been far from precise. Over a period, she imagined, it would not be difficult to pick a hole or two in it. It would be nice to bundle Studdy off somewhere and eventually to turn the place into a chic home for the aged.

8

Studdy stood in a doorway waiting for the grey Morris Minor of Mrs Rush. He passed the time with a matchstick, breaking it in half, breaking the two pieces again, mashing it up in his fingers until it was a mass of grey shreds.

Studdy took a second match from his box. It was not of the sort called safety matches: it was short, with a pink tip that could be struck on any material that would create friction with it. 'The smoker's match,' said Studdy to himself, quoting words he had seen on the side of a bus. He wondered what it meant, saying a match was a smoker's match. He wondered if it was supposed to light cigarettes better.

Studdy inserted the match into his mouth, holding it by its pink tip. He began on the lower jaw, working from tooth to tooth, clearing out lodged food from gaps and crevices. His roving tongue picked up the particles.

As he was lifting a fresh match from the box he observed Nurse Clock approaching slowly on her bicycle. He swore quietly: he guessed she was coming to visit Mrs Maylam. Hastily he turned up his coat collar and lifted a hand to shield his face, pretending he was lighting a cigarette. He watched her out of the corner of his right eye. She brought her bicycle to a halt, propped it against the curb, looked around her, noticed him immediately and waved cheerily. Studdy did not respond. For a moment he thought that this was perhaps a mistake, that she would now be doubtful as to the identity of the crouching man and might cross the road to sort matters out. Fortunately, she did not seem interested. She unstrapped her black nurse's bag from the carrier of her bicycle and without further ado entered the large red-brick building that contained Mrs Maylam's two rooms. A moment later Mrs Rush's grey Morris Minor drew up, neatly hemming in Nurse Clock's bicycle.

'It is my bounden duty,' said Nurse Clock, a smile radiant upon her face, her small fingers busy within her nurse's bag.

The floor creaked as she crossed it, and the noise caused Mrs Maylam to shift her gaze from the nurse's face to the black stockinged calves that traversed her worn carpet and were attached to the instruments of the disturbance. 'It is my bounden duty,' repeated Nurse Clock 'to see that you achieve the goal that He has set you. Remember, dear, it is His life. Not yours, nor mine; ours but to rent, ours but to borrow –'

Mrs Maylam emitted a cry, and accused the nurse of being mentally deficient. But Nurse Clock only laughed, implying a kindly scorn thrown upon the old woman's words.

Mrs Maylam laughed too, joining her laughter to Nurse Clock's; then, ceasing it with abruptness, she snapped:

'I am up to your tricks.'

'Tricks, dear?'

'Remember old Mrs Fishon?'

'Yes, dear, I remember Mrs Fishon.'

'She died intact at one-oh-one.'

'She died in her sleep, Mrs Maylam. A peaceful death. 'Twas better that way. Her mind, you know.'

'Her mind was as sound as yours. You could not break her spirit.'

'Now, death is worrying you, Mrs Maylam. You have lost your family and we must see that all that does not cause you fret. Try to be cheerful, my dear.'

Mrs Maylam was silent for a moment and then broke into swearing. Finally she said:

'Take that morbid nurse's chatter elsewhere. Frig off, Nurse Clock.'

In silence Nurse Clock walked to the window, having taken small offence and wishing to display it. But the scene she saw in the street below cheered her enormously and held her entranced.

Janice Rush, who had been Janice Brownlow, the belle of many a flannel dance, was middle-aged now, forty-four and a bit. Her face had lines, not many but clearly the precursors of many. The skin of her neck bore a goose-flesh look, though only when the light fell directly upon it. Her husband, Martin Henry Rush, had married her nineteen years ago, one hot day in August in the church of St Cyril, the church of a south-western suburb. The Reverend Hamblin had conducted the service and a Mr Pryse, St Cyril's official organist, had played *Jesu, Joy of Man's Desiring* as she walked up the aisle on her father's arm. Janice Rush thought constantly about the occasion: she had a thing about her wedding day.

Studdy knew nothing of this. He saw a woman leave the driver's seat of the car and approach the front of it. He saw her fiddling with the catch of the bonnet as though not quite sure how it operated.

Disturbed by the arrival of Studdy's letter and its consequent preying on her mind, Janice Rush thought about her wedding day as she stood by the prow of her car seeking to release a catch. It was a memory that had never ceased to comfort her: she liked to think of herself then, that day at the altar of St Cyril's and later on the lawn of the hotel, because she saw the occasion as the ultimate blooming of her innocence and the end of her girlish optimism; she saw it decorated with the lupins that had just reached their greatest beauty in the flower-beds, and her happiest memory was one in which she stood against the lupins, at her mother's request, while a bearded photographer captured the image from many angles. Later that day, when Janice and Martin Henry were in an aeroplane, the lupins began to wilt and by the following morning were well past their prime. For Janice the process was longer drawn-out; but she knew quite soon that she had lived until her wedding day and had then begun to die.

On that day Janice had shaken hands in the sunshine on the hotel lawn; she had listened to the speeches and with the help of her spouse had cut into the wedding cake. On the hotel lawn she walked and talked and glanced about her. She had noted the colours and patterns of satins and silks. She saw and recognized women like sandcastles, simple monolith shapes with grey hair dyed blue or severely waved. She saw herself as one of these when the years took hold of her, and vowed, as she stood, that the years instead must wreck her, must pull the flesh from her bones and leave her like a rake. Better, she thought, to seem like a rake than to be built up into the sloop of a sandcastle.

She released the catch of the bonnet and lifted the thing up, balancing it on a metal rod attached for that purpose. She peered at the machinery of the engine, not understanding anything of it, wondering what would happen now. She remembered, as often she did, that in church the Reverend Hamblin had looked tired and crumpled as he received their vows and she wondered if that had made a difference. She had thought at the time that his cheeks might have been shaven closer or might at least, to mark the moment, have received the razor at a later hour. She had counted rust marks on his surplice and had held that against him too. Janice Rush had never had a child, and for a long time now her marriage had been loveless.

Studdy threw away his match and walked slowly across the road. His eyes were on the woman and the open engine; he did not notice the man sitting in the seat beside the driver's seat.

'In trouble, missus?' Studdy said.

'No, no.' She looked at him quickly, feeling nervous. She began to tug at the metal rod that held the bonnet up.

'Mrs Rush née Brownlow, espoused to Martin Hen –'

The man from the car stood beside Studdy. He bent his hand into a fist and struck him hard on the side of the jaw. Studdy shivered. He was knocked off his balance but remained on his feet. He felt one of his teeth move.

The man, who was not Mrs Rush's husband, hit Studdy again, on just the same spot. Then he lifted his other fist, the left one, and punched at Studdy's nose. Mrs Rush dropped the bonnet of the car. She said 'Don't' once, in a weak voice, and then she climbed behind the steering wheel. 'Never try that again,' another voice said, speaking to Studdy, but Studdy could hardly hear it. He was aware of pounding in his ears. He thought there must be blood all over his face: he thought his eyes must be covered in it. A stone seemed to have found its way into his mouth. Muzzily, he imagined that the man had hit him and then put a small stone in his mouth. He spat it out and did not look to see that it was the major part of a tooth.

The engine of the Morris Minor gave a quick roar and the car sped away. Mrs Rush changed from second to third gear without glancing at the man beside her. She should have said thank you, because it was she who would have suffered. She said nothing at all. She felt heat soak through the flesh of her body, seeming as if it had been generated within her. She knew she had been weak and afraid: how much better it would have been to refuse to pay the man money and let him simply do his worst. The car crossed the Thames, moving east, heading for the centre of the city.

For Studdy, bewildered on the pavement, the adventure was over; the Mrs Rush who had offered him a fifty-fifty chance of financial betterment, or so it had seemed, passed for ever from his life. All he had ever known about her was that she had once a week carried a tray of cooked food to Mrs Maylam and that the old woman had regularly complained of its quality. It was true that Studdy would have relished knowing more, a few more details of a practical nature, but beyond that he would never have cared much. It was Mr Bird, that tireless collector of people, who would have been moved by the condition of Janice Rush at forty-four.

Studdy lay on the uncomfortable horsehair sofa in Mrs Maylam's sitting-room.

'Open your mouth,' commanded Nurse Clock. 'Shall I call a policeman?'

He opened his mouth and then tried to speak, to prevent the police from coming, but Nurse Clock had put a pair of tweezers in his mouth and was feeling around. She took them out and Studdy said:

'The fellow tried to put a stone down my throat.'

'A stone? Are you sure? Did you swallow that stone, Mr Studdy?'

Studdy said he had spat it out. 'He's been in a rough and tumble,' said Mrs Maylam.

'The nose is all in order. You're lucky, Mr Studdy. A blow like that could have deformed you for life. Damage to the bone; I've seen it happen. You lost half a molar.'

'A molar? Half a –'

'Half a back tooth, Mr Studdy, right in the back, downstairs: you can feel with your fingers.'

Studdy felt with his fingers and found the sharp edges where a piece of the tooth had come away.

'Have the root out,' advised Nurse Clock. 'Don't go hanging on to that thing. That tooth was cracked before the accident. A blow on the cheek could never break up a tooth.'

Nurse Clock was dabbing about on Studdy's face with a piece of cotton wool. She wiped away the dried blood beneath his nostrils.

'Fighting like a mad thing,' said Mrs Maylam.

Studdy felt a heaving in his stomach. He asked Nurse Clock to cork up one of her bottles because the smell was upsetting him.

'There now,' said Nurse Clock.

Already the shame of the whole undignified incident was beginning to bite into his soul. He tried to sit up. He saw Nurse Clock's face beaming close to his. He felt her hand restraining him.

'Extraordinary,' said Nurse Clock. 'In broad daylight.'

'They were after the wallet.' He patted the area of his clothes where his wallet found a home. 'I beat them off.'

Nurse Clock, who had watched the whole incident from Mrs Maylam's window, was surprised to hear this lie. She wondered why he should not say what had happened: that he had spoken to a woman in trouble with a motor-car and that another man had struck him.

'Did they get nothing at all?' she enquired, enjoying herself.

Studdy reached into one of his trouser pockets and brought out a handful of coins. He counted them. He said:

'I'm short a sixpence. They had a tanner off me.'

Nurse Clock soothed him. She said he must lie still for another few minutes as she feared unfortunate after-effects. 'May I make a cup of tea, Mrs Maylam?'

'I'm all right,' said Studdy.

Mrs Maylam said: 'You can't watch them,' and Nurse Clock went into the kitchen to make tea.

Of Studdy Mr Bird had written:

S. J. Studdy (53) answered an advertisement in the *Evening Standard* in 1952. He came without baggage, though he has seemingly acquired baggage since. He is a species of petty criminal, with his hair-oil everywhere and his great red face. Yet how can one not extend the hand of pity towards him? Anyone can see that poor old Studdy never had a friend in his life.

'A nice cup of tea,' said Nurse Clock.

Studdy took the cup from her hands and sipped at the scalding, buff-coloured beverage.

'Now that Mr Studdy is here,' said Nurse Clock, 'we can talk about the old potato.'

'Shocking,' said Mrs Maylam. 'Mr Studdy's at death's door.'

He began to blow at the surface of the tea. He blew too hard and the tea spattered the skirt of Nurse Clock's uniform. She saw it happening and looked at him sharply. She turned to Mrs Maylam and said:

'Mrs Maylam, Mr Studdy came to realize the uselessness of that potato you wear. He says there's no point to it at all. Mr Studdy's made a mistake.'

'What?' asked Mrs Maylam.

'There's no possible point to the potato around your waist. So Mr Studdy was telling me. It's a big mistake.'

'The potato's a cure. For me. Injections is a thing of the past, Nurse.'

'Mr Studdy made an error. Mr Studdy, tell Mrs Maylam.'

'Well, the fact is now –'

'That potato is an aid to me, Mr Studdy. I'll swear that to Christ.'

Nurse Clock shook her head. She said: 'No, Mrs Maylam dear.'

'I haven't felt better in the length of my life. These old bones are hopping me round like a two-year-old.'

'Well, the fact is,' explained Studdy, 'that what Nurse says isn't far wrong. I'm only afraid you'll lie flat on the potato and it'll stick into your flesh, maybe damage an organ. D'you know what I mean, missus?'

'You told me bind the potato there, Mr Studdy. Your lips said the words. Fix a peeled potato on a length of string, you said it clear as day. I'm ninety next spring, Mr Studdy, remember that.'

'That's it,' said Studdy. 'That very consideration. Will we take the potato away and have done with it? You might crack a rib with it. I wouldn't like to be held responsible. Nurse says the Medical Council maybe will get after me, to do a thing like that, crack the ribs of an old lady. D'you follow me?'

'I do not,' said Mrs Maylam. 'How could the potato crack a rib? That's a lot of bloody mularkey, Mr Studdy.'

'You hear these things,' said Nurse Clock. 'A woman in Kew died with a magnet in her bed, put there to rid her of the cramp.'

'Is that so?' said Studdy, finishing his tea and swinging his two legs from the sofa to the floor. 'Mrs Maylam, did you hear that? A woman with a magnet in the bed with her.'

'Ho, ho,' cried Mrs Maylam, laughing loudly at some private joke.

'That potato is sour and bad,' Nurse Clock said to Studdy. 'She's had it there a fortnight.' She raised her voice. 'It's dirty having a potato on your body day and night.'

'I wouldn't mind a bit of dirt if it's a certain cure. If it's dirt that's worrying you, don't waste your time with it. My stomach's ingrained, as well you know. Am I embarrassing Mr Studdy?'

The conversation continued. Studdy was interested in Nurse Clock's story about the woman who had died with the magnet in her bed. He questioned the accuracy of this, seeking details. Mrs Maylam relapsed into a world of her own, not answering questions, refusing to discuss the matter of the potato further.

'Workers' Playtime,' said Mrs Maylam after a time. 'Put on that wireless, Mr Studdy, like a good old warrior.'

Studdy rose from the sofa. His overcoat was unbuttoned

and the belt hung loosely by his sides. He twisted the knobs on the wireless and in a moment the room was filled with the noise of applause and laughter. Mrs Maylam threw back her head and laughed heartily herself.

9

Major Eele had once been married. Ten years ago, when he was fifty-nine, he had met a woman called Mrs Andrews at a party given in a hotel in Amesbury. 'Who is this sleeping soldier?' he had heard a voice cry, for he had fallen asleep in an arm-chair, and then had felt a pressure on his head which turned out to be Mrs Andrews' hand. The courtship was brief, and in retrospect a totally inexplicable turn of events. The marriage itself lasted only the extent of the honeymoon.

'I have come again,' said Mrs le Tor, and immediately Major Eele thought of Mrs Andrews. The two women spoke alike, he thought: they had the same intonation, the same way of placing their words in a certain order.

'Mrs le Tor,' said Major Eele, about to leave the house, en route for a West End film, *Hot Hours*. 'I fear you are out of luck today. There is hardly anyone in the place just now. A bad time of day, the afternoon. Only Studdy and I are usually about, and Studdy is taking it easy. Surprisingly, he was involved in a brawl.'

'Heavens!' said Mrs le Tor, interested.

'Ruffians, it seems, attacked the man in the full light of day, while Studdy was simply going about his business. In confidence, though, there is more to this than meets the eye.'

Mrs le Tor was wearing her white gloves and a carefully ironed white blouse. On top she wore a coat and skirt of what the manufacturers called petal green. Her finger-nails were burnished and made to seem pink. They were long and pointed, like the finger-nails of Mrs Andrews, who had protested often lest he in passion should damage one. The Major smiled, wondering if Mrs le Tor would protest likewise. She said:

'I do not think I met this Studdy. What an odd name! Is he the boots?'

Major Eele giggled to himself, savouring this misconception and thinking how best to release it in the television lounge that evening, perhaps embroidering a bit. 'Mrs le Tor thought Studdy was the bootman and Nurse Clock a tweeny.' He laughed aloud.

'Alas, Mrs le Tor, I must inform you that we have no boots here. Boots are tended to by the residents themselves. There is no molly-coddling in our boarding-house.'

'Do you mean that all those people, men and women, polish and keep in trim their own footwear?'

'That is so, Mrs le Tor.'

At this point it seemed as if the conversation would come to a halt unless it were at once rekindled. Smiles were exchanged. Major Eele, the time of his cinema performance harping on his mind, made a motion to descend the steps that led from the front door. Mrs le Tor fell into step with him.

'Which way are you walking, Major Eele? It seems my journey has been a fruitless one.'

The Major thought: She intends to accompany me. That will be awkward, sitting down beside the woman for *Hot Hours*.

'I am walking to the West End,' he said.

'But Major dear, that is eight miles.'

'I generally take a bus the last bit.' He did not care for the way in which the woman had seen fit to address him. He remembered Mrs Andrews' hand upon his head, how he had woken up to find it there, hearing her cry: 'Who is this sleeping soldier?'

'What a lovely day,' remarked Mrs le Tor, and the Major thought that the time had come to be direct. He stopped abruptly, while she continued to walk on a pace or two. She turned to face him, her eyebrows raised.

'Madam,' said Major Eele, speaking with deliberate clarity, 'I must inform you that I am not in the market.'

'Oh,' said Mrs le Tor. 'What market is that?'

'I am not in the market for what you are offering this afternoon. I am on my way to an art film; my time is limited. Excuse me, madam, you are not my sort.'

Mrs le Tor, who had been married twice and had in her

lifetime suffered many a setback and many a fright, looked hard at the man who claimed to have been a military major. She wondered for a moment if this boarding-house might not be an asylum for the mentally deprived. She had received two letters, one with the offer of a donkey carved in bog-oak, the other incomprehensible. Now there was this man in a summer hat saying he was not her sort, exclaiming that he was not in the market.

'There is some misunderstanding,' said Mrs le Tor, feeling the words to be weak, unable to think of better words or words more suited to her bewilderment.

'No misunderstanding,' cried Major Eele, striding off. 'Bye-bye, Mrs le Tor.'

'Oh, no, Major, do not go. You have not explained. I think it is my due, an explanation, some little explanation –'

'I would wish you to leave me, madam. I wish to be on my own. Try other houses this afternoon. There are many others in Jubilee Road. A warm day like this –'

The situation now was that Mrs le Tor had laid her right hand on Major Eele's arm and was restraining his forward movement. She interrupted his reference to the prevailing weather by ejaculating incomprehensibly.

'Unhand me, madam,' cried the Major, having always wished to use the expression. 'Unhand me,' he repeated. 'Leave me be.'

The sun was shining brightly. The sky, pale blue, was clear of clouds. That afternoon in London the swimming pools were crowded.

Mrs le Tor, grasping the material of Major Eele's jacket, spoke again. Her teeth flashed in the strong sunlight, glistening, close to his face. He heard her voice and saw the bright red lips open and close, keeping a kind of time with it. He did not know what she said.

As he stood on the pavement, frightening pieces of his disastrous marriage surfaced and clogged together. Pictures invaded his mind, and he had not the power to prevent them.

In a cinema that Mrs Andrews had taken him to a woman had objected to the fumes from his pipe. In Dickens and Jones he was asked again to put out his pipe and was abused by a woman whose stocking, she said, he had damaged with his foot. An altercation had arisen between them, and when Mrs Andrews had returned from the knitwear department the woman was loudly demanding money and people were looking at Major Eele. He, having forgotten the rule, was lighting his pipe again. 'No smoking,' cried an official person in black. 'What has happened?' asked Mrs Andrews, then Mrs Eele, but never seeming so to the Major, who thought of her still as Mrs Andrews, who had never used her Christian name, although she had told him that it was Grace. 'What's up?' said Mrs Andrews, puzzled by the scene. 'He kicked me,' said the woman with the damaged stocking. 'Nonsense,' said Mrs. Andrews. 'My dear, give her ten shillings.' But he was unwilling to give the woman ten shillings and indignant at being accused of kicking. 'Settle this, please, on the street,' said the official person, shooing them off in a bunch, as though the incident were a private disagreement that they had chosen to act out in the store. 'The stockings cost sixteen and eleven,' said the woman, and Mrs Andrews gave her a pound and did not ask for change. 'Watch where you put your feet,' she said to her husband as she marched him off. 'I do so hate embarrassment.'

The pictures were like nightmare flashes. At the social occasions beloved by Mrs Andrews, tall women in horn-rimmed spectacles spilled their cocktails over his clothes and did not apologize. In a cellar in Chelsea that Mrs Andrews said was a Portuguese restaurant he had spat a forkful of food on to the floor. Afterwards he explained that something had moved in his mouth. 'You have a prejudice against eating in restaurants,' accused Mrs Andrews. 'This menu is famed all over London.' But Major Eele had been adamant. 'I will not eat live food,' he said.

He was new to London in those days, and he had not liked it. He had not cared for the intensity of the traffic, or the underground trains that were full of a human smell and of people who lit up tipped cigarettes and pushed with their elbows. When the honeymoon was over and the marriage had collapsed he returned to the country, but later, when he retired, he came to live in the boarding-house. He had given up smoking his pipe and had developed interests that were metropolitan.

'My husband,' Mrs Andrews was saying, introducing him to a barman in the Berkeley. 'What will you have, my dear?' 'What was the stuff I had last night?' 'Sherry, my dear?' But he said it wasn't sherry, but something coloured red. A discussion followed, a fruitless one in a way because what he wished to make clear was that he did not care to have the red drink again. 'It gave me diarrhoea,' he told the barman, and Mrs Andrews laughed loudly and said in jest that he should not use that word in mixed company.

Major Eele shuddered.

'Are you well?' asked Mrs le Tor. 'You are not acting well.'

Mrs Andrews has disguised herself, thought Major Eele, looking at her; and then he remembered that this was Mrs le Tor, a local tart.

'I am not up to anything today,' said Major Eele, greatly debilitated by the memories of Mrs Andrews. He had married her because of a single urge. 'My dear, I've just had my hair done,' Mrs Andrews had been wont to say at night. Major Eele shuddered.

'You've had a seizure,' said Mrs le Tor. 'Can I get you a glass of water? It's this heat.'

Major Eele shook his head.

'Shall we return to your nice boarding-house and I'll rustle you up a cup of tea. There's nothing so good as a cup of tea –'

He could not struggle against the hand on his arm and the relentless driving voice. 'I am going to the cinema. I'm sorry, I have very little money just now.'

'You poor dear man. Here, let me lend you a pound. Come now, take a pound and you shall pay me back when funds have looked up.'

'I do not want a pound. Why should I take a pound from a strange woman? Why are you pressing all this on me?'

'I am only trying to help you, Major Eele.'

'I am on my way to a cinema. I'm sorry, but I don't at all want any help. I do not wish to take your money or your help. I came to the door of the house, about to leave it and you were there. You have attached yourself like a barnacle to me, though I have made it clear I do not require your services. Bye-bye, Mrs le Tor.'

'Oh, Major Eele, you have had a seizure. You have had a seizure here on the street and I held you up. I assure you you are not fit to walk eight miles. But please yourself, for goodness' sake. You have been rather rude, you know.'

'I apologize –'

'Why say I attached myself like a barnacle to you? I did no such thing. I wished only to discuss a letter I had received which seemed to refer to my visit to your boarding-house. I am not used to receiving anonymous letters.'

She pushed the letter at him and he took it and examined it.

Dear Mrs le Tor,
I put it to you...

He read the letter, and it dawned on him then, for a reason he could not fathom, that Mrs le Tor was a genuine and respectable woman. 'Good God,' said Major Eele aloud, thinking of the words he had used to this woman, how he had drawn her attention to his lack of money, how he had advised her to ply her trade at the doors of other houses in the road. He had said that she had clung to him like a barnacle.

'I have never heard of the boarding-house or of the dead Mr Bird,' said Mrs le Tor. 'And then I came and met you all, to try and find an explanation. And then this other letter. And then I meet you and you are rude. Are you the guilty one, Major Eele? Is this a play of yours?'

'No, I am not the guilty one, and I must tender my apologies: I fear I have laboured beneath a misconception. I took you to be otherwise than what you clearly are. I find myself greatly embarrassed, Mrs le Tor. I can only bid you good day.'

The Major was not at all himself. The images of life with Mrs Andrews, the hot sun striking mercilessly at his back while he stood and talked, the woman's face with its glistening teeth: all these combined with the awkwardness he felt to make him feel, as well as awkward, distressed.

'I am worried about you. Can I let you walk away into the

sun, eight miles on your feet on an afternoon like this? You are not a young man now, Major Eele.'

He had found a pair of socks, long after he and Mrs Andrews had broken up, a pair of socks marked with Mrs Andrews' previous husband's name. It had hurt him, even then, that she had taken it upon herself to add to his wardrobe in this way, thinking he would never notice.

'Will you have tea with me one day?' he asked Mrs le Tor. He spoke impulsively but he uttered the words deliberately, standing straight and firm on the pavement. 'One day next week.' And he mentioned the name of a tea-shop in a near-by high street.

'Well, that is kind –'

'I cannot offer you tea today, because I am otherwise engaged. But I would deem it an honour, and more than an honour, if you would join me next week. It is something I would quite look forward to. We can discuss those letters. I feel sure we shall arrive at an explanation.'

She is finer looking than Mrs Andrews, he thought; she has better bones, and more calf to her leg.

He has asked me to tea because I said he was not a young man, thought Mrs le Tor: how sweet!

'Let us say that then,' said Major Eele, inwardly complimenting himself on his keen politeness. I would quite fancy this one, he thought; I would fancy her more than Andrews in her time.

'How kind,' murmured Mrs le Tor.

The arrangements were made and the two parted, with many assurances on Major Eele's part that he was in good health, and had never had a seizure in his life.

Dalliance, though Major Eele, in a new mood: no need to get caught up, no need for wedding bells. He remembered again the socks that had once been the property of Mr Andrews; he remembered the moment he had lifted them from a drawer and pulled the two socks apart and noticed the name-tape. He could quite see her coming across them somewhere in her flat and putting them with his things, not thinking he would mind even if he did notice.

'Holy gun,' said Major Eele as he walked down Jubilee Road, 'there was a woman for you.' On that last night, that tenth night, he believed she had made an attempt on his life. It was never easy in her flat to get a plate of food, and on this particular night, he insisting that he would eat at home, she prepared for him a repast which she had discovered in a tin, left behind, as afterwards she confessed, by previous tenants. Shortly after midnight he awoke with an ache in his stomach. He tried to wake Mrs Andrews to tell her, but she, who had already explained that she had had her hair done, rejected him with an expression that was new to him. He lay in the dark, thinking; and then, at three o'clock, he sat upright and put on the light. He filled his pipe and struck a number of matches before it got going. 'What the hell is this?' asked Mrs Andrews, waking in discomfort and fumbling beneath her body. 'For God's sake, there are used matches in the bed.' He explained that he had a pain in his stomach and had thought a smoke might ease it. 'A smoke? For God's sake, take a look at the state of my sheets.' An early morning quarrel had ensued, in the course of which Mrs Andrews, wishing to cause him concern, had confessed that the food she had given him that night had been in fact a cat's preparation. He had leapt from the bed then and dragged on his clothes, and had later quit the flat for ever.

Major Eele walked slowly, though he knew that the slower he walked the sooner he would have to take a bus. In the distance he could hear the noise of traffic, coming from an area that was more used by motor-cars and lorries and buses. It was quiet where he walked; no sound came from the open windows of houses: children were having their afternoon sleep, mothers were resting. In one house only in Jubilee Road a lover came to visit his housewife mistress. He let himself into the house without a sound, and when the two met they spoke in whispers, for somehow it was that kind of afternoon, an afternoon that was full of silence, with only Major Eele abroad.

In his *Notes on Residents* Mr Bird had written:

Major Eeele (69) came to me only seven years ago. He had had the misfortune to embark upon a marriage with a woman of forty-odd years, a marriage of which he has repeated to me various yarns. Major Eeele is greatly given to chat, but like most of the people here he is not always accurate. After all, I am not always accurate myself: inaccuracy is a symptom of our condition, I suppose, and I do not begrudge the old Major his little embroideries. Major Eeele has often dropped into conversation with me in the afternoon and referred to me as a man of the world. By this I deduce that he is seeking information. I have, in fact, engaged the Major upon a practical course of education in the hope that in the future he will leave me in peace, as I particularly dislike people coming to my door at all hours, though naturally I make a point of saying I do not mind. I would not like to have to ask the Major to move on.

'I would like to go into that bar in the Berkeley with Mrs le Tor upon my arm and look out for Mrs Andrews' face.' He said this aloud, and began to laugh at the thought of it: how now, ten years later, with his new sophistication, he would march up to the bar and order two Camparis, and carry them back to a little table where Mrs le Tor awaited him with a smile. She was a smart woman, he thought; a smarter woman than Mrs Andrews any day. There would be Mrs Andrews, perched on a high stool, up at the bar with no one to talk to except the barman, eating a little white onion. 'Heavens,' he would whisper to Mrs le Tor, 'd'you see that woman, the one with no calves to her legs? D'you know who that is? That's Mrs Andrews, one time a wife of mine.' Major Eele paused in his walking to survey the scene more closely. 'Why, Mrs Andrews, my old heart, what a thing this is, running into you here.' Again he spoke aloud, but nobody heard, for the pavement was still deserted in the heat of the day.

10

On chosen days the delivery vans of the big stores crept through the district of SW17, delivering almost anything that one could hope for: the green vans of Selfridge's, Barker's with stripes, Harrod's with a prominent coat of arms, by Royal Appointment. They carried assorted meats and clothes, groceries, furniture, hardware and haberdashery. They brought out specially, for long established customers, for the older families of the district and beyond it, special tins of smoking tobacco and special blends of tea, and free-range chickens already slaughtered. The men who drove them knew their way about and enjoyed that knowledge, because to them it was more interesting to know a bit about a place and to memorize certain weekly details. They knew where to leave their parcels if a house seemed empty: around the back as previously arranged a year or so ago and kept to as a rule ever since, or on a basement window-sill, or in a garden shed. The men who drove the vans could tell you a thing or two, but they probably never would, guarding their inside information because it was their business and not yours.

In the quiet roads, daily driving lessons took place. The men with the vans knew the instructors by sight and did not envy them their chore. They saw the cars with L plates and the notice of a motoring school crawl jaggedly from drive to avenue, from lane to crescent. Often, their goods delivered at a door, they paused to watch the practising of the reverse gear, cars going backwards round a corner, tyres rasping on the pavement edge.

At eleven o'clock every day, until the day he took to his ultimate bed, Mr Bird had banged the door of the boarding-house behind him and had set off to walk the neighbourhood for an hour. To the driving instructors and to the men of the delivery vans he had become a familiar figure, walking alone with his stick, moving slowly because of his size and his bad foot. Often they waved a hand at him and as often as they chose to do so he waved a hand back. 'A boarding-house keeper. Two Jubilee Road.' More than once one driving instructor had thus informed another. The men, who cleared the dustbins bade him good day as he passed, addressing him without much respect but without ill-will either. And the brothers of St Dominic's smiled at him, and received in turn their special due: a greater gesture, reserved for their cloth.

Mr Bird had come to know the pets of the area, the dogs and cats of Jubilee Road and Peterloo Avenue, of Mantle Lane, Crimea Road and Lisbon Drive, and of other places too. He knew the animals by sight and often paused to stroke them, though he was not himself an animal-lover and had never owned a pet of any kind. He knew which windows held goldfish in a tank or caged birds, canaries and budgerigars, a parrot that said its name was Hamish. He liked to see the brewery dray horses; unnecessary, he thought, in a mechanized age, yet pleasant to watch going by: some kind of publicity stunt, he reckoned. In Jubilee Road, by the front gate of number fourteen, there was a collection box built into the form of a large dog, with a notice on it that mentioned the National Society for the Prevention of Cruelty to Animals, and asked for alms. Mr Bird never dropped anything into it and wondered if anyone ever had. He had often thought that a suburban road seemed an unprofitable site for an artificial dog, begging.

In the mornings, when Mr Bird took his constitutional walk, Jubilee Road was at its quietest. Earlier, with people going to work, with bicycles and a few cars passing along, it had a small buzz. Women rubbed at brasses on hall-doors, someone might sweep a step; curtains were dragged back and roller blinds released with an early morning twang. But by eleven o'clock all that was over. Jets screamed above, but between their screams it was still and calm in Jubilee Road; except on Tuesdays, when the dustmen clattered and shouted out, and that was anyway later in the morning, nearer lunchtime.

Sometimes women, pushing prams or deep baskets on wheels for shopping, nodded to him when they met; children were heard, even by Mr Bird, to remark upon his limp or his slow progression, and mothers smiled more openly at him then, smiling their apology, trusting he understood. A few such women knew him by name and addressed him, remarking on the weather or the noise of the jets or something that might have occurred, like a road accident.

Major Eele, Studdy and Nurse Clock, the three residents who were regularly about in the mornings, had occasionally met him on the streets strolling along or leaving the shop where his habit it was to buy a tube of Rowntree's Gums, his favourite sweet. Nurse Clock's bicycle would carry her on her way, popping gently while she sat motionless on the saddle, only her lips at work, murmuring the verses of a hymn. She had had the engine added at Mr Bird's suggestion, for he often had noticed her labouring against a wind or up a long hill. It pleased him whenever he heard the familiar two-stroke tone and occasionally he would ask her about it and remind her to add, now and again, the necessary oil.

When Mr Bird died Studdy took to walking in the mornings as Mr Bird had walked, banging the door at eleven o'clock, buttoning his overcoat and doing up the belt as he passed down Jubilee Road. By nature, Studdy had never been a hard worker and it suited him well to slip into Mr Bird's role, venturing unhurriedly out at a set hour, saluting the dustmen and the van-drivers, saving a word for the brothers at St Dominic's and becoming familiar with the local pets. Studdy in time came to walk the roads and the avenues like a king, peeping at the windows, noticing everything. He felt that the area was his to know as Mr Bird had known it, with an intimacy that was reserved for those who were interested in the houses, who liked to watch and were curious.

But for some days after his altercation with the man in Mrs Rush's Morris Minor Studdy did not go walking, nor even appear in the public rooms at the boarding-house. Nurse Clock gave him codeine, warning him that the pain in his face would become intense if he did not dose himself regularly. 'A rest can do you no harm at all,' pronounced Nurse Clock, taking his wrist to feel his pulse and making him think of the pin in his lapel.

Studdy lay on his bed and did nothing. It was the first time that such a thing had happened, that a venture had resulted in so unfortunate an outcome. He saw that in future he would have to tread with greater care, yet he could not see that he had been foolish in any way. He had been quite subtle, he thought, asking the woman if she was having trouble with her car, as though he were about to help in a natural way, and then coming firmly to the point. In future he would have to see that men were not about, hiding in motor-cars or loitering near by.

Of late, Studdy had been observing Miss Clerricot and he greatly regretted this interruption, these three days hidden away on his own. Since the night Major Eele had passed on to him the information that she had been taken aback by the advent of Mrs le Tor in the television lounge, Miss Clerricot had been a source of mounting interest. Before his accident he had begun to watch her closely, and he thought he recognized a new liveliness about her eyes. 'That woman is up to something,' said Studdy to himself, and on the first day that he allowed himself to be seen in public again he pursued her to her place of work.

Studdy was used to following people about. Often on the street he would notice a man or a woman with a guilty look about the face and would follow his suspect for an hour or so, into shops, on to buses, sometimes to a distant suburb. Once he had followed a man who was acting in what he considered to be a dubious manner, sidling along close to shop-fronts, peeping around pillar-boxes, walking slowly and quickly in turn. This man, it had turned out, was himself following another man, and the three of them ended up sitting side by side in a news cinema.

Miss Clerricot turned into a large building, and Studdy remained outside. He stood about for a while, watching other employees arrive. A few of them looked at him, a notable figure on a hot August day: a man in an overcoat with the collar turned up, with a hat, and a scarf that obscured part of his chin. He kept looking at his watch as though waiting for someone, and after a few minutes he drank a cup of tea at a café near by. He paid for this with a two-shilling piece and questioned the change, stating at once that he had handed over half-a-crown. In the end the cup of tea, priced at sevenpence, cost Studdy a penny. 'Sorry about that,' he said as he left, and the girl behind the counter said not at all, it was her mistake. She seemed so sure that it was she who had been in error, and smiled so affably, that for a moment he considered trying the ploy again. He contented himself with commenting on the high quality of the tea, adding that he would certainly return one day. 'Always delighted,' said the girl, and Studdy left.

He walked for a while, piecing together a plan of campaign. At eleven-thirty he approached the reception area of the building that Miss Clerricot had entered. 'Have you got a Miss Clerricot at work here?' he questioned, taking care to keep his voice low in case the woman should suddenly appear.

'Certainly, sir,' the receptionist said briskly. 'You have an appointment?'

'No, no. No, I don't wish to see her today; it's just I was establishing her place of work.'

'Can I help you, sir?'

'Ah no. It's just a little surprise we're arranging for Miss Clerricot's birthday. D'you know what I mean?'

The woman behind the reception desk raised dark eyebrows and did not smile. She said she did not know what Studdy meant.

'Miss Clerricot passes out here at lunchtime, does she?'

'Why ever should she not?'

'No reason, missus –'

'Excuse me, sir, if you wish to see or speak to Miss Clerricot I can phone through. Otherwise –'

'Ah no. No, it's a little surprise we've all got together at her place of residence for Miss Clerricot's birthday. Only you see, I thought I'd come down here and see what the situation was. We're all going to be waiting for her outside the entrance there on the big day. In two taxi-cabs –'

'Well, that will be nice for Miss Clerricot. Now, sir ...'

Studdy saluted the woman, bringing his open hand smartly up to his forehead. He spent the rest of the morning watching the entrance from the other side of the street.

At one o'clock Miss Clerricot appeared, accompanied by a man of advanced middle age. The latter hailed a taxi. Studdy, with no means to follow them except by the hire of such a vehicle himself, watched the cab move off, mechanically noting its number. He crossed the street and inquired of the woman in the reception area if Miss Clerricot had left. 'I thought I had seen her,' he explained, 'only I wasn't sure. I called after the taxi-cab. Was that Sir John with her?'

'Sir John?'

'The gentleman who was with Miss Clerricot. I thought he looked like Sir John.'

'I'm sorry, sir, I know no Sir John.'

'Ah well, no, I'm not saying you do. Only that the gentleman with Miss Clerricot there –'

'That was Mr Sellwood, sir.'

'Sellwood. Mr Sellwood. Ah, of course it was. Good-bye now.'

Studdy hastened away.

'The Pearl Assurance Company,' said Mr Sellwood, 'has branches all over the country, yet its organization is extremely simple and extremely efficient.'

Miss Clerricot thought about that, but found it hard to formulate a reply. Then she said:

'I see.'

'Now, what will you take to eat? Minestrone soup, chicken *à la maison*? I shall take fish myself. With fresh garden peas and new potatoes. Yes, I think that should do. What do you say, Miss Clerricot? The chicken? Well, that is that, then. Melon? Good. Oh, they know what they're doing at the Pearl.'

For a moment there was a silence. Mr Sellwood was making a calculation in his head. Miss Clerricot had seen him making calculations like this on and off for twelve years. She watched him reach a final figure.

'Do you know how the Pearl Assurance Company works?' Mr Sellwood asked.

'You mean, how it plans its policies and decides on premiums?'

Mr Sellwood drove his fork deep into a slice of melon.

'Decides on premiums? I think, you know, that that is a secret thing. Yes, I rather think that that is a matter that is not revealed. Business is like that, you understand. One cannot give away secrets. Business is built upon the other chap not knowing. You see?'

Miss Clerricot was thinking of his life in Sevenoaks, trying to visualize it, seeing him in an arm-chair in a sitting-room, his wife in the same room sewing a piece of cloth, his two sons reading boys' magazines. She wondered what the family talked about: what Mrs Sellwood said to Mr Sellwood, what the boys said and what their interests were. She wondered whether the talk ever touched upon the Pearl Assurance Company.

'Yes,' she said. 'I follow you.'

'Private enterprise is like a military campaign.'

She imagined the two boys, years ago when they were small, hearing stories about private enterprises that were like military campaigns. Lloyd's and Barclay's, the Westminster and the Midland and the National Provincial. She had read somewhere recently that the National Provincial Sports Club had done well in a rowing competition. Perhaps that was something that the boys could join in about: perhaps they were interested in rowing and had followed the National Provincial to victory. She began to worry about the boys: what if they did not have a rowing interest, what then? How would they pass the hours and the years with their father out in Sevenoaks? How could a good relationship flourish?

'The Pearl Assurance Company,' said Mr Sellwood, 'has branches throughout the country, in the major provincial towns. The Company is well distributed.' He stopped and then continued: 'I have to go to Leeds next week. Perhaps you would care to come? The food is excellent in Leeds; there are numerous kinds of local dishes. What do you say, Miss Clerricot?'

She did not know what to say. She felt a voice in her mind, struggling to gain ascendancy, whispering hoarsely that she was a fool even to consider the proposition, even to be here having lunch with her employer. It was the dead, lugubrious voice of Mr Bird, bidding her to say no, quoting Pope at her.

'Oh, but,' said Miss Clerricot, pausing after the two words, hoping for an interruption. But Mr Sellwood was eating a trout, making faces as he disentangled the flesh from the bones. So she ate some fish herself and let the unfinished sentence hang limply in the air.

'Quite useful you'd be in Leeds,' said Mr Sellwood with a bone caught in his teeth. He gave a nervous laugh, reminding her of Venables. It wasn't fair, thought Miss Clerricot, to assume that the little bout of laughter was connected in any way with what he was saying. He was not, or so she assumed, laughing at the idea of her usefulness in Leeds. Later, over coffee, he said again:

'I think – I rather think, you know, that if you were to accompany me to Leeds, Miss Clerricot, you could be quite useful.'

Miss Clerricot became carried away. What does he mean by 'quite useful'? she wondered. He was asking her to go away with him to Leeds, for a night or two nights, she did not know which. She did not know what was in Mr Sellwood's mind, but she knew, or guessed, what was in his subconscious. It would not be; she could not ever let it be. She could never take a man from a wife and from a family: that was not her role. Yet Mr Sellwood had made the gesture; he had issued an invitation and she had never before in her whole long life received such an invitation, or indeed any invitation that was couched so subtly.

'I have made a study of the subject,' Mr Bird had said. 'I know what I am doing. I am open to criticism, that I admit, but at least I am abnormally honest.' Mr Bird said he had studied the condition of loneliness, looking at people who were solitary for one reason or another as though examining a thing or an insect beneath a microscope. The memory of Mr Bird was bitter at that moment, and the words he spoke in her mind were unwelcome there, for they were cruel in their wisdom.

'I have never been in Leeds,' said Miss Clerricot.

'Then you must join me next week. We can work together on the train.'

'Yes,' said Miss Clerricot.

'You ventured out?' enquired Nurse Clock, smiling. 'You're feeling OK, Mr Studdy?'

Studdy replied that he had never felt better.

'Well, I have had a field day,' Nurse Clock went on chattily. 'After my calls I set to tidying in Mr Bird's room.'

Studdy paused in the act of running his fingers over his bruised jowl. 'Tidying,' he said.

'Shoes and clothes for the refugees, old magazines, trousers' presses – you've never seen such a load. Gallelty and I tied cloths around our hair and did a great old turn-out.'

There were two suits of Mr Bird's that Studdy coveted; two worsted suits with stripes, and a couple of pairs of shoes in excellent condition. He had often noticed them on the living man and had recalled them afterwards. They would not fit Studdy himself, nor could he very well wear them here in the boarding-house, but he knew where he could dispose of such remains for a reasonable sum. He kept calm. He said:

'You've made a pile of the old stuff, have you? I can borrow you a hand-cart to transfer it to the refugee woman. You didn't burn anything? Some of those old mags might make a bit of interesting reading.'

'Magazines for the hospitals, Mr Studdy. I have the whole thing organized. Mrs Trine is calling round tonight for the clothes.'

Studdy nodded. He fingered the point of his lapel. He said:

'A decent woman, Mrs Trine. Excuse me now, Nurse.'

The time was five o'clock. The boarding-house was empty save for Nurse Clock, Studdy and the two in the kitchen. Studdy climbed to the top of the house and entered the attic room of the late Mr Bird. The bed was stacked with clothes: suits and socks, ties, shirts, underclothes. On the floor, magazines were tied into bundles. Seeing all this, Studdy swore savagely. He lit a cigarette to calm himself. Caught between the pages of an old *Wide World* en route for a hospital was Mr Bird's *Notes on Residents*.

Studdy sorted out the suits he required and looked about him for shoes. He found them, all with shoe-trees in them, in a large cardboard box. He tucked three pairs under his arm, picked up two suits still on their coat-hangers, a few pairs of socks and four shirts. He walked with care to his room.

He wrapped the clothes in sheets of newspaper and packed them into the back of his wardrobe. He put the shoes in one of the drawers of his dressing-table. Then he lay down on his bed for a moment, to think about the problem of replacing their bulk in Mr Bird's room. It took him fourteen minutes to arrive at what appeared to be a workable solution.

Mr Scribbin had always seemed to Studdy to be a man who possessed a variety of clothes. Nurse Clock, he felt sure, had not made an inventory: it would be necessary only to add a couple of Mr Scribbin's shirts and a suit to give the impression that the stack on Mr Bird's bed had not depreciated.

Mr Scribbin's room was on the same floor as Studdy's. He crossed the landing to it, treading softly. He knocked in case the man should be inside, but received no response. He turned the door-handle and entered. The room was neat. The big gramophone was mounted on a stand close to the window, records were ranked in racks on either side of it. On the walls were many unframed photographs of railway engines. Studdy had never been in this room before; he found it interesting, but he moved at once towards the wardrobe, intent upon his task.

He chose a long blue suit with a white stripe, that seemed in need of sundry small repairs. Studdy wondered if Mrs Trine attended to such details before forwarding the clothes to the refguees. He selected two shirts, and as an afterthought slipped into Venables' room for a pair of socks and three ties. It took him less than a minute to transfer everything to Mr Bird's room and to pick up some magazines. He stretched himself on his bed and read a *Picturegoer* that had been issued in February 1937.

II

'I shall be away next Tuesday night,' said Miss Clerricot. 'Possibly Wednesday too. I am going to Leeds on business.'

Studdy's self-trained ear caught the statement, and his brain absorbed it with excitement. 'Leeds, by dad,' he murmured to himself.

'Well, that will make a break for you,' he heard Nurse Clock say, and then he coughed and descended the stairs.

'Miss Clerricot's going to Leeds on Tuesday,' said Nurse Clock. 'I'm saying that will make a break for her.'

Studdy smiled lazily. 'A fine city,' he said. 'Better than many another. Happy times, Miss Clerricot.'

Miss Clerricot, he noticed, had gone the colour of a cut beetroot.

'I have never been to Leeds,' she said, and gripped the banister and ascended the stairs at speed.

From the television lounge came the sound of loud voices and the occasional chuckle from Major Eele. The door was half open: Studdy could see Mr Obd in his shirt-sleeves and Rose Cave knitting a length of grey wool into a rectangle.

'A nice cream from top to bottom,' said Nurse Clock.

Studdy was no longer looking at the half-open door of the television lounge; he was running the thumb-nail of his right hand beneath a finger-nail of his left. He shifted a small wedge of dirt which in turn became lodged behind the thumb-nail. He removed it from this latter with the little finger of his right hand.

'A nice cream,' repeated Nurse Clock, watching the grime move from finger to finger.

'Cream?' said Studdy.

'I'm saying we should have the place done up, painted out a nice clean colour. You understand me?'

'That would cost a fortune. Sure, the old place –'

'Now, now, Mr Studdy.'

'Ah, I'm only too pleased to meet you half way. I'm an obliging man, Nurse Clock. Only is there enough in the till for that kind of thing? I mean, we'd have to be careful now. No good trying to run before we can walk.'

'We have a spare room now, Mr Studdy.'

'We must consider that.'

'We'll burn a candle in there tomorrow; it's the thing to do after a death; a fumigating candle to clear the air. Then a woman can scrub the place out. In no time at all it'll be a comfy little den again.'

'We might let it for a trifle more, after the trouble you're going to. Isn't it only fair to rent it at a price that covers the cost of candles and that?'

'To be honest with you, I thought we'd let it to some poor soul, some case maybe I'd meet on my rounds.'

Hearing this, Studdy became at once alarmed. Nurse Clock, it seemed, was bent upon turning the place into a charitable institution. He questioned her at once.

'We would take a fair rent,' explained Nurse Clock. 'I am not trying to be unbusinesslike. We would charge what you and I deemed to be a fair and reasonable sum. All I am saying, Mr Studdy, is that the room would make a happy place for some poor soul.'

'There's people I know myself,' said Studdy, 'who would be glad of it. I must make a few enquiries.'

Nurse Clock, seeing awkwardness ahead, smiled to ease it away. She said, still smiling:

'We must be careful not to let it in two different directions. Imagine you bringing up one of your cronies one night and finding some poor soul in bed there already!'

She implied a picture of Studdy, surrounded by good friends in a congenial setting, suddenly turning to one who was looking for new lodgings and generously offering what he had at hand. Her subtlety was lost on him; he said that that would never do and agreed that such a contretemps must be indeed avoided.

'You must meet all sorts,' he said.

'Indeed I do. All sorts and every sort. Nursing is a varied life, and the nurse on the bike gets all that's going.'

'Rich and poor,' said Studdy. 'The elderly?'

'Oh, many an elderly folk.'

'Are a lot of them helpless? Tied to their beds, is that it?'

'Not all that should be. You'd be surprised to see how many get up when they should be seeing their lives out on their backs.'

'You have a hard time of it, Nurse, dealing with all that kind of thing.'

Nurse Clock replied that this was her vocation, that she had agreed to the work voluntarily.

'You do a lot outside your duty, do you? Making a cup of tea in the kitchen, drying dishes and that? I've heard tell from Mrs Maylam.'

'One does one's small best, Mr Studdy.'

It surprised Nurse Clock that Studdy had apparently developed an interest in the nursing profession. She listened to him, wondering about it.

'Do you ever do a bit of spring cleaning at all? I'm thinking I could give you a hand. You know, I like a bit of charitable work. Like I call round now and again to sit with Mrs Maylam.'

Nurse Clock decided to say nothing. She smiled, giving him a chance to go on.

'You must come across a lot of old treasures. Things in drawers. Photographs. Letters. Isn't it surprising the way people store things up? D'you ever think that?'

With truth, Nurse Clock said she didn't know what to think.

'Well, be seeing you, Nurse.' He drew himself up, saluting her. She thought he was probably out of his wits, wearing that heavy coat in a temperature like this, saying he liked charitable work.

In the television lounge Mr Obd watched a man with a long bow launching arrows at a girl who held balloons in her mouth. Since none of the arrows missed the balloons, Major Eele said it was a put-up job. Music played, and the audience applauded. Rose Cave counted the grey stitches of her knitting.

'Now we have cyclists,' said Mr Scribbin, reading the details in the *Radio Times*. He nodded at Venables. 'Cyclists', he repeated.

Major Eele said:

'Has anyone ever come across a woman called Hammond who performs with a flock of waltzing birds?'

Nobody had. Mr Obd changed the channel on the television set. A handsome man was drilling a hole in a road. Seeing the camera turned upon him, he laid the drill aside and spoke of the breakfast that his wife had earlier prepared for him. He smiled and returned to work.

'What has it to do with fixing our roads?' Major Eele asked, and again nobody could supply him with an answer. He was a little on edge. He had felt that inviting Mrs le Tor to tea was the least he could do, since he had behaved so badly towards her: now he was not so sure that he had not made a mistake. He felt a little spasm of anger at his own folly, and then felt something else: a touch of excitement and a small offering to his pride.

'Hammond, like the organ?' enquired Rose Cave, remembering that no one had answered the question and thinking that it was perhaps unkind to show no interest at all.

Venables was watching the television screen. He quite enjoyed the advertisements, especially the dashing ones about cigarettes and pipe tobacco. He tried not to think about what was uppermost in his mind: that the boarding-house might close now that Nurse Clock and Studdy were running it. He did not like the prospect of making a change. He had been before in a house where young men from an estate office had poured golden syrup on the handle of his door every Saturday night; he had had to leave another place because the landlady, drunken one day, had struck him on the head with a soup-spoon. Venables thought that somehow or other Nurse Clock and Studdy were bound to fall out. What would happen then? A prick of pain came in his stomach, low down, on the left.

'Just like the organ,' said Major Eele. 'An American lady. She does the most remarkable things. I think I am right in saying that she organizes the birds to storm and capture a castle.'

'A castle?' asked Mr Scribbin, suddenly interested. 'You don't mean a real castle?'

'There's a ventriloquist next,' said Mr Obd, referring to the television.

'You changed the channel,' said Major Eele. 'Just when our interest is whetted Sambo changes the channel.'

'Major Eele!' Rose Cave spoke loudly, feeling outraged and making that clear. 'Major Eele, you cannot say that.'

'Why not? The channel has been changed. Why can't I say that? Just when our interest has been whetted –'

'Major Eele, you cannot address Mr Obd in that way.'

'I did not address him. I said he had changed the channel. One minute we are looking at trick cyclists and next it is an advertisement for a plateful of breakfast food.'

'I changed back,' Mr Obd explained. He did not much mind how Major Eele referred to him. He was used to Major Eele by now; he did not expect too much and he did not receive it. He was trying hard to be cheerful, flashing his smile about, turning the television switches. That same afternoon he had bought a dozen roses and carried them to the flat of Annabel Tonks, but when he rang the bell there was no reply and once again he had been obliged to lay them on the doorstep with the letter he had already prepared.

'You cannot call Mr Obd names.'

Mr Obd looked at the carpet. The pile had been worn flat. Like the wallpaper in the hall, the pattern had almost disappeared; the overall effect was a stained and dingy brown.

'Sorry, there,' said Major Eele.

Mr Obd shrugged, smiling slightly at the carpet, noting that one of the larger stains looked like a can-can dancer. Mr Bird had written of him at length:

Tome Obd (44) came to London twenty-five years ago, a fresh-faced Nigerian seeking to discover the secret of our legal systems and to return a knowledge king to his native soil. Well, it was not to be. Mr Obd studied the law assiduously but could make no impression on the examiners at his college. Over many years he attempted the course set for him but was finally obliged to sever his academic ambitions for ever. He had left his country with a promise on his lips, and without having attained the machinery with which he might fulfil it he had not the heart to return. I believe I correctly deduce when I state that Tome Obd was smitten by shame. He felt the dishonour of returning empty-tongued too great. He would settle in England, he said, and wrote to his family that he was already a successful lawyer. What excuse he gave them I cannot fathom, except perhaps that he may have spoken of his new sophisticated ways, of his fear that such ways were not the ways of Africa; or perhaps he had said that already he was wedded to a white girl who would not easily be received by the home community. Whatever the truth is, Tome Obd made his peace as best he could and took on clerkly employment, perforce rejecting the allowance that his family had set aside for his long education. Who knows, these simple people may have worked themselves to their Nigerian bones, saving and scraping for the youth who would be a lawyer. Who can blame Tome Obd for not returning?

Eleven years ago, in 1953, a place was found for Mr Obd in my boarding-house by a certain Miss Tonks. This lady, unknown to me until I heard her voice, telephoned to inquire after a room for a friend, giving Mr Obd's case as I have given it above. I was at once suspicious. I did not care for this voice on the telephone, nor was I certain where it was that she had heard about us. A boarding-house proprietor cannot be too careful; one never knows what people will try to turn the place into, and I confess that my immediate reaction was that naturally I did not wish to have anyone black about the place. For some time past such elements had been infiltrating the neighbourhood and I had always been staunch in my disapproval, though I am not of course in any way a public man. My inclination, on hearing the request of Miss Tonks presented in terms that were clearly employed to appeal to my better nature and in accents that certified Miss Tonks as a one-time inhabitant of an urban settlement in the Midlands, was to refuse peremptorily to have further dealings with her. That, I say, was my inclination. But I was touched, or must have been touched, by some detail that this lady had revealed in passing. In retrospect, I can do no better than to suggest that it may have had to do with a reference to Mr Obd's interest in the game of table-tennis, a sport of which, if Miss Tonks' story is to be believed, he had never wholly mastered the rules. The image of Tome Obd darting about at one end of a ping-pong table, striking back the little white ball, clearly went to my heart. Perhaps the confusion that I sensed in the man's mind touched me and moved me to listen further to the now irrepressible Miss Tonks. I use the word 'confusion' advisedly; for what can the man have felt, this stranger to our country, to find himself taken up by women from Birmingham or thereabouts and placed at one end of a table and told to hit over a stretched net a light ball of an inch and a quarter in diameter? Must he not have wondered at the reason for this ceremony? Must he not surely have been puzzled by the loud cries that greeted each of his muffed attempts, at the numbers that were called out, and at the eventful news that once again victory had eluded him? Did he know what victory they spoke of? Did he perhaps not think to himself that this was some kind of scorn poured upon his colour, that the game was a chastisement of the African soul?

Be all that as it may, the fact remains that I said to Miss Tonks on the telephone: 'Send your Mr Obd round.'

'Welcome to our shores, Mr Obd,' I said. I stretched out a hand. I addressed him in this way, with a welcome, because I saw it as the polite thing to do. I knew he had been in England for many years now, yet something told me, I think, that no one had ever put into words that simple sentiment.

I am sorry to say that Mr Tome Obd did not acknowledge my greeting. He did not smile graciously; he did not show gratitude through the medium of speech. Instead he said, as though it were the simplest matter in the world:

'I am told that surely you have a room.'

This odd piece of language construction was given no questioning tone. It was present to me as a statement. I said nothing.

'I am informed from a reliable quarter,' continued Mr Tome Obd.

I looked stern. I observed Mr Obd. His ebony face seemed strange and immensely remote in my small room. I said quietly:

'I am always glad to welcome an imperial cousin.'

'An imperial cousin?' He questioned me as though I spoke in a mysterious way, as though he did not understand our language. I said, more slowly:

'There is no skin prejudice in this house.'

He, as though repetition were his forte, repeated the words.

'Skin prejudice?'

'But I must add,' I said, 'that those who come here are recommended from the highest sources. I confess it straight away, Mr Obd, we have had foreigners here in the past. Ambassadors of foreign powers are not unknown in the precincts of the boarding-house, nor are the world's potentates, oilmen, religious leaders, mystics, men of politics, men of royal blood. The four winds have swept the great and the little, the good and the evil, into our midst here in the boarding-house –'

'Precincts?' queried Mr Obd.

'That is difficult to explain,' I said. 'Where were you at school, Mr Obd?'

Thus we went on for some time, for I delight myself by talking in this manner. I drew useful information from Mr Obd, and in the end I offered him a room, planning in my mind to ask a Miss Bedge to vacate hers. I had always looked upon Miss Bedge as a stopgap, and I was not displeased at an opportunity to move her on. In the meanwhile, I impressed upon Mr Obd that there were full toilet and washing facilities in my boarding-house, and there and then pointed out the lavatories and bathrooms to him. After all, one is never quite certain of the habits obtaining in these far-off parts. To drive my point home, I remarked quietly as I pulled one of the w.c. chains: 'When in Rome do as the Romans do, eh?'

I said no more to Mr Obd that day except to explain that I had once held a post in the travel business and was thus conversant with the many appeals of his country.

He came a fortnight later and has been with me ever since. His face has grown more dismal over the years, and he has never done much, nor said much, except to write lengthy letters to that same Miss Tonks, many of which I have perused in an unfinished state in his room. He is fighting a losing battle, only he will not see it, and of course has mentioned nothing of this to me. I feel immediately downcast when I meet him, and offer when I can a word or two of gloomy sympathy. I fear he is heading for disaster.

'You don't mean a real castle?' Mr Scribbin asked again, leaning forward in his chair, sloping his narrow back towards Major Eele, who said: 'A model castle, I think. Though for all I know it may have been otherwise.'

'There was a film recently,' said Venables, 'in which the birds took over.'

Major Eele thought that it need not be a lengthy business: he would sit down to tea with her in the Cadena and leave after nine or ten minutes, claiming another appointment.

'Mrs Hammond's birds?' he said. 'Mrs Hammond's birds took over, did they? Well, that doesn't surprise me in the least.'

Venables felt the warm blanket of pain beginning in earnest in his stomach. Sweat broke on his forehead. 'Birds of the air,' he said. 'Just any birds. Nothing to do with Mrs Hammond. Just all the birds – the birds of the air.'

'Untrained birds?' asked Major Eele. 'How very odd. Are you sure you have got your facts right, Venables?'

'I think it was trick photography. The birds attacked people. It was really rather too much.' Venables sat still and was aware of his stomach moving. There was a sourness down there and the ache spread from his lower abdomen up to the base of his lungs. He had never been able to face the prospect of going to a doctor. He thought of long hospital trolleys and white-masked men and sharp young nurses in starched linen. He saw a blade cutting through his flesh, and the steel instruments entering the delicate passages of his tubes.

Major Eele said: 'Not parakeets? I think Mrs Hammond operates with parakeets.'

'Parakeets?' repeated Mr Scribbin.

'They are birds, Scribbin, a breed of bird.'

'I know ...' Mr Scribbin was becoming intrigued by the picture of trained parakeets storming and capturing a castle under the guidance of Mrs Hammond of America. He wished to show he understood what parakeets were, and then to ask a few more questions of Major Eele since Major Eele knew about the matter. But Major Eele interrupted him, speaking to Venables.

'Are you sure it was trick photography? It could not have been some other kind of trick? Mrs Hammond's parakeets, for instance, disguised as day-to-day birds – seagulls, crows, pigeons, what-have-you? Could it have been that, Venables?'

Venables said he didn't know, and Major Eele sighed, and Mr Scribbin began again.

Rose Cave knitted on, occasionally glancing at the television screen, occasionally saying something. It was warm in the room, and rather gloomy. Long curtains held out the daylight, hanging from brass rods. There were three windows in the television lounge and thirty yards of net curtain. As well, there were other curtains, drapes of brown velvet that were there for conventional decoration and could not, in fact, be pulled to. When the electric light was put on roller blinds were used to prevent people from seeing in.

Rose Cave had become used to the appearance of this room, although it was not an appearance that she herself, given a free hand, would have favoured. When first she had come to the boarding-house she had noticed things in the room: the Wedgwood plates on the walls, the pottery ornaments, the ash-trays made into the shapes of other objects and those that once had been sea-shells. There was a stuffed woodpecker in a glass case and a heavy writing-desk that nobody ever used, that was covered with travel literature. She had noticed the coloured antimacassars, the chipped grained paint of the skirting-boards and the window-frames, the flowered dado that ran around the four walls, high up, about ten feet from the ground. Almost everything in the room, except the travel literature, dated back to the time before Mr Bird had inherited the boarding-house. The wallpaper and the paint had remained unchanged for forty-three years; the arrangement on the mantelshelf of four china mermaids, an ebony elephant, a clock, two ashtrays shaped like boats, two brass vases and sundry smaller details had altered little in the same span of time. Mr Bird had seen no reason for change; he had been the most conservative of men.

'I remember as a child,' said Mr Scribbin, 'being brought to see an exhibition of performing fish.'

Rose Cave, her fingers moving fast, the grey wool coagulating and taking useful form, remembered how she and her mother had cycled from Ewell to Dorking one Sunday afternoon during the war. They had made the journey to see some exhibition, though not of performing fish. Why, she wondered, had Mr Scribbin said that about fish, and then it came back to her that previously the men had been speaking of performing birds, and there was of course an obvious connexion. She remembered now, the other exhibition had been one of flower arrangements from Japan. 'Look,' her mother had said, reading a notice from a local paper, 'there is an exhibition of Japanese flower arrangements in Dorking on Sunday.' They had filled a thermos flask with tea and wrapped up sandwiches and scones and put a little milk in a blue Milk of Magnesia bottle, and had set off on their bicycles. Ten miles: it had taken them hours.

'Scribbin is on about fish now,' Major Eele remarked. 'Has

anyone ever seen a film in which the fish take over? Whales and haddock waddling through the land, shellfish in the ears of kings and emperors?'

Venables did not reply, although the Major was looking at him, expecting some reply, expecting a conversation.

'It is quite a theme,' said Mr Scribbin.

Venables, his stomach quietening down, could feel the beginning of a laugh. He made an effort to control it.

'What?' asked Major Eele.

'The fish taking over, like Mr Venables' birds.'

'Look out for the Rainbow Men,' warned a gay voice from the television set.

'Ha, ha,' said Venables, and Major Eele asked him what the matter was.

'Cocoa,' said Gallelty at the door, standing with cups on a tray and cocoa in a jug. There was a mixture of biscuits, a few of them iced but the majority rather plain.

Rose Cave put her knitting needles aside, stuck them into the knitted piece and then into the ball of grey wool. She took a cup and saucer from the tray.

'Who else?' said Gallelty.

They drank a cup each and ate a few biscuits; and one by one they went to bed.

12

'I suppose you can go in and out of a house without anyone bothering?' said Studdy. 'A nurse would have keys to places? It must be that fascinating.' He wagged his head, suggesting an inner marvelling at the work she did.

'It is a coincidence that we are both so fond of the aged,' said Nurse Clock. 'That gives us something in common.'

'Oh, definitely it does.'

'Funny, really, that both of us should have met up over Mrs Maylam. Do you read to her at all? I have a few books that might interest her –'

'Ah, to tell the truth, I don't read much to the old lady. The occasional devotional extract, nothing exciting. No, I'm more useful making a cup of tea or frying a chop – the practical man.'

'We have stymied Mr Bird,' said Nurse Clock. 'Are you aware of that?'

Studdy lit a cigarette from the remains of his previous one.

'What d'you mean?'

She watched him trying to press the cigarette stub into the carpet in a clandestine manner and immediately drew his attention to it. She said:

'Mr Bird thought to spread disaffection and anger. He thought that you and I would fight like cat and dog, Mr Studdy, and that all in the boarding-house would suffer in the encounter. Mr Bird was a man of bitterness.'

'Glory be to God,' said Studdy. The hatred was still there between them, but it no longer raged; it was no longer on the brink of violence, because something stronger, something like self-interest or greed or small ambition, had put it into its proper place.

They looked at one another, their eyes meeting for once, and they recognized the hatred they had shelved away, and between them was the feeling of Mr Bird's miscalculation.

'Those are my clothes,' said Mr Scribbin.

Mrs Trine and Nurse Clock paused to look at him.

'What are you doing,' demanded Mr Scribbin, 'taking away my clothes?'

Mrs Trine glanced at Nurse Clock, suspecting something, thinking that Nurse Clock in her zeal had taken the law into her own hands. But Nurse Clock said:

'These are the clothes of Mr Bird. They were left behind by Mr Bird in his room. How could they be yours, Mr Scribbin?'

'That is my suit.' Mr Scribbin had seized a trouser-leg and tugged it. Some of the clothes fell from Mrs Trine's arms.

'Oh, Mr Scribbin, Mr Scribbin.' Nurse Clock was angry, down on her hands and knees sorting out the confusion of the floor. She felt embarrassed that Mr Scribbin had behaved like this in front of Mrs Trine, in the hall of the boarding-house. She wondered if Mr Scribbin went in for necrogenic excitement; she had heard before of people who are interested in the clothes of the newly dead. 'You've had your gift from Mr Bird,' she reminded him. She turned to Mrs Trine. 'Mr Scribbin got left a lovely little ormolu clock.' This in fact was not strictly accurate. The clock that had come into Mr Scribbin's possession was a large black object built in the shape of a temple, with an inscription on a brass plaque that read: *To Charles Edward Burrows on the occasion of his retirement, from his friends at Walter and Peacock. February 24th, 1931.*

Mr Scribbin had a narrow tuft of moustache, a ragged, though noticeable, addition to his upper lip. The shape of his jaw was narrow too, so that his teeth protruded in an acute semicircle. To counteract the effect, the moustache might better have served its purpose had it been grown in a more profuse and extended way, but nobody had ever told Mr Scribbin this, and he, having cultivated it, had not thought of experimenting. On his head his hair grew ragged too, difficult to manage, inclined from an early age to stick out at the sides and on the crown. All this gave Mr Scribbin an untidy appearance, although in fact he was a tidy man in other ways.

'My shirts. Those are my shirts. Nurse Clock, what on earth is going on ? Why is this lady taking away my clothes ?'

'I have told you already, Mr Scribbin. These clothes were the property of Mr Bird and are now the property of Mr Studdy and myself, who have between us deemed it right that they should be handed over to the refugees.'

'To refugees ?'

'We send them all over the world,' said Mrs Trine. 'To the East and to Africa; to Europe, South America and the Middle East. The situation is bad in the Middle East.'

'I did not say, Nurse Clock, that my clothes could be sent away. Why do you keep talking about Mr Bird ? I did not give Mr Bird my clothes. Mr Bird did not own the clothes of everyone in the boarding-house. You have socks here belonging to Venables. Look, it says so. T. O. Venables. Just as mine say J. Scribbin.'

'Good God,' said Nurse Clock.

'There has been some error, has there ?' Mrs Trine enquired, trying to keep cheerful. She had driven over specially for these clothes, and now apparently they were the clothes of living people in the boarding-house. Mrs Trine said to herself that Nurse Clock was unreliable.

Nurse Clock was thinking that any moment now the hall would fill with residents, wondering about the commotion. They would all pick clothes from the pile in Mrs Trine's arms and the scene would resemble a draper's shop. She felt considerably embarrassed and she thought of a similar moment, in the Lord-Bloods' basement flat, when Mrs Cheek had thrown the pot of jam and the Indian had complained about the noise.

'I do not know what to say,' said Nurse Clock. 'Something has gone wrong.'

'Did we pick up the wrong pile ?' asked Mrs Trine. 'Are these for dispatch to the laundry or the cleaners ?'

'My shirts are clean,' cried Mr Scribbin, holding them to his chest. 'My shirts do not require the laundry. What is she talking about ?'

A scene then took place. Major Eele, a man with a feeling for all trouble, appeared in the middle of things. Behind him Nurse Clock could see Miss Clerricot in the television lounge and a little beyond her Mr Obd. Mr Obd was doing something that had never been done before: he was sitting at the large writing-desk with an open fountain pen in his hand. There was no paper on the writing-desk; the pen was poised in the air; Mr Obd's head was at an angle, his eyes aimed upward, indicative of thought.

'Your shirts are clean?' said Major Eele. 'Clean?'

The garments that Mrs Trine had been holding were now on the hall table. Owing to Mr Scribbin's continued interference they were in some disarray. Coat-hangers had become displaced; sleeves hung down, collars were twisted this way and that.

'What's this?' asked Major Eele, picking up something that had been in fact Mr Bird's.

Nurse Clock took it from his hand, saying it was a medical thing.

'What's going on?' said Major Eele, a smile touching his lips, looking at neither Nurse Clock nor Mr Scribbin nor Mrs Trine but at the clothes on the marble-topped table. 'Is somebody buying second-hand clothes?'

Mrs Trine began to explain, saying that she represented a refugee organization. She said that she had called around for the clothes of Mr Bird and that some mistake had happened.

'I have various things,' said Major Eele. 'Ties I have never used, underclothes, a pair of plus-fours. How about that, madam? Can I interest you? Shall I fetch what I have to offer?'

'Mrs Trine, this is Major Eele,' said Nurse Clock. She was looking through the clothes, trying to establish what belonged to whom. Mr Scribbin had taken his things. She laid aside the ties and socks of Venables and a glove that seemed to be a female glove. She still felt acutely awkward.

'How kind,' said Mrs Trine, speaking to Major Eele, employing a smile she reserved for such occasions.

Major Eele went quickly off. Nurse Clock said:

'I am so sorry about this. I really cannot think what has happened.'

She could not think how it had come about that the clothes which she had cleared from Mr Bird's room had become confused with the clothes of Venables and Mr Scribbin. She herself had sorted everything out: she had placed the suits and the shirts and the other things on the bed while Gallelty had cleaned around her, mopping the floor with Ajax and hot water.

'Venables,' called Mr Scribbin at the door of the television lounge, 'they are taking away your clothes.'

Mr Obd, whose pen was no longer poised but who still sat at the writing-desk, heard the reedy voice of Mr Scribbin call out to Venables that his clothes were being taken away. Rose Cave heard the same, and Miss Clerricot and Venables himself. It was an unusual thing for them to hear at this time of night in the boarding-house, or at any time. They came to attention; they raised their heads to listen further; Venables rose and walked across the room and entered the hall.

'What?' said Venables.

'There are socks and ties of yours,' said Mr Scribbin, 'that this lady was about to make off with to the Middle East. There was a suit of mine too, and a couple of pairs of shirts. It is all in the name of charity, but you may not wish to give socks and ties to the Middle East.'

'How about these?' cried Major Eele, arriving out of breath, bearing another armful of clothes, more than he had said he had gone to fetch. He placed them on top of the pile on the table and held them up one by one.

'Whatever is going on?' asked Venables.

Mr Obd had come to the door of the television lounge and was watching the happenings in the hall. 'Everyone is bringing clothes,' he reported to Miss Clerricot and Rose Cave. 'The hall is full of clothes.'

Miss Clerricot and Rose Cave joined him at the door. Venables was rooting through the pile, looking for his property.

'That is my glove,' said Miss Clerricot, seeing the grey glove laid aside on the marble-topped table.

'Any good?' asked Major Eele, holding up a pair of plus-fours.

Nurse Clock clapped her hands.

'There has been a mistake. Somehow or other a few articles of clothing have got mixed up with Mr Bird's old clothes which Mrs Trine was kindly taking away for the refugees. No one knows how it has happened. Well, we must not worry. Major Eele, let us just sort out what is what before you add your offering. Mr Scribbin, you have what is yours?'

But Mr Scribbin said he did not know. What he held in his arms, he explained, was his, but he did not know if other clothes had been taken from his room or how often Mrs Trine had previously called at the boarding-house.

'This was a good pressed suit,' he complained, displaying the limpness of the material he held.

'Any good?' asked Major Eele, holding up a handful of ties. 'I haven't worn them once. They would cut quite a dash.'

Nurse Clock had collected together a pile that seemed indubitably to have been Mr Bird's. 'Nothing here is yours, Mr Scribbin.'

Mr Scribbin nodded.

'And Mrs Trine has never before been here, so nothing else can possibly have gone the way of the refugees. Mr Venables, are you content too?'

Venables shrugged; then thinking that that was ungracious, smiled.

'Now, Mrs Trine,' said Major Eele, 'how much for this?'

Major Eele was again displaying his plus-fours. They had braces attached and seemed in good condition.

Mrs Trine laughed. She thought it best to laugh, feeling a little at sea, not knowing whether the Major was being playful.

Nurse Clock knew he was not being playful. She said: 'Mrs Trine is collecting for the refugees of the world, Major. She is not paying for our clothes.'

'Who is paying then? Isn't Mrs Trine authorized to name a price?'

'The clothes are a gift. We are giving them to the clothesless in the Middle East. This is an act of charity.'

Major Eele laughed sharply.

'*I* am not giving my clothes away,' he said. 'Come now, Mrs Trine, these are first-class garments. The ties have never been worn, the trousers only once or twice.'

'The lady has come to buy old clothes,' said Mr Obd, still standing at the door of the television lounge.

'No, no, no,' cried Rose Cave, for Mr Obd was already mounting the stairs to his room.

'Why is my glove there ?' Miss Clerricot asked again.

Rose Cave perceived that Mrs Trine had come for Mr Bird's clothes and would convey them to the refugees. She saw that in some way Mr Bird's clothes had become confused with other clothes in the boarding-house, and that Major Eele had misunderstood the situation and was now offering his wardrobe on a commercial basis. She knew about Miss Clerricot's glove because she herself had earlier found it on the floor of the hall and had placed it on the table.

'I am so sorry,' she said now, 'I had meant to tell you. I imagined it must be yours. What has happened is that the clothes were placed on top of it.'

Miss Clerricot stepped forward and received her glove.

'Fifty shillings,' said Major Eele.

Nurse Clock looked harshly at him. She had found a piece of string in the pocket of her skirt and was tying the bundle together.

'I have had these since first I came to England,' said Mr Obd at the bottom of the stairs. 'The material is most excellent. It has been in moth-balls.'

Mr Obd stood in his tribal robes. They were white, with decorations stitched in red and black. He held up his arms to display the large quantity of material involved.

'Bravo! Bravo!' cried Major Eele.

Nurse Clock had tied the bundle and had placed a hand on Mrs Trine's arm, about to propel her to the door.

'They will be most welcome, those robes,' Mrs Trine said. She spoke in a low voice, addressing the observation to Nurse Clock, feeling that Nurse Clock should know what was in her mind before she made it public, since it was Nurse Clock's boarding-house.

'Are you giving them to the refugees?' Nurse Clock asked Mr Obd.

Mr Obd slipped the robes over his head and stood in trousers and shirt.

'I thought the lady was buying clothes. But the refugees may have them. They are no use to me.'

'Mr Obd has pieces of bone for the nose,' said Major Eele. 'Very valuable.'

Mr Scribbin uttered a cry. He approached the bound bundle in Mrs Trine's arms and pulled out a shirt.

'Another shirt,' he cried.

The string broke and the clothes descended to the floor. Major Eele, overcome by the drama of the situation, threw up his hands, releasing his plus-fours and his ties.

'Wrap everything in Sambo's robe,' he cried, already busy on the floor, picking things up and throwing them about. Mr Scribbin put down his clothes a safe distance away and hunted afresh through the collected garments for further evidence of his belongings.

'Cocoa,' said Gallelty, coming up from the basement with her tray.

'Mrs Trine, have cocoa and biscuits, do,' said Nurse Clock. 'Come and sit down, my dear, while this awful old chaos is sorted out.'

She led Mrs Trine away, into the television lounge, where promotion for margarine was taking place.

'Modern England, modern England,' murmured Mrs Trine, glancing nastily at the screen and hearing some falsehoods proclaimed.

'It is not always like this,' said Nurse Clock, thinking her guest referred to the incidents that had taken place in the hall. 'Mr Scribbin was upset. The Major likes a joke.'

'No, no,' said Mrs Trine. 'I was thinking of –' She indicated the television screen but did not complete her sentence.

'Sugar?' said Nurse Clock.

In the hall Major Eele had laid Mr Obd's robe on the floor and was piling the clothes on to it. Miss Clerricot and Rose Cave had returned to the television lounge and were drinking cocoa with Mrs Trine.

'Mrs Trine, Miss Cave, Miss Clerricot,' introduced Nurse Clock.

Mr Scribbin and Venables, satisfied that nothing of theirs now remained with the clothes for the refugees, returned also to the television lounge. Mr Obd and Major Eele were left to tie everything into Mr Obd's robe.

'These may go to your native Africa,' said Major Eele, setting aside his plus-fours; and Mr Obd wondered who in Africa would wear the big baggy suits of Mr Bird, and then he thought how surprised they would be to see his robes come back.

Major Eele put his plus-fours for safety on the stairs. As he did so he noticed another heap of clothes on a higher step. He reached for them and threw them to Mr Obd, saying they must have been dropped.

'Biscuits, Mrs Trine?' said Nurse Clock.

'It must be interesting work,' Rose Cave remarked, herself taking a biscuit. 'I suppose the clothes go all over the world?'

Mrs Trine said again that the clothes went in all directions: to the distant East, to Africa, South America, Europe and the countries of the Middle East.

Mr Scribbin said: 'I mean no offence, Mrs Trine. I only regret I cannot spare my suit and the shirts. It is simply that as far as I can see my bedroom has been looted.'

Nurse Clock laughed, and Venables, socks and ties folded upon his knee, laughed too. Earlier, in the hall, Mr Scribbin had turned to him and said, 'What do you imagine these two are up to? There is no normal explanation for this.'

'The African clothes will be most welcome,' said Mrs Trine.

In the hall Major Eele secured the bundle by seizing the ends of the robe and winding string around it. He tied an effective knot.

'That should do,' he said to Mr Obd. 'I'm afraid everything has fallen out of its folds,' he warned Mrs Trine as she approached from the television lounge. 'Everything has got knocked about, but no doubt that doesn't matter to a starving man.'

Mrs Trine said it was marvellous to get so many clothes, and Nurse Clock apologized again for the delay and the confusion.

'Where are my clothes?' cried Mr Scribbin, staring at the stairs where he had left them in safety.

Nurse Clock heard Mr Scribbin say this and could not believe it. Her intention now was to get Mrs Trine, a local woman of standing, out of the house and into her car. She ushered Mrs Trine; and Major Eele and Mr Obd between them, at the Major's instigation, picked up the bundle and made for the hall-door.

'Where have my clothes gone?' cried Mr Scribbin on the street.

'Now, Mr Scribbin, you have had your clothes,' explained Nurse Clock. 'We have been through all that.' But Mrs Trine, one foot on the pavement and one within her small car, paused, for she did not wish to be responsible for the pilfering of clothes.

'My clothes have disappeared from the stairs,' said Mr Scribbin. 'Somehow or other my clothes have got into Mr Obd's robe.' He approached the robe and drew a penknife from his trouser pocket. With this he cut the string. The robe, held by Mr Obd and Major Eele, fell asunder and once again clothes fell to the ground.

Nurse Clock ejaculated. Major Eele laughed. Mr Obd looked startled. Mrs Trine said, or began to say, that perhaps she should call around another day. Venables had come to the door of the boarding-house: he now called back to Miss Clerricot and Rose Cave that further trouble had broken out. Mr Scribbin rescued his clothes.

Studdy, about to enter Jubilee Road, watched from a distance and held himself in the shadow of a tree. He heard Mr Scribbin's cry and Major Eele's laugh and sounds of protest from Nurse Clock. He watched for five minutes while Mr Scribbin satisfied himself that all was well, or almost well, for his clothes would now require attention. He saw Mrs Trine wave and drive away with Mr Obd's gay Nigerian robe in the boot of her car. He heard the door of the boarding-house bang, and he walked slowly up Jubilee Road.

In this manner, amidst chaos and excitement, did the clothes of Mr Bird, his most personal things, leave the boarding-house on the night of August 26th.

13

It was a dreaming season in London, that long warm summer. In a magistrates' court a man who had been charged with the theft of spoons from Woolworth's claimed to have been guided towards the action in a dream; he said the dream had left him with the compulsion, that for days he had gone in fear of death – for death, he said, was his destined lot unless he stole the spoons.

On the night that Mrs Trine called at the boarding-house two old men in Wimbledon dreamed of their schooldays and discussed the scenes that had happened over breakfast; for they, too, lived side by side in a boarding-house, though one that was vastly different from the one that had been Mr Bird's. They talked far into the day, comparing notes and marking the coincidence; and though they did not say it, they hoped that that night too it might be given to them to dream again of their schooldays.

Not far from where the old men dreamed in Wimbledon, Janice Rush, who had been Janice Brownlow, dreamed of Studdy. She saw his face swollen to monstrous size from the blow her friend had struck him. She saw him conveyed along hospital corridors to an operating theatre that was peopled with characters from a television serial. 'His heart will not take it,' said one of these, and cast a grim order at a nurse. The man will die, thought Janice Rush, waking up confused. And then it came to her that this was most unlikely. She switched the light on and slipped from bed, noting the form of her slumbering husband and feeling no emotion at the sight of it. In her kitchen she smoked a cigarette and thought about her marriage day, pretending it was not the slumbering husband she had married but someone else, someone she did not know and could not ever meet. She felt the solitude that would have excited Mr Bird, and sighed at the feeling; for she, who in her day had been the belle of flannel dances, who had been beautiful and dearly loved, had never come to terms with her loneliness and never would now. She hadn't grown to see it and accept it, as his people of the boarding-house had, or would in time.

Studdy dreamed that he had entered local politics and was asked to become Mayor of SW17. 'Together again,' cried Nurse Clock, sitting beside him in the Mayor's parlour, for somehow she was Mayor as well. In his dream he greeted her and touched her shoulder, and planned a terrible vengeance.

Mr Scribbin dreamed that once he had been a wild man, bare-footed in the street. He, whose night in a way this one had been, since he had made himself felt over the matter of his clothes, dreamed, too, that he was at the controls of the double-chimneyed *Lord Faringdon*. Beside him stood Mrs Trine, pulling at his overalls, asking for his tie. 'We are late,' he cried. 'We are late, we are late, Mrs Trine.' He spoke with the rhythm of the wheels, forcing on her the urgency of the circumstances, but she laughed and asked for his tie. 'We are bound for King's Cross,' cried Mr Scribbin, trying to push her off. 'I cannot hear you,' laughed Mrs Trine, and then the cab was filled with people: Venables and Major Eele, Nurse Clock and Mr Obd. They held him back while Nurse Clock and Mrs Trine opened the fire and threw in his clothes. His own moans of distress woke him, and when it was difficult to return to sleep he rose and listened to *Narrow Gauge on the Costa Brava*. Of him Mr Bird had earlier written:

Joseph Scribbin (55) is a lone man, an example of the species. As a child, I imagine, he must have towered over boys and masters alike. Possibly, he had not the strength to match his height, since the height would incline to sap it away. One may imagine the gangling Scribbin tormented by smaller youths, tripped up, knocked over, sworn at by his mentors, who would expect of so high a fellow intelligence to match. He was the sort of boy, I would guess, whose beard grew early, who wore for years on his chin and upper lip a thick mat of down on which food of all descriptions left generous debris. He works today in some position where his body takes sedentary form, since this to Scribbin is an essential thing. I have ceaselessly attempted to cheer him out of his obsession, to offer him, in fact, practical tips as I offered Major Eele, though naturally of a different nature. I have suggested that he should walk with a slouch, affecting a crablike motion. In this way, I claim, his inordinate height would pass unnoticed, though of course the crablike motion might not. He takes no heed of me in any case, just looks dumb and goes away to play his gramophone. I weep when I think of Joseph Scribbin's life, and the emptiness thereof.

Rose Cave's mother was in the television lounge, sitting on a chair in the centre of the room, eating a sandwich. 'I asked for chicken vol-au-vent,' she cried. 'Rose, little child, I asked for vol-au-vent and you have brought me a tongue sandwich. Whatever has gone wrong with you?' 'I'm sorry,' said Rose Cave and lifted the sandwich from her mother's hand and ate it herself. 'That is unkind,' cried her mother, 'to take the bread from a mother's mouth. What has gone wrong with you? Are you ill? Are you mad? Have you got the change of life?' 'Yes, I have got the change of life,' said Rose Cave, and wept in front of everyone.

Venables was telling Mr Bird, as often in the past he had told him, of his position in the business world as traffic controller in a firm of merit; he was trying to explain what traffic controller meant without detracting too much from the ring of the title, and Mr Bird, as always, was patient and discreet.

'"Fools rush in",' murmured Mr Bird in the ear of Miss Clerricot, '"where angels fear to tread." That's Alexander Pope, Miss Clerricot.' She looked at him and said she never knew that Alexander Pope had written those words. She would not discuss the matter that Mr Bird was hinting at, and in the silence that fell between them she felt herself going redder in her dream. 'To err is human,' murmured Mr Bird, smiling before he died.

'You did not record my ultimate observations,' said he to Nurse Clock in the only dream of Nurse Clock's life. 'You informed no newspaper that William Bird died by degrees, a process that began with the feet. I have scanned the British Press and seen no mention of the matter. I call that callous, Nurse Clock; after all, I left you a boarding-house.'

'And Studdy too! What kind of trick? They will roast you for that, sir, to do so awful an action. Ill nature I call it, Mr Bird: a trick you've played on all of us.'

'I took you in, Nurse Clock, when the Lord-Bloods had ground you to the dust. I left my house to my grandest residents. How could I leave it to you alone? You would turn it into a home for the old.'

And Nurse Clock, who of a sudden was sitting in the death room of her late landlord, took no notice and read her magazine.

Major Eele saw Mr Bird in the distance, sitting on a park seat, his bad leg stretched on the seat in front of him. Mr Bird seemed to be dozing, but Major Eele suspected that he was watching to see if Mrs le Tor should pass by.

Mr Bird lived on, that night and for nights and days to come, in the minds of them all, but most marvellously in the mind of Mr Obd, who dreamed that Mr Bird had risen from the dead.

Tome Obd, who had sat at the writing-desk in the television lounge, a thing that no one had done before, who lay now dreaming of the risen Mr Bird, had again taken flowers to the flat of Annabel Tonks. Miss Tonks, however, was absent, or so it seemed, and once again Mr Obd found himself on the stone landing outside the door of her flat, standing with flowers and feeling dejected. He had rung the bell and had heard it ringing. He had knocked with the small brass knocker and then in an agony of sorrow had cried aloud: 'Oh, Annabel, why do our paths never meet?' When he telephoned her the wires seemed always to cross. 'That number has been changed,' an official of the telephone service had informed him recently, but when he enquired for the new number the voice had said: 'I am not at liberty to divulge it,' and had added, 'sir'. It was a long time now since he had laid his pale eyes on the girl he had played ping-pong with in the past. Yet always his flowers had gone when next he called, and not just the flowers but also the accompanying letter. 'Don't you know you have an establishment in my heart?' cried Mr Obd, quoting inaccurately from a beautiful poem. 'Annabel, Annabel, this is Tome Obd.'

It had never occurred to Mr Obd that Annabel Tonks might possibly have moved away from her flat at the top of all those stone stairs. It had not occurred to him, as it rarely does in such circumstances, that she might have gone quietly and told the tenant who replaced her that she wished her forwarding address to be kept away from a man from Africa who would call with flowers. It did not pass through Mr Obd's mind that another woman might be taking his flowers week after week and settling them in a vase, and reading, or not bothering to read, his letters in black ink.

'Open the door,' cried Mr Obd, beating the door with the palms of his hands. 'Annabel, Annabel.'

'Are you Mr Obd?' asked a girl with fair hair, not his Miss Tonks, but a girl all the same who had opened the door of the flat from the inside.

'Yes, yes. I am Tome Obd. It is Annabel I wish to see. Look, I have brought her a selection of dahlias.'

'How lovely,' cried the girl, burying her face in the bunch. 'What delicious flowers! Mr Obd, I'm sorry, Miss Tonks has moved away.'

'How do you mean that? Moved away? She is out? I may wait. Are you a flat-mate? I have known others. How do you do; my name is Tome Obd.'

Smiling, Mr Obd held out his hand.

'No,' the girl said, 'Annabel Tonks has taken herself to another flat. She is somewhere else in London. I do not know the address.'

Mr Obd shook his head. 'No, no, you can't understand. I am a long established friend of Annabel. She would not go somewhere else in London without first telling Tome Obd. What is your name? There are bonds between Annabel Tonks and myself, as I dare say she had told you.'

The girl, whose name was Josephine Tonks, being a sister of Annabel, noticed with interest that Mr Obd's teeth were not his own. She had, perhaps naturally, never before thought of dentures in an African mouth. She rather imagined she had assumed, without going into it, that the African smile was a real one all the way to the roots. As she reported afterwards, she was quite taken aback at the little gum-line of pink plastic that was included with Mr Obd's.

'I'm afraid I know little of Miss Tonks' life,' said Josephine Tonks. 'I cannot answer for her.'

Mr Obd had read in a magazine that girls who live together were often jealous of each other's men friends. He suspected a case of this now. He knew that Annabel Tonks still belonged in the flat because he could see one of her coats in the hall.

'You have often left flowers, have you?' said the girl carelessly. 'Certainly flowers were occasionally taken away by the caretaker. No one knows where Miss Tonks has sped to. She has vanished into thin air.'

'Now, that is not true,' cried Tome Obd. 'That is far from the honest truth and you surely know it. What is that there? It is my Annabel's coat hanging upon a hook. Annabel, Annabel, you have an establishment in my heart.' Mr Obd raised his voice for that last sentence, and Annabel Tonks, seated in front of a looking-glass with a beauty preparation on her face, sighed heavily and wished he would go away. Her sister, who was many years younger, was quite enjoying the drama of the encounter and thinking how romantic it was really, a black man saying he had an establishment in his heart. But Annabel herself, who never quite knew when it was safe to open the door, was bored by now with the drama and the romance of it. It was twelve years since she had last accompanied Tome Obd to the cinema, and two years before that they had played their final game of table-tennis. Surely he could understand, since they had met at a club called the Society for the Promotion of Commonwealth Friendship? Surely he could see, or should at least have seen by now, that she had been promoting Commonwealth friendship and only that?

'It is absolutely no use whatsoever,' explained Mr Obd, waving the bunch of dahlias. 'I must stand here all night if needs be. When have I last seen Annabel? Six months ago. We have got out of touch; it is a poor state of affairs.'

'Maybe,' said Annabel Tonks' sister. 'Maybe that is very

true, but what can we do, for goodness' sake? I am only another tenant. I fear you must take your troubles elsewhere.'

'You are jealous,' cried Mr Obd. 'You are a jealous young girl.'

'In fact I am,' she said. 'I have a jealous nature, it says so in my horoscope. But what has that to do with anything?'

'You are envious of my friendship with Miss Annabel Tonks. You are her flat-mate and are envious. I know that to be true.'

'It is not true at all. I see no reason to be envious of you. Frankly, half the time I don't understand what you're saying.'

'Now you are wounding me,' cried Mr Obd. 'You have wounded Tome Obd with your cruel tongue, and you will not even tell me your name.'

'Go away, please,' ordered Annabel Tonks' sister, and shut the door with a swift movement.

'He will come again,' said Annabel Tonks, 'and then I shall see him myself. I have said to him to his face that he is an obtrusion. Next time I shall say that the police will arrest him. You can have that done, you know, with people who are a persistent nuisance.'

Mr Obd did not hear this, for it was said in the depths of the flat, far from the closed hall-door. He wept on the stone landing and the tears rolled down his cheeks and dripped on to his stiff white collar.

'It is a large house,' Nurse Clock said. 'I often thought it could be put to greater profit.'

Studdy watched her, easing cigarette smoke through his nostrils, interested in what she said.

'It is big, certainly.' He watched the ash fall on to the dark fabric of his overcoat, and then shifted his eyes back to the nurse's face.

There was a short silence, a stillness that was broken only by Studdy's smoking. Eventually he said:

'Have you plans?'

She knew she needed this man's co-operation. She saw what Mr Bird had been up to. She nodded, and after another silence spoke again.

14

'I have new responsibilities,' said Studdy. 'I may not be around too often, missus.'

'What's that, Mr Studdy?'

'I say I may not be around too often. I have fresh fields to plough –'

'What's that?'

Studdy turned the wireless down.

'I have fresh fields to plough. The boarding-house takes up a bit of time. It's hard to make ends meet above there.'

'I've no more money, Mr Studdy.'

'It's not that, missus. It's just I won't have too much time to be visiting you. I think –'

'Aren't you coming again, Mr Studdy? Are you deserting me, is that it?'

'Ah, not at all, Mrs Maylam.'

'Nobody comes here now, did you know that? The woman with the dinners hasn't been since last week. My bed isn't clean. Did you hear that, Mr Studdy? Are you deserting me?'

'Nurse Clock will come, missus, to give you the injections. Take the injections, now, that way you'll get rid of your old trouble.'

'You were ever on my side, Mr Studdy. You're letting an old woman down.'

'Ah no, not at all.'

'Back to the land, is it? You're going out ploughing, are you?'

'Ah no, Mrs Maylam, that's only a figure of speech. Will you be all right now?'

'You've sucked me dry, Mr Studdy. There isn't another penny in me. No wonder you're going. Get to hell out, now.'

'That's no way to talk to a friend. Haven't I always been a help to you?'

'Turn on my old radio, Mr Studdy. You're a bloody philanderer.'

Later, Nurse Clock said:

'No nonsense now, Mrs Maylam: let's throw away this filthy old potato. Lift up your skirt like a good girl and I'll slip in this nice injection.' And she, whose greatest joy was to keep the elderly alive and alert, dabbed a portion of Mrs Maylam's eighty-nine-year-old leg with iodine on cotton wool, and jabbed in her needle.

On quiet afternoons he seemed to be everywhere in the boarding-house: in the rooms upstairs, the private bedrooms and in the public rooms and the basement; in the hall, dim with brown paint, and on the staircase with the carpet that once had been a blaze of light and was now a dark gravy. In the coolness of that hall, as one entered and glanced at the Watts prints and the flights of china geese, one was especially aware of the deceased Mr Bird. The house was not haunted by the ghost of a dead man but by the needling memory of a living one. A stranger in the hall might have felt a vacuum, might have felt perhaps an absence rather than a presence, or a stranger in a hurry might have felt nothing at all.

In the hall there was a mirror that showed Miss Clerricot her face and caught the length of Mr Scribbin as he passed it. In the television lounge there was a wedding photograph that Mr Bird had bought because he thought it a suitable thing to have. So he had said, coming into the television lounge late one night and placing it on a side table, saying he did not know who the people were but that he had bought it, frame and all, for one and sixpence. The frame, he said, was worth a fortune. It had stood there since, reminding Rose Cave that wedding bells had never come her way, and had not come the way of her mother either. It reminded Major Eele of his marriage night, and the nine nights after, although in fact he had not been married in such splendour.

'May I speak to Major Eele, please?'

'I think he's in,' said Studdy, laying down the receiver, interested. 'Major, there's a woman for you on the phone.'

'A woman?'

'She gave no name, sir.'

Major Eele was hurrying across the television lounge, thinking wildly, wondering if Mrs Andrews for some reason wished to see him and had ferreted him out. He paused in the hall and beckoned Studdy with his forefinger. Whispering, he said:

'Ask who it is, will you?'

Studdy ran his fat tongue around the inside of his mouth. He swallowed a few crumbs of fried bread. He said:

'The Major wishes to know who it is, madam.'

'Mrs le Tor,' said Mrs le Tor.

'A Mrs le Tor,' said Studdy.

'Hullo, Mrs le Tor,' said Major Eele.

'I was simply wondering, Major, whether it mightn't be a better idea to meet for lunch. Rather than tea, you know. Lunch is more of an occasion, isn't it now? That is, if you can spare the time.'

Studdy was standing close to Major Eele, trying to hear what the voice was saying. 'Do you want something?' asked Major Eele.

'You remember we arranged to have tea. You had kindly invited me.'

'No, no. I was speaking to someone else. Mr Studdy is at my elbow; I made the query of him.'

Studdy moved away. He felt the leaves of the rubber plant, taking them in turn between thumb and forefinger. To lend greater authority to this action he spoke in a low voice, addressing some argument to himself.

'Well, that would be fine. If lunch is your preference, Mrs le Tor, lunch it shall be.'

'There is a five and sixpenny lunch at the Jasmine. Quite good value. Do you know the Jasmine, Major Eele?'

'In the West End,' said Major Eele for Studdy's benefit, knowing that the Jasmine was a local café run by the Misses Gregory.

Mrs le Tor laughed and said that the Jasmine was not in the West End at all but was a local place run by the Misses Gregory, who were quite good friends of hers. She gave directions for getting there, and Major Eele nodded, visualizing her long legs and red barbaric finger-nails. When she finished he said:

'Since we have moved away from tea, why not go the whole hog and have dinner? Dinner is the thing nowadays.'

Mrs le Tor allowed a pause to manifest itself along the wire.

'How very kind of you, Major Eele. Alas, though, I fear the Jasmine does not do dinners.'

'Well, somewhere else then. Somewhere in Jermyn Street,' he added, with his hand over the mouthpiece. 'Or round the Curzon Street area. There are one or two places I frequent.'

'There is nowhere else round here, really,' said Mrs le Tor. 'Unless we were to go into London. Chelsea perhaps?'

'I do not care for that.' He thought she was becoming like Mrs Andrews again: he remembered the cavern restaurant where he had spat out the Portuguese food. He slipped his hand over the mouthpiece again. 'What about the Colony in Berkeley Square? All the big business boys go there. Would you care for that kind of thing?'

'I know,' said Mrs le Tor. 'The Misses Gregory will cook us a dinner if I have a word with them. I'm sure they will. They're kindness itself. Think of it, we'd have a lovely quiet dinner in the Jasmine, just the two of us. I'll ring them up and call you back. Cheery-bye, Major Eele.'

Mrs le Tor rang off, and Major Eele said into the dead receiver: 'Young Armstrong-Jones might well be there.'

He walked past Studdy, writing busily in a diary he had had for many years.

'An old folks' home,' said Studdy. 'That's what's in your mind, Nurse. Am I any way right?'

She nodded.

Studdy lit a cigarette of his own manufacture. He smiled, showing teeth in need of repair. He said:

'You cannot fool me.'

Nurse Clock, caught up with his teeth somehow, held by what she considered their unsavouriness, brought her eyelids firmly down and blotted out the sight. With closed eyes she turned her head away and spoke.

'I did not wish to fool you, Mr Studdy.'

'Ah no, we are in this together.'

'You have often spoken of the aged. You would be a help to me in an old folks' home, doing all the practical things. And the house is ours to share.'

'Oh, definitely.'

'We would make a bit of money, and if you did not take to the work I could buy you out.'

'Ah no, that type of work suits me very well.'

'A smart appearance would be vital, Mr Studdy.'

'Ah, we'd definitely have to smarten up.'

'Cleanliness is essential in a thing like this.'

'Oh, certainly.'

Nurse Clock hummed two bars of Hymn Thirteen.

'A coat of paint all round, as once you said, Nurse.'

'I was meaning, really, personal cleanliness.'

'Personal cleanliness. Ah yes. You're quite right.'

Nurse Clock hummed again. 'The late King's favourite,' she said.

'Pardon ?'

'*Abide With Me*, the late King's favourite.'

'Certainly,' said Studdy. 'We'll sing that here, Nurse, on a Sunday morning and again at night, with all the old dads joining in. Sure, it'll be the happiest –'

'Mr Studdy, if you were occasionally to brush your teeth it would help to give that overall appearance of cleanliness and a smart appearance.'

There was a pause, after which Studdy said:

'Teeth ?'

'Do not take offence, Mr Studdy. Remember, this is a business relationship. We are setting up a business partnership. We cannot be remiss about mentioning something that will help us both. I'd like it to be an elegant place.'

Studdy scratched at his teeth with the nail of his right forefinger.

'I will brush my teeth with a tooth-brush,' he said, saluting her with his open palm; and felt the hand itching to touch the pin. He wondered if the rewards were going to be worth it, and consoled himself with a series of images: his hands opening old biscuit tins full of incriminating letters, his voice talking subtly to a whole houseful of richer Mrs Maylams, discussing a line or two in a will. He wagged his head and began to smile. Then, remembering what Nurse Clock had said about his teeth, he desisted, locking them behind his lips.

'They'll have to go, every one of them,' said Studdy.

'Oh, no, I'm sure that is not necessary. Brush them often, as you say. Perhaps visit a dentist.'

'Pardon?'

'It is surely not necessary to have your teeth taken out. I did not mean that, Mr Studdy.'

'I will brush my teeth with a tooth-brush. I have promised that.'

'Good.'

'I was speaking about the residents. I was thinking they would have to go.'

'Oh, of course, Mr Studdy.'

15

Miss Clerricot and Mr Sellwood caught the seven forty-five train to Leeds.

'Breakfast?' suggested Mr Sellwood.

Miss Clerricot had had an early breakfast at the boarding-house. She had risen at half past five because she could not sleep.

She suggested coffee, but there was trouble about that because breakfast was being served and a cup of coffee by itself was not breakfast. She returned to their compartment, leaving Mr Sellwood with a newspaper, awaiting a plate of bacon and eggs.

Studdy, who had pursued Miss Clerricot from the boarding-house to King's Cross, saw the train move off and went to have a cup of tea in one of the large cafeterias. He had left the boarding-house without having had time to shave, and as he carried his tea to an empty table his overcoat fell open, revealing evidence of hasty dressing. He sat for a while in thought and drew eventually from an inside pocket his lined writing pad and a pencil. He wrote:

Dear Mr Sellwood,

I put it to you that your lady wife would be more than interested to learn that on the morning of August 28th at seven thirty-three precisely you were seen to mount a Leeds-bound train in the company of a woman. I put it to you that you subsequently spent two nights in the city of Leeds with this same woman, *and reputedly with others*, and were observed by sworn witnesses to act in a profligate manner. My assistants and I have compiled a sworn dossier that when published will cause you to leave these shores. If you wish to prevent this unhappy event, please leave two pounds in an envelope addressed to M. Moran at the reception desk of your office, to be collected on September 7th. The money will be invested on behalf of a religious organization.

Respectfully,

A friend to decent morals.

He sealed the envelope, marked it *Urgent and Personal*, and dropped it into a letter-box without the addition of a stamp. Despite his recent failure with Mrs Rush, there was little doubt in Studdy's mind that Mr Sellwood's immediate reaction to his message would be to place two pound notes in an envelope and address it hastily as requested.

'Our railway system is still ahead,' Mr Sellwood commented. 'Egg, bacon, sausage, fried potatoes, fried tomatoes, coffee, toast, butter, marmalade. Where in the world would you get the equal of that?'

'The United States of America,' replied a man sitting opposite, who from his voice hailed from that country. 'The United States has built an empire on personal service.'

Mr Sellwood, taken aback, said that he had been to the United States.

'Name of Bone,' said the man, and added further details. 'Pleased to meet you, sir.'

'I am interested to hear you say service,' said Mr Sellwood. 'Private enterprise –'

'Personal service on airlines,' said the man called Bone. 'Trans World Airlines. Have you been on Trans World Airlines, sir?'

'I have not,' confessed Mr Sellwood.

'One of the truly great airlines,' said the man.

'Have you come over on holiday?' Miss Clerricot asked, feeling obliged to contribute.

'Holiday!' shouted Mr Bone, a small, almost round man with spectacles. 'Holiday!' he repeated.

'I am particularly interested in community services,' said Mr Sellwood. 'For example, our banking here is rather interesting: perhaps you have had time to study it?'

'You in that line?' asked Mr Bone.

'Oh no, not at all. It is just that as a service to the nation banking absorbs me greatly. We have here what we call our

Big Five: Lloyd's, Barclay's, the National Provincial, the Westminster, and the Midland. I do not put them in any particular order, they all provide a highly efficient service.'

'I,' said Mr Bone, 'bank with Chase Manhattan. It has never let me down.'

'We have as well,' said Mr Sellwood, 'Martin's Bank, a most interesting foundation, dating from 1563; and Coutts and Cox's. But it is not the quantity of our banks that I wish to draw your attention to, it is the quality of the service they give. The same, Mr Bone, whether you are in the heart of our capital or in any market town.'

Miss Clerricot did not speak again until the train drew in at Leeds. She said then, because she felt she should remind Mr Sellwood of her presence on the train:

'What a pleasant journey!'

'Interesting about the Chase Manhattan,' remarked Mr Sellwood.

Major Eele collected his dark flannel suit from the Tip Top Cleaners and bought himself a small rosebud. He walked slowly back to Jubilee Road, considering imaginatively the evening that lay before him. He laughed to himself over his early error: taking Mrs le Tor to be a tart. His train of thought led him deep into the past, and he was put in mind of Bicey-Jones, who years ago had caused such excitement in the dormitory with his tales of a motherly French tart he claimed to have picked up one afternoon in Piccadilly. She had, so Bicey-Jones reported, kept on much of her underclothing, but what had always seemed more interesting to Major Eele was that while Bicey-Jones was extracting his money's worth this elderly Frenchwoman had occupied herself by squeezing blackheads from his face. Ever since Major Eele had come to live in London he had been periodically tantalized by this story, unable to decide whether or not to believe it. If he met Bicey-Jones tomorrow he would ask him straight away if in fact the woman had removed his blackheads, and if so whether she had done so at his bidding.

That afternoon the Major rested, reading *Urge* in the television lounge. He had arranged the volume within the green plastic cover that the boarding-house supplied for the *Radio Times*. He dropped off to sleep about four o'clock and when he woke half an hour later he suffered a small shock, because for a moment he imagined that he was still married to Mrs Andrews. 'Meet me in our Berkeley bar,' she seemed to have said, going off to have her hair done; but then he remembered that it was Mrs le Tor he was to meet that evening and he gave a thankful sigh.

'Well, Miss Clerricot, would you care for a cocktail?'

Miss Clerricot said she would. She had spent the afternoon walking about Leeds while Mr Sellwood had conducted his business.

'A gin and tonic, Miss Clerricot? Or a gin and bitter lemon? Or a gin and – What would you like?'

She said she would like sherry. Mr Sellwood said that was a capital choice. He paused before ordering it: he had seen the creation of sherry, he said, while on a family holiday in Spain. He told Miss Clerricot about it.

Mr Sellwood drank sherry too. 'A good sherry,' he acclaimed it after a sip. 'A good sherry,' he repeated to a passing barman, and the barman bowed.

In a huge, elaborately framed mirror Miss Clerricot saw the image of Mr Sellwood and herself. The mirror was some way away, and she did not at first recognize the woman in a black suit and the thin, slightly stooped, bald man. Then the woman's head moved and Miss Clerricot saw her own mouth smiling and quickly looked away.

'What a pleasant hotel,' she said.

'It is one of a vast chain,' Mr Sellwood explained. 'A chain that is, I always hold, run on the most excellent lines. Are you interested in hotels, Miss Clerricot?'

She found it difficult to answer this question. She had never thought very much about hotels: she rarely stayed in them.

'The organization of a big hotel,' said Mr Sellwood, lighting a cigarette, 'is absolutely fascinating.'

She wondered if he ever went to the cinema, or to the theatre, or to an art exhibition. She wondered what he did on his family holidays besides observing the manufacture of sherry. He stayed in hotels, she imagined, and noted their organization, while his wife, whom she saw silent beside him, drank, perhaps, a great deal of gin.

'The heart of any hotel,' said Mr Sellwood, 'is its kitchen. It is what happens in the kitchen and what comes from the kitchen, and the briskness with which it comes, that put hotels into their categories. Mind you, I'm not for a moment saying that lounges and the writing-rooms must not be well-appointed.' Mr Sellwood talked on, and said after five minutes: 'What was it we were drinking?'

One expected, Miss Clerricot thought, a fresh aspect of a person when circumstances changed; when Mr Sellwood, for example, rose from behind his desk and took her out to lunch, not once but several times, and took her to Leeds and gave her glass after glass of sherry to drink. But Mr Sellwood scarcely changed at all. This is a case of Jekyll and Hyde, thought Miss Clerricot: in a moment now, or later on, Mr Sellwood would froth a little at one corner of his mouth, his eyes would glaze and his hands develop a strength like steel. She thought he might pale, and she saw in the glazed eyes small specks of blood.

'Two more sherries,' said Mr Sellwood to the barman. 'I am going to time this,' he added to Miss Clerricot, 'and see how long it takes.'

Miss Clerricot thought: He will get drunk and fall about, and then one small thing will lead to another; I shall see his hands become taut and cold, I shall watch his face for the white foam and the glazing of the eyes and then the flecks of blood.

'Thirty seconds,' said Mr Sellwood, and to the barman: 'Well done, sir.'

The barman, amazed, hurried away with Mr Sellwood's ten-shilling note, expecting a notable tip, and was disappointed when the moment came.

Miss Clerricot laughed to herself at this vision of Mr Sellwood in her mind: she knew she was having a private joke, she didn't for a moment believe that Mr Sellwood would change his nature. What was he like as a boy ? she wondered.

'Interesting about the Chase Manhattan,' said Mr Sellwood. 'I had no idea about any of that. One does meet some interesting fellows on trains.'

'Yes,' said Miss Clerricot. 'Did you have a satisfactory afternoon ?'

'What's that ?'

'Did all go well this afternoon ?'

'I met a man,' said Mr Sellwood, 'on a train once, whose brother had written the history of one of our smaller insurance companies. It happened that the man was reading the book at the time; that is how the conversation came up. I afterwards wrote to the man's brother, having read the book myself in the meantime, and said how much I had enjoyed it, and added in a postscript that I had met his brother on a journey from Aylesbury to London.'

Miss Clerricot smiled, offering encouragement.

'I had a most civil letter in reply, but to my utter astonishment the fellow said he had no brother at all, and was in fact an only child. I wrote at once to apologize, explaining what had happened and describing the man on the train. He was a smallish man, with sandy eyebrows, I remember, and a rather red face. He had been wearing a waterproof coat, one of those plastic things. I thought it odd at the time to wear a plastic coat in a first-class compartment, but of course I said nothing. Well, this second fellow, the author of the book, dropped me a postcard, thanking me for my letter and making some joke, I've forgotten what it was.'

'How very odd,' said Miss Clerricot.

'I thought it odd. Well, frankly, it preyed a bit on me, and a month or so later I wrote to this fellow again, just to ask him if anything had come to light. I thought perhaps that the man in the train might have been arrested or something, for posing as the other fellow's brother – well, not arrested perhaps, but at least brought to task . . .'

'What happened then ?'

Mr Sellwood did not reply. He seemed to have become locked

between wedges of deep thought. He was looking into the middle distance, his mouth set, his eyes screwed up.

My God, thought Miss Clerricot, they are glazing over.

'I did not get a reply to that letter,' said Mr Sellwood. 'I did not hear another thing.'

'How curious.'

'I thought it curious. Especially since the man had been courteous in the past. Yes, I found it most curious indeed. Are you hungry? Should we eat, Miss Clerricot?' She thought he spoke as though it were in doubt whether or not they should eat at all. She felt he might have it in mind to sit in the lounge all evening, until eleven o'clock or so, ordering glasses of sherry and timing the waiter's alacrity.

'I am hungry,' said Miss Clerricot. 'Well, I mean, quite hungry.'

'They do you well here,' he said, but did not rise. 'Let's just try this fellow again. Would you mind ordering while I do the other?'

She assumed that this must be a regular practice of his. She ordered the drinks while he kept his face bent over his wrist. The barman, noticing everything, seemed to lose composure. She thought she saw him quiver as he stood there with his silver or mock-silver tray, picking up the empty glasses and an ash-tray. What is the barman thinking? she wondered; what on earth is there for a man to think in circumstances like this? Yet Mr Sellwood was not being rowdy; he was very quiet in his madness. She watched the barman cross the floor and hurry up a couple of steps to the bar. While he waited for the drinks he spoke to a man standing there. That is the manager, thought Miss Clerricot; he is dressed like a manager; the barman is complaining, he is greatly distressed.

She watched Mr Sellwood, seeing a face she knew very well. She closed her eyes and played a game: she tried to think whether or not Mr Sellwood had a moustache. There was something on his upper lip, some mark, she was sure of that. She tried to visualize a small grey moustache, but somehow it didn't seem to fit. She thought then that it must be black, a thin charcoal line of closely cropped bristle. That, somehow, didn't seem right either. Then fantasy gripped Miss Clerricot and she imagined Mr Sellwood with a huge curling growth, with pointed ends waxed and dangerous-looking. She reflected seriously again, closing her eyes tight: there was something on Mr Sellwood's upper lip, she knew the lip was not bare; there was something there, something one took for granted like a nose.

The barman, returning with two glasses of sherry, saw his motion being timed by the man, and the woman sitting with her eyes closed. He thought she seemed to be swaying back and forth, and he wondered if the two were indulging in some ceremony. In silence he placed the glasses and a fresh ashtray on the table between them.

'Two minutes thirty-four,' said Mr Sellwood. 'Something has gone wrong with the fellow.'

Miss Clerricot opened her eyes and saw the familiar moustache, Home Counties grey, with strands of darker fibre in it. She saw the barman standing near by, pretending an interest in another table. Mr Sellwood said:

'An up-and-down performer.'

In the boarding-house at that moment Mr Scribbin was turning on the television set. Behind him Rose Cave sat down with her knitting, and Mr Obd, sighing and moaning within himself, hung about by the doorway. In the dining-room Gallelty brushed crumbs from the tables, thinking about nothing at all, intent upon the crumbs. Venables, still in the dining-room, sat sick and pale, his right hand playing with the plastic ring that held his napkin. The pain in his stomach caused sweat to form all over his body. He could not move, but he knew that in a minute or two the pain would cease and he would succeed in rising and would pass some remark about the weather to the maid.

Mr Sellwood leaned back in his chair and lifted his sherry glass to his lips. 'What a pleasant way,' he said, 'to spend an evening.'

The Misses Gregory had done wonders with the Jasmine Café. They had cut flowers from their own garden and had placed them, pleasantly arranged, on the table reserved for Major Eele and Mrs le Tor. They knew Mrs le Tor of old; she had possibilities as a customer, and it was not often that a request was made for a special dinner for two. Deliciously curious, the Misses Gregory were touched by the romance of it.

'Well, this is quite delightful,' said Mrs le Tor, looking around her at twelve unoccupied tables set for morning coffee. The tables had checked cloths, red and white, but their own table, in honour of them, had a plain starched cloth of pure linen, left to the Misses Gregory by their mother in 1955.

'Have you brought the wine, Major Eele? I do like this. Look, they have written out a special menu.'

Two candles burned on their table, two slim red candles that did not at all remind Major Eele of the candles in the cavern restaurant. Mrs le Tor, he considered, was looking radiant. Her cheeks seemed more flushed than usual; he thought it suited her and wondered if he should say so. He glanced at her legs, shimmering and making a noise when she moved them. He said:

'Wine?'

'Oh, my dear, didn't I say? I meant to say. What on earth can I have been thinking of? The Jasmine isn't licensed. We have to bring our bottle.'

Major Eele clicked his teeth. 'Well, we haven't.'

'Could you not slip out to the place at the corner? Sauterne or Chablis or something. Let me go halves.'

But the Major refused this offering and made the journey to the corner of the street.

'He has just slipped out for wine,' said Mrs le Tor to the Miss Gregory who was hovering near. 'He will be but a minute.'

'A charming man,' the other replied. 'How straight and gallant he walks.'

'The old school,' said Mrs le Tor, looking at the menu. 'A brigadier.'

'I have a brother,' said Mr Sellwood, 'who is in the hotel business. I do not see him often.'

They walked from the bar towards the dining-room. 'Excuse me for a moment,' Miss Clerricot said in the hall.

Mr Sellwood, who had not absorbed the import of Miss Clerricot's request, turned around a moment later to find her gone. He was by then on his way across the dining-room, led by a waiter.

'Where is she?' Mr Sellwood asked, stopping in his tracks. 'Where is the lady?'

The waiter made a polite gesture of the lips, a waiter's smile.

'Where?' repeated Mr Sellwood, looking about him.

The waiter indicated the table he had reserved. 'A table for two,' he said. 'Your friend will join you, sir?'

'Where is my friend?'

'You came in alone, sir.'

'I came in with Miss Clerricot. Certainly I came in with Miss Clerricot. I had better hunt for her.' And Mr Sellwood walked away, leaving the waiter with his arm outstretched, pointing to a table for two. Later that night this same waiter was heard to say: 'There is a lunatic in our midst.'

'I am looking for the lady who was with me just now,' said Mr Sellwood in the bar. 'We had arranged, I thought, to go together to the dining-room, yet when I reach there she is no longer by my side. I thought she must still be here.'

But the barman whom Mr Sellwood had earlier timed shook his head and did not smile as the waiter had smiled. 'I am not here to be clocked by customers,' he had already complained, though not to Mr Sellwood.

Miss Clerricot in turn was led to the table reserved for Mr Sellwood.

'Where is Mr Sellwood?' she asked, seeing that the table was empty. The man did something in the air with his hand, a skilful movement that suggested that Mr Sellwood was on the way. Miss Clerricot guessed he was in the lavatory.

'Find the gentleman,' the waiter said to a lesser waiter, speaking in a low voice. 'He will be mooching about the hall.'

Mr Sellwood, however, feeling rather cross, was still in the bar, where he had ordered a further glass of sherry. He shot his watch from beneath his cuff and regarded the minute hand.

'Three shillings, sir,' the barman said.

Mr Sellwood still could not understand how it was that once the time taken had been half a minute and on the other two occasions it had been two minutes and thirty-four seconds and two minutes ninety seconds respectively. It annoyed Mr Sellwood as he sat there, drinking his sherry. For a moment he had forgotten about Miss Clerricot.

'Sir,' said a youth beside him, and Mr Sellwood looked up and saw a child of twelve or so in elaborate uniform. 'Mr Sellwood, sir, they are looking for you in the dining-room.'

'I am Sellwood, yes.'

'The waiters are looking for you, sir. Your wife has arrived at your table in the dining-room.'

'My God,' cried Mr Sellwood, leaping to his feet, standing on them and appearing frightened.

'I do not much care for this,' said Mr Scribbin in the television lounge. 'Why are we watching an operation on a stomach ulcer?'

'Nurse Clock wanted it,' said Rose Cave. 'She will be angry if you turn to something else.'

'Nurse Clock is not here.'

'No, Nurse Clock is not. She is seeing to what blankets should be laundered. I gave her an offer of help. She has a lot on her hands, now that things have changed.'

In his room Mr Obd wrote a letter, the longest and most poignant he had ever written to Annabel Tonks. He was not shy on paper: all that was in his heart came out.

'Tell me all about yourself, Major Eele. What life is like in your boarding-house, how you improve the shining hour. What gorgeous fare the girls are treating us to! Let me just run away and say so.'

Mrs le Tor, flushed with wine, encased in a patterned silk dress, dashed to the back of the café, to a region she seemed familiar with. Major Eele heard voices raised in praise and admiration, of the food on Mrs le Tor's part, of her dress and accessories on the part of the Misses Gregory. When she returned to the candle-lit table he saw the faces of the ladies smiling around a partition.

'What do you do all day?' Mrs le Tor asked him. 'Does time hang heavy? Of course, you're a great walker. You go to the cinema, you said.'

'I am a cinema-goer, yes. Foreign films mostly. When Mr Bird was alive we used together to attend theatrical productions.'

'How nice. I am always at the theatre, the upper circle. Now that your friend is dead you have no companion? Poor Major, how sad.'

'Now that I think of it I believe Mr Bird only accompanied me once. He gave me a feeling for the thing, you understand. I like to go alone.'

'On your owney-oh? Oh, no. How sad.'

'I find it better so. I do not mind that at all. I am a solitary bird, as Mr Bird would have said.'

'You never married, Major Eele?'

'I have been married.'

'And I, Major Eele,' cried Mrs le Tor. 'And I too!'

Major Eele coughed. He found her red finger-nails fascinating. He thought he might be wrong, that she was maybe a tart after all. A scarlet woman, he thought; how amused they'd be in the boarding-house to see him sitting here with a scarlet woman in an empty café.

'Major, shall we get some more wine?' cried Mrs le Tor, full of enthusiasm for the project. 'Let's make an evening of it!'

He rose and bowed to her, and walked again to the public house at the corner of the street.

The uniformed child, who imagined that Mr Sellwood would press into his palm a many-cornered threepenny piece, blinked his eyes, looking at the stooping man who was hunched in a chair beside him. His instinct was to take this man by the arm, or at least by some portion of his clothes, and lead him to the dining-room, but his training prevented so natural an expression. He stood there, small and enthusiastic, a child who was later to rise to heights in the hotel business, and said nothing further.

Miss Clerricot read the menu and noticed that there was salmon in a sauce, that there was no choice of soup but that if she did not wish to have soup there was paté or grapefruit or, surprisingly, lasagne. There was cold chicken and cold tongue, and ham and pork and other meats. Potatoes were creamed or fried or new. There were broad beans and French beans, or garden peas, or asparagus, or celery hearts.

'Madam ?' said the head waiter.

'I had better wait,' she murmured, blushing.

'Where on earth did you get to ?' demanded Mr Sellwood. 'I hunted for you everywhere.' He sat down and took the menu from her. She felt quite close to the waiter who had hovered about her, who knew the details of the confusion. She felt that if she looked up now and caught his eye he would smile or cast an upward look.

'Paté and salmon,' said Mr Sellwood. 'They do you well here.'

I shall have soup, she thought, and then salmon with new potatoes and broad beans. Mr Sellwood will order a bottle of wine, and afterwards he will offer a liqueur with my coffee and I shall say cherry brandy because I like the taste.

'Soup,' she said, 'please. And salmon, I think, with new potatoes and broad beans. Delicious, Mr Sellwood.'

She had done no work. So far he had not mentioned work. After dinner in the lounge, over coffee and liqueurs, when Mr Sellwood would smoke a small cigar, he would touch her knee with his hand, as if by accident.

'Do not do that, Mr Sellwood.' She would stare at him askance; and then perhaps he would beg her and she would explain, shaking her head, saying she could not take the responsibility of doing anything wrong. She thought of his wife at Sevenoaks watching the television as they were watching it in the boarding-house. She saw his wife laughing over some witty thing in the Dick Van Dyke Show, and drinking gin.

'What did you say ?' Mr Sellwood asked.

'Nothing. I did not say anything.'

'Where on earth did you get to, Miss Clerricot ? I could not see you anywhere. One moment we were walking into the dining-room and the next I was all alone being presented with an empty table.'

'I slipped away in the hall. I said I was going.'

'To post a letter? You went out to post a letter?'

'No, no, I did not go out at all. I was still in the hotel. I'm sorry about that.'

'But where in heavens did you get to? Did you have a headache? I searched the whole hotel.'

'I went to the lavatory, Mr Sellwood.'

'The lavatory?'

The waiter reported the conversation in the kitchen. He was a waiter who quite often had little patience with the people he served. Men in the past had offended him. He had been asked to leave employment once because he spat upon a plate of steak. 'They talked about going to the lavatory,' he said, 'while I served the woman with beans. We are getting a rough crowd nowadays.'

Mr Sellwood was looking at his watch again. 'Summon the wine waiter,' he requested, 'and let me tell you how long it takes the fellow to reach us.'

Miss Clerricot waved her hand above her head, not knowing which of the waiters was the wine one. The head waiter returned. 'Something, madam?' he said, pushing up his eyebrows. 'Wine,' she said, and the man snapped his fingers.

'One twenty,' revealed Mr Sellwood, taking the wine list. 'What do you recommend, young fellow?'

Wine was brought and the meal commenced. In the course of it Mr Sellwood spoke of familiar topics: the Pearl Assurance Company and the banks. Miss Clerricot said little. She knew she had made a mistake. She knew by now that nothing could come of this trip to Leeds except perhaps her dismissal from Mr Sellwood's employ. She did not even know why she had undertaken the journey.

'What is Sevenoaks like?' she asked.

'Sevenoaks?'

'What kind of a town –'

'Are you interested in Sevenoaks?'

'No, no, I simply wondered since you live there, Mr Sellwood. I only wondered what kind of a place it was to live in.'

He let a silence fall, looking at her. Then he said it was a good place to live in. He told her part of the history of Sevenoaks and explained about the train service between Sevenoaks and London. 'I myself generally catch the eight-five,' he said. 'And then the five-forty on the way home. But of course there are many other equally suitable trains I could catch. We are richly served in Sevenoaks.'

'Yes, I imagine it is an excellent service.'

'I have just remembered, Miss Clerricot: a page said my wife was here. I have just realized: he imagined you to be my wife. Ha, ha, ha.'

She was embarrassed by this. She felt the blood roaring in her face and neck. She bent her head, scooping up a spoon of cream of chicken soup with simulated care. She did not at all know what to say. 'I wish the floor would open and suck me down': she remembered saying that as a child, one awful afternoon when there had been a party because it was her birthday. The other children had been interested and intent, loving the food and the occasion, shouting for sardine sandwiches and more tinned fruit. She, in the chair of honour, eight years to a day, had sat there feeling groggy in her spectacles, and had afterwards been sick in the lavatory. 'Excitement,' her mother diagnosed; but she knew better. Terror, she thought.

The waiter lifted her soup-plate away, and Mr Sellwood's eyes fell again upon his watch. She considered the waiter's broad back, clad in the conventional garb of his calling. She watched him move between the tables, and it came to her suddenly why she had agreed to come to Leeds.

'Your marriage did not work out, Major Eele,' said Mrs le Tor. 'Well, we have both had our share of misfortune in that direction.'

'My marriage was an interlude I rarely consider,' he said. 'There is no point in raking over the ashes. Mrs Andrews and I were together only a matter of days, and neither of us wished to prolong the issue. Do you watch the television, Mrs le Tor? I would prefer to talk of something else.'

'I have no television.' Her voice was high-pitched now. He thought he detected a querulous note breaking into the gaiety. He drank more wine. He said:

'Cheer up, madam. The television is not much. God knows, there is little enough worth seeing except advertisements –'

'The theatre, though. You said you were a theatre man. Well, so am I a theatre enthusiast. Lavish musicals are very much my line.' She was happy again, smiling generously at him, gesturing, her eyes dancing about. 'Musicals,' repeated Mrs le Tor, 'and anything historical. And you?'

'More intimate theatre really.' He was feeling good. He did not often drink wine. He relaxed in euphoria, seeing Mrs le Tor a little blurred but pleasantly so.

'Revues and that? How modern of you, Major.'

'African ballet is what I like. I will travel a long way to see a black ballet.'

'I do not think I have ever come across the like. You don't mean the Black and White Minstrel Show?'

Major Eele laughed loudly and poured the rest of the wine.

'No, I do not mean that. If it were not a bit late I would suggest we went along to an African ballet tonight.'

'We have come to the end of another bottle. Should we finish up and go together to the corner for a nightcap? Though if you like I will take the African ballet in my stride.'

'You might not like it, madam.' Major Eele coughed and giggled, thinking about the man with the flashlight, and the one-bar electric fire to keep the girls from getting cold.

'Well, what about it? Shall we pay up here and make our way to the upstairs lounge at the corner? I am not a drinking girl myself, but somehow it would pleasantly round off the evening.'

'Brandy would be nice,' said Major Eele. 'Surely these ladies have brandy laid on? Twice I have been out for bottles.' He banged the table lightly with a spoon, though not as lightly as the Misses Gregory would have wished.

'Brandy,' he repeated, speaking to the sister who had served them, who shook her head, reminding him that the café was not licensed.

'Slip out for half a bottle of a good brew, that we may drink it with our coffee. What do you say, Mrs le Tor?'

She clapped her hands together, playfully admiring his go-ahead ways. 'Brandy would be lovely,' she said. 'Couldn't the ladies join us over a bottle, Major, since they have laid on such a feast?'

Major Eele heard these casually spoken words and did not much approve of them. He could not say so, since the woman still stood by the table. He said to her:

'Well, can you get it? Half a bottle of Martell or something?'

Miss Gregory smiled and seemed at a loss. She said she'd ask her sister.

'What on earth did you say that for?' cried Major Eele, rounding on his guest. 'We don't want these women drinking with us. Don't mention it again, and we'll hope they won't have the neck to press it.'

Mrs le Tor said she had meant it only as a gesture, a sign of appreciation, since everything had been so well arranged and seen to. She touched the back of Major Eele's hand, implying apology. 'I never knew anything about African ballet,' she said, giving in to him, making the point that he was the richer in experience and *savoir faire*.

'I'm ever so sorry,' said Miss Gregory. 'We think it is too late to go out for brandy. We're ever so sorry.'

'You run a restaurant, don't you?' Major Eele demanded roughly. 'I myself have messengered twice tonight. What are we paying for?'

'We're very sorry –'

'Think nothing of it,' cried Mrs le Tor. 'Bring the bill, my dear, and we two night birds shall be smartly on our way.'

In the upstairs lounge of the public house they settled down in a corner over their brandies. After his second Major Eele said:

'I thought you were a pro, you know.'

'This other man,' said Mr Sellwood, 'the one with the monkey's face, is by far the swifter operator.'

She wanted the thing to happen; she wanted it to happen once, so that in the future she could think that it had occurred, that a man had tried something on.

'The monkey-faced waiter of the people beside us took only fifteen seconds. Ours took twenty-two.'

She wanted him to make the gesture, to make it finally clear that he had for weeks been leading up to this, that all the conversations about the Pearl Assurance Company and the banks had an end in an hotel in Leeds. It was not that she desired it in order to rebuff Mr Sellwood: the rebuffing would not be easy; it would put her in the wrong, making her seem a grasping kind of woman, and Mr Sellwood might well demand an explanation. She would not enjoy that side of it: Mr Sellwood at a loss for words, issuing his nervous laugh that reminded her of Venables in the boarding-house.

'Ha, ha, ha,' said Mr Sellwood. 'Miss Clerricot, do you know that joke about the couple who arrived at heaven's gate unmarried? "Some vicar here will do the deed," the man said, but St Peter only laughed and said that the vicars seemed all to go elsewhere. Do you understand that, Miss Clerricot?'

She nodded, smiling slightly, still thinking.

Mr Sellwood said: 'I suppose that is what you would call humour by implication.' He looked at his watch, and his eyes darted restlessly about the dining-room.

His wife will not listen to him, she thought. His wife sits there with her ears closed to all his speech. *Efficiency* and *organization* are words that have rung in the wife's ears and which will ring no longer because they are words she will not have in the house. She looked at Mr Sellwood and saw all this in his face, above the moustache, in his eyes and in the lines about his eyes, below it at the corners of his lips.

'Mr Sellwood?'

He did not hear her. She sighed slightly and kept her silence. Instinctively she knew that often in the past he had timed her too. She saw him sitting at his desk, his eyes surreptitiously on the minute hand of his watch, while she walked to the filing cabinet and opened it and sought inside for papers. She wondered if half the time he had really wanted the papers at all, if for twelve years she had not been performing chores so that Mr Sellwood could calculate her speed.

I am sitting with a grown man in a hotel in Leeds, thought Miss Clerricot, and he is playing a game, playing time and motion study with a series of waiters and assuming I take an interest.

'One thing that puzzles me about the Pearl Assurance Company,' Miss Clerricot said, because she felt she had to stop the other thing.

While he talked about the Pearl Assurance Company, in the dining-room and later over coffee in a lounge, she knew that he would not try anything on. He was far away from trying something on; he had never, even, had such a thing in his mind. And she, when she left Leeds and returned by train to London, listening to talk about efficiency in business, would still be what she had been: a woman whom no man had ever taken a liberty with.

'I have a misery of a face,' Miss Clerricot said, meaning not to say the words but only to think them. Mr Sellwood, pulled up in the middle of his subject and startled by what he heard, allowed himself to examine the face referred to and thought that there was not a great deal wrong with it. His secretary had become a little tipsy, he thought; which was rather a pity because he had been about to suggest that they should go out for a short walk. He thought it might be pleasant to walk about in Leeds, looking at cameras in the lighted windows of chemists' shops: he was a keen photographer.

He has taken me to lunch, she thought, and he has taken me with him to Leeds for one reason only: because I listen to him, because I have never said: 'Mr Sellwood, you are boring me.' He has purchased me as an audience.

In the boarding-house the television screen went blank and a high-pitched noise filled the television lounge. 'Wake up, Mr Venables,' cried Nurse Clock in her dressing-gown and soft slippers. 'You can hear that all over the house. I thought it was Mr Scribbin's trains.'

'I thought we might amble out for a stroll,' said Mr Sellwood. 'Are you feeling OK?'

Perhaps she had not said the words, she thought. Perhaps she had just imagined that she had spoken them when all the time they had only been in her mind.

'A stroll?' she said.

'A walk around the shops.'

This is some new piece of tediousness, she thought. There will be a reason for a walk around the shops, perhaps to see if all the shops are locked and safe, perhaps to check that the police of Leeds are doing their job.

'I do not think so.'

'You have a headache, have you? Are you feeling unwell, Miss Clerricot?'

Miss Clerricot shivered and then she wept. She bent her head down so that he should not see her face, which was worse now than ever, contorted and out of control. Her sobs were loud, and when they ceased words tumbled out of her and she told Mr Sellwood all the things she had thought that evening, while he had talked of banks and insurance and had timed the waiters. To Mr Sellwood it sounded confused, but what he made of it was that his secretary loved him in some way and had assumed that he loved her too. 'I am a listening box to you,' she had cried in her emotion. 'A wireless in reverse.'

Mr Sellwood said nothing except that it was an awkward situation, but Miss Clerricot said it was more than that. She went in misery to her room and put her belongings back in her suitcase and took the night's last train to London.

16

Mrs le Tor did not take kindly to Major Eele's admission that he had imagined her to be a prostitute.

'Why?' she enquired, sitting away from him. 'Why did you think that of me?'

'Why not? I can tell you truly, Mrs le Tor, I felt embarrassed that day in Jubilee Road when the truth dawned on me. You will find it amusing, I know: I had imagined you were pressing your services on me.'

Mrs le Tor did not find it amusing and said so.

'It is horrid of you, Major Eele,' she cried.

He reached out to touch the back of her hand, to proffer some small comfort. His eyes were laughing: to Major Eele the misunderstanding was still funny. He said:

'Come, now; anyone can make a mistake.'

But in a sulky manner Mrs le Tor withdrew the hand he sought. 'Get us some more brandy,' she ordered. 'You have behaved disgracefully.'

'Come now,' he said again, and shambled off, affected by her displeasure, to fetch more brandy.

Mrs le Tor took against Major Eele after that. When he returned to her she exclaimed:

'Well, I forgive you all.' She smiled at him and let him touch her hand. She knew what she would do, and watched him becoming a little drunk. 'How odd those letters were. Why did you write those letters? Was it just to give us a chance to meet? You had admired me from afar, had you? I must say your courting ways are a wee bit irregular.'

'I did not write you letters.'

'You wrote to say your Mr Bird had left me a donkey in his will, asking me to call at the boarding-house. And then again saying to put a postcard in the window of a tobacconist's shop.'

'I did not –'

'Let's have no secrets, Major. Why deny it? The second letter accused me of what you had in mind, of the horrid thing you said just now. Let's have another drink. It seemed to me you were attempting to extort some money. Dear Major, you are welcome to all I have.' Mrs le Tor laughed, nudging Major Eele with her eyes, playing a vengeful part.

'Shall I tell you about those ballets?' he asked.

'*Boeing-Boeing* is more my line. Have you seen *Boeing-Boeing*? A superb farce.'

'It is a little club I go to, introduced there by the late Mr Bird –'

'Mr Bird,' she cried. 'Mr Bird, Mr Bird – one hears of nothing but Mr Bird.'

'He took me to the Ti-Ti and signed me in – they created me a member on the spot. The black ballet is a non-stop performance from midday until two o'clock in the morning, though I confess I have never sat it through.'

'A strip club,' cried Mrs le Tor.

'Ha, ha, ha.'

'You frequent a strip club. My God, Major Eele, you're a shady customer!'

He grinned, looking down.

'Am I safe out with you?' Mrs le Tor demanded. 'What would the Misses Gregory say if they knew their fine old soldier was a degenerate? Am I safe with Major Eele?' she called to the man behind the bar. 'He goes to stripping clubs.'

Other people laughed, and Major Eele laughed too, after a pause, straightening his tie.

'No wonder you took me for what you did,' she whispered to him. 'You know no other women, I dare say. Heavens above, what are you up to? Are you trying to get me into an organization?'

Major Eele saw the room move. The shining bottles behind the bar, and the tables and the barman, and Mrs le Tor and the other people present, all moved around, as though the place had suddenly been launched on to a sea.

'These are on me,' announced Mrs le Tor, making for the bar with their two glasses. 'Doubles,' she said.

'What are you thinking when you watch the girls, Major Eele? Tell me about it. What kind of a place do you attend?'

He tried to tell her, but his sentences fell over one another. He spoke of the cinemas he went to; he told her about Bicey-Jones and the motherly tart of fifty years ago. 'She took his blackheads out,' he said.

Mrs le Tor had Major Eele well placed in her mind by now. He was, she saw, a sexual maniac who had insulted her and who would pay for that. She swiftly wrote him off as a companion and felt doubly bitter because a companion in the neighbourhood would have been rather nice. She had heard of many aberrations, among them, she supposed, the writing of incomprehensible letters with an undertone of sex. She thought he could be had up by the police for writing letters to women implying they were prostitutes.

'You are a filthy man.' She laughed as she spoke, implying that his filth had a gay aspect.

Major Eele laughed too. He said:

'You are twice the woman of Mrs Andrews.'

'Now, now, Major.'

'I mean it, madam. I wish it had been you who put a hand on my head in Amesbury. We would have got on very well – I can see us, you and I, laughing our heads off at some joke. You would not always be getting your hair done.'

She whispered: 'Is this a proposal, my dear?'

'Proposal?'

'You are making me blush,' cried Mrs le Tor. 'A proposal of marriage has taken place,' she exclaimed aloud so that all might hear, and eyes were turned on Major Eele.

'On the house?' she said to the barman. But the barman, who had come across such excitements before, shook his head.

A man with another man and two women called out:

'What are you drinking?'

'Oh dear, brandy,' said Mrs le Tor.

The man bought them brandies and invited them to join his party.

'Come on,' said Mrs le Tor, not smiling at Major Eele but smiling at the man. 'Come on, then.'

He was reminded of Mrs Andrews again. Mrs Andrews had always been involving him with other people, people she knew, in restaurants and other public places. There was always somebody in the Berkeley bar, and in the cavern restaurant a man had winked at Mrs Andrews all through a meal once, and she had winked back. He had sat there watching them, his wife and a strange man winking at one another every few minutes for an hour or more.

'Let's stay here,' he said.

'He's bought us a drink. The gentleman has bought us a round.' She walked to the other table, and he followed. 'My newly betrothed,' she said, 'was trying to get out of buying a round.' Everyone laughed except Major Eele. 'Are you sick?' asked Mrs le Tor, and he shook his head, trying to smile. 'A terrible fellow,' she said to the others. 'He tried to bring me to a strip club.'

'Paddy, Joan, Edwin, Kate,' said the man, making introductions.

'Maria,' said Mrs le Tor, 'and Bill.'

'Hullo, Bill,' said the two women together.

'Bill?' said Major Eele.

Mrs le Tor remarked that it was quiet this evening.

'Strip club?' said one of the men, quietly to Major Eele. 'Strip club, Bill? A local place?'

'What?'

'The lady said a strip club. Do you go to a strip joint, Bill? I was wondering, was it local?'

'Why are you calling me Bill? I do not know you, sir.'

'Sorry, old boy. I thought the lady said Bill. What then?'

'I am Major Eele.'

'Our round,' cried Mrs le Tor. 'Now, what is everyone having?'

She walked to the bar and ordered the drinks, returning while they were being poured to ask her escort for a pound.

Major Eele, intoxicated, remembered something he had done a few years ago and which he had never really been able to account for. He had long since put it from his mind, but now, unable to control something, the whole scene rose before him and depressed him further.

'Maria and Bill,' said the man called Paddy, the man who had invited them to join his party. 'To Maria and Bill.' He held his glass in the air and the others clinked theirs against it in an expert way, as though similar occasions often arose.

'Speech,' the others cried, and there was a pause and someone said: 'He's past it.'

Through the mist Major Eele saw himself walking into St George's Hospital at Hyde Park Corner. He could not remember the details of what he had said or what anyone had said to him, but in his sober moments the words were all there, engraved with accuracy.

He had, that day, a hot autumn day in 1961, made at once for the outpatients' department and then had walked straight ahead, towards a counter divided into sections. He approached the area marked *New Patients*.

'May I see the doctor on duty?' Major Eele had said, keeping his voice low.

A young woman in a green overall smiled at him, or half smiled at him, putting him at his ease. She asked if he were a casualty.

'No, no. I would just like to see the doctor in charge.'

The young woman smiled further, enticing him to present information, trained in her job. 'Could you be,' she said, 'a little more explicit? The nature of the ailment?'

'I need advice,' said Major Eele. 'I need advice on a medical matter. It is simply a question of a consultation with a doctor. This is an affair of urgency – I have come today in the heat for that very reason.'

'I understand,' explained the young woman, 'only you see, I cannot really help you unless I know a few more facts. This is a very large hospital; the whole establishment is subdivided. You see, it's very difficult –'

He leaned forward and spoke into her ear. His lips were

touching her brown hair. 'I suspect a venereal infection,' said Major Eele. 'What d'you say to that?'

The young woman said nothing immediately. She withdrew her head and handed him a blue card. She pointed to a row of chairs. 'Come back on Wednesday afternoon,' she said. 'Sit there; a chap in a white coat will look after you.'

After a few more words Major Eele left. There was a number on the blue card. 'That is your number,' the woman had said, and he had queried this with her, saying he did not wish to have a number but would prefer to see his name on the card, arguing with her that his name would have been there before the Health Scheme. 'Treatment is given under conditions of secrecy,' said the young woman. 'It has always been so in my time.'

Major Eele was on his feet again, approaching the bar, asking for more drinks. He fought against the moving room, determined that he should not fall down. He spoke to the barman clearly: he heard his own voice give the order, prompted by one of the men at the table behind him.

'Hurrah!' someone said when he returned to the table with the first couple of drinks. He was aware that he was spending money which he had set aside for other purposes. He sat down and raised his glass, smiling, since they were all doing that: raising their glasses and smiling. He drank some brandy, and the interior of St George's Hospital was clear again in his mind. He recalled quite perfectly the West Indian doctor, a big man with curly black hair, and this time he remembered every word that had passed between them. The encounter took place and he could not stop it, as he swayed in his chair and was ignored by Mrs le Tor.

'Are you married?' asked the doctor.

'Indeed.'

'For how long?'

'Twenty-one years. Well no, twenty-one years this February.'

'Children?'

'Children?'

'Have you any children?'

'Four. Three girls and a boy. The eldest, Monica, is now at Cambridge.'

'Intercourse was extra-marital?'

'With a woman of the streets. I am ashamed of this.'

'When, sir?'

'Many times. I do not know. I do not know the exact occasion. You understand me, Doctor; I am depraved. My name is Major Eele. I am an old soldier, I am shameful in this sin –'

Two minutes later the doctor said:

'We will give you a blood-test, sir. But I would not worry: there is nothing the matter with you. Come back in a week for the result of this test.'

'My name is Major Eele,' he said to a young man in the queue for the blood-tests, but the young man did not seem inclined to exchange pleasantries.

He left St George's Hospital and did not ever return, knowing the test would be negative.

'Let's get him home,' the others said. 'We've got a car.'

'How sweet of you,' said Mrs le Tor. 'Poor old boy, he lives in a dreadful boarding-house, Jubilee Road.'

Mrs le Tor rang the bell at the boarding-house and hammered with the knocker. Her vengeance was full; she felt sweet and warm. She rang and hammered again, and Nurse Clock, earlier disturbed by the high-pitched television sound and now by noise at the hall-door, appeared in her night attire.

'One old sweat, the worse for wear,' cried Mrs le Tor, standing back to reveal Major Eele supported by two men.

'Mrs le Tor!' said Nurse Clock.

'Hi,' said Mrs le Tor.

'Best get him up the stairs,' said one of the men.

'Beddy-byes,' said Mrs le Tor, and giggled hysterically.

The men pulled Major Eele up to his room and laid him out on his bed. One of them loosened his tie and unbuttoned his collar.

'What a frightful joint,' said Mrs le Tor when Nurse Clock had closed the door. 'You'd think they'd offer you a cup of tea.'

She had done her worst, yet she felt still a surge of bitterness against the man whose victim she imagined she had been. He had seen her and desired her in his ugly, unhealthy way, and had written her appalling letters. Well, he would not do that again. She walked away from the boarding-house, refusing a lift from the people who had brought the man home, and felt glad that her escape had been so painless.

17

Studdy removed the pin from the point of his lapel and threw it away.

Nurse Clock said:

'There will be a lot of work in this, straightening the place out. Will you be available, Mr Studdy? What work is it you do at present?'

'I'm concerned with a religious organization.' As he spoke he determined to write no more letters, nor to fritter away his time following people about. He resolved to become a new man, to turn his talents to the success of his newest and most promising venture. The old would go, thought Studdy, and leave behind them money for the home that had cared for their long last hours. The old died more than others: there would be wreaths and funerals often.

'If Bishop Hode had had a place like we plan, Mr Studdy, he might have seen out further days in greater peace.'

'And been duly grateful,' he reminded her. But Nurse Clock pretended not to hear, knowing well what he meant.

'You are the practical one,' she suggested. 'By the terms of Mr Bird's will the house should remain a boarding-house as on his death, even though he left it in our keeping and would have welcomed our better idea. Still, we have people to think about. How shall we go about that, Mr Studdy? There are legal technicalities.'

'Some will take money to go. We could object to others, as Mr Bird himself objected down the years. I think that's the best way. To say a word or two on grounds of unsuitability, and in difficult cases, like the Major, to offer a small sum. The Major would argue the toss.'

'We could get that back garden into trim, for the old folk to sit out in in deck-chairs. What d'you say, Mr Studdy? There's enough in the kitty. A man could come and do it. Mrs Trine mentioned someone to me the other evening. Unless you'd prefer to do it yourself. Are you a gardener, Mr Studdy?'

Studdy replied in the negative. He added:

'Mr Scribbin should go on account of complaints received about noises at night.'

'A useless man,' declared Nurse Clock; and they fell to, making plans.

The season changed, and a misty, mellow autumn crept over all England. The damp leaves scattered, were swept and carted and lost their crinkle. In Gloucestershire the last of the plums already were stored, apples in lofts sat quietly in rows, none of them touching. The trees they came from looked naked in the wind, the backs of their leaves caught and exposed.

In London the air was sharp and pleasant, the evenings drew in, and in a month or so the clocks, put back an hour, would make it winter. In the district of SW17 the season made its mark, on the common land of the area, on the heath, and in front and back gardens where grass was brown now, where summer flowers gave way to wallflowers and michaelmas daisies. At St Dominic's the brothers greased the garden tools and laid the bulk of them away for months to come. The blades of St Dominic's lawn-mower were lifted from their place and carried, an annual thing, to Mr Evans, an ironmonger. He it was who would sharpen them when next he had a moment, or counsel a replacement which the brothers in conclave would discuss. In Jubilee Road the name of Mr Evans was mentioned also and in a similar context. 'Spades we need,' said Nurse Clock, 'and forks and secateurs and all garden implements. Make up a big order, Mr Studdy, and see if Mr Evans will perhaps knock off a shilling or two. Mrs Trine's man is coming on Wednesday: that garden shall bloom this spring.' And she promised herself that in the summer months, in June and July and August, a year after Mr Bird's death, old people would take their ease in canvas garden-chairs and be happy to greet their ninetieth year.

In the centre of London on September 7th a small boy, idling on the streets near the office block where Miss Clerricot worked, was approached by a heavily-built man in a woollen overcoat and was asked to perform a simple chore. Five minutes later the boy handed the man an envelope marked *M. Moran* and received fourpence for his trouble. Studdy, who had watched from a convenient doorway, who had seen the boy enter the reception area that he had once entered himself and a moment later reappear with the envelope in his hand, took the envelope to another place and opened it. He read:

Dear Mr Moran,

I fear I must bring you at once to task.

Your information re my recent visit to Leeds is gravely at fault, and I can only assume that I have been contacted in error. My secretary, Miss Clerricot of 2 Jubilee Road, SW17, who accompanied me on that little excursion, returned to London on the night of our arrival and will vouch for all I claim.

Through this information you will readily agree that the morals you fear for in your letter do not enter into it. In the circumstances I regret that I am unable to contribute to your organization the amount you suggest.

Yours truly,
H. B. Sellwood.

Studdy had met with reverses before and had not succumbed; nevertheless, he felt glad that the boarding-house was soon to be turned into a source of greater profit. He crumpled the letter, typewritten on Mr Sellwood's business paper, and made a small ball of it and threw it lightly towards the edge of the pavement. At least, he reflected, he had gleaned some useful information: Miss Clerricot had left Leeds unexpectedly, and in the middle of the night. She had said she would be away for a day or two. Had she and this Sellwood fallen out? Certainly, there was something there that looked fishy enough to be a lever in the eviction of Miss Clerricot from the boarding-house.

Mr Sellwood had coughed and said it was best that she should move to another department, and she had apologized, saying she could not think what had come over her, saying she did not deserve the indulgence of the Company. 'Tut, tut,' said Mr

Sellwood. He never again spoke to her of the Pearl Assurance Company, and often failed to recognize her when by chance they met.

The dead Mr Bird murmured in the mind of Miss Clerricot, some words of Pope that were a repetition of what he had murmured to her more than once in life. Hearing them, Miss Clerricot thought of death, because the words were to do with it. She thought of death and of her own in particular: the death of her body and the death of her face.

The first leaves of autumn floated down past the barred windows of the boarding-house kitchen. The days were fine, but the sun, weaker than a summer sun, did not entirely illuminate the area of the room. It did not cause the jugs and cups, hanging in long rows on a green dresser, to glisten and glow with summer highlights. But at least it showed off the new season's onions, purchased at the door from a man who came every year from Normandy. They hung on long strings from nails on the sides of the dresser, and they gave the kitchen a harvest look.

'Summer is out,' said Mrs Slape, preparing herrings.

Two other women, the daily women at the boarding-house, who were now drinking tea at the kitchen table, nodded wisely, agreeing with the observations. Gallelty said:

'It has been a good summer.'

The women nodded again. Mrs Slape glanced at Gallelty. 'What are you doing?' she asked.

'I am polishing this.'

The three women looked and saw her polishing a medal.

'What is that?' one asked.

'A medal,' said Gallelty. 'A medal presented to Mr Bird.'

'Never,' said Mrs Slape, firmly, conclusively.

'A medal presented in 1913.'

'Mr Bird in the war?' asked one of the women.

'The war had not begun,' corrected the other. 'The war began in 1914.'

'The medal then?'

'What is the medal, Gallelty?' asked Mrs Slape.

'For the breast-stroke.'

'Swimming!'

'Mr Bird told me of this day, when he won the medal for the forty yards' breast-stroke.'

'Not Mr Bird?'

Gallelty looked at the three women, for all of them seemed to have said the name of Mr Bird in this questioning way.

'Mr Bird showed me the medal,' Gallelty said.

'Mr Bird's foot,' one of the daily women reminded, a woman with an eye for detail.

'He could never swim,' said Mrs Slape. 'How on earth could Mr Bird have swum?'

'He won the race,' Gallelty declared, disturbed at the doubt about the medal. 'Forty yards of the breast-stroke.'

Mrs Slape put a herring half gutted on the draining-board. She wiped her fingers on her apron. 'What for heaven's sake is all this?'

'Mr Bird's medal,' Gallelty repeated, 'for proficiency at the breast-stroke.' She read aloud the words on the medal: '*R. I. Twining, second, 1913*. He said it was the breast-stroke.'

'Who is R. I. Twining?' one of the daily women asked.

'That is not Mr Bird's medal,' the other said. 'Why do you think that is a medal won by Bird?'

'He showed it to me. He talked about it.'

The women laughed, all three of them, hearing Gallelty admit her lack of evidence.

'You cannot believe what you hear,' one of them said.

'Not all you hear,' the other added.

'Put away that medal now,' ordered Mrs Slape. 'Tidy up, Gallelty, there are other things to do.'

'I didn't read the words,' Gallelty explained. 'I found the medal in a corner of a drawer and thought it was the same one. It must have been a different one, a different medal.'

The two women returned to the drinking of their tea and Mrs Slape to the gutting of the herrings. Gallelty put away the cleaning materials, and put the medal with them, since now it seemed to have no merit, being the medal of R. I. Twining, a figure whom no one knew. She thought of R. I. Twining swimming the breast-stroke in 1913, not winning but coming second, to cries of lesser adulation. Somewhere, she felt, there was a medal awarded to Mr Bird for a similar performance, or even for a greater one, in 1913 or thereabouts, before he had had a bad leg, or foot, or whatever it was he had suffered with.

The medal went into a cupboard box that once had contained six small bars of soap and was now the depository of cloths and a metal cleaner. Mrs Slape shook her head over the herrings, reflecting that Gallelty was romantic, thinking that you could not believe much of what she said. The daily women rose from the table and rinsed their tea-cups but did not wash the saucers they had stood on.

Afterwards one of the daily women was only a little sceptical, while the other was certain and adamant. Mrs Slape said that her eyes had not been raised from the herrings, but Gallelty, who was doing only an idle thing with half her mind on it, said that she had clearly seen what there was to be seen, although her story did not at all tally with that of the daily women. Gallelty announced news of the visitation calmly, with neither tears nor fuss. As soon as she had finished speaking, the daily woman, intrigued by the whole idea, chimed in with a version of her own:

'He came into the kitchen and stood at the door, just inside the door, with his panama hat on, smiling about and leaning forward.'

'He was at my elbow,' said Gallelty, 'contradicting about the medal. He said he had won a silver medal and pointed out that this one was only bronze. He laughed over R. I. Twining, saying he was never any good. He used a rude expression.'

Mrs Slape laughed then, using an expression that was not quite rude but was one not generally employed. She did not for a moment believe that Mr Bird had entered the kitchen and had stood with his hat on by the door and had whispered a message to Gallelty.

'I do not believe in things like that,' she said, but did not explain what things these were.

'Fancy,' said the second daily woman, the one who had been bent over a tea-cup at the sink, who had had her back to all that now was claimed to have taken place.

'As clear as day,' the other woman said, and asked for brandy or other household alcohol. 'Anything at all,' she said. 'I am come over faint.'

Gallelty sat down and looked ahead of her at the dresser, at the onions fresh from France and the great collection of bric-à-brac.

'Gallelty is in a trance,' said the daily woman who had not seen anything.

'Gallelty!' cried Mrs Slape.

'He was here as clear as day. He was smiling and he gave a laugh. He was amused about the medal. He is far beyond medals now, poor Mr Bird. He is in the land of his fathers.'

'Gallelty hardly knew him,' said Mrs Slape, feeling jealous that she herself had received no visitation. She had known Mr Bird for eighteen years, she had served him well.

'We are not psychic, dear,' said the daily woman who had been at first only a little sceptical and was now not sceptical at all. 'It seems he passed amongst us and we missed him. Think of that, it could be happening all the time.'

'I don't believe in that,' said Mrs Slape again. 'Neurotic.'

An argument ensued between Mrs Slape and the woman who claimed to have seen Mr Bird, the woman saying that she was certainly not neurotic. She threatened to give in her notice, to complain to Nurse Clock.

'I was not frightened,' Gallelty reported. 'He stood beside me, a man of death, and I never turned a hair. I welcomed him in my heart and then he faded away, like a mark you put Dabitoff on. Mrs Slape, I have never enjoyed so rich an experience.'

'Like Aladdin,' said she who had shared this experience. 'Gallelty, you were rubbing the medal like Aladdin rubbed his lamp and suddenly Mr Bird appeared, though we saw him different. I saw him by the door and you by your elbow. What a story to tell!' Carried away by the drama, she had forgotten that a moment ago she had been offended by Mrs Slape. Then, seeing her, she remembered. 'It will not do, Mrs Slape. If you are jealous that you have been left out, I cannot help. Neither Gallelty nor I can help it in any way at all. It is not our affair, but you must take back what you said. I do not come here to be called a nerve case.'

'I spoke in haste,' said Mrs Slape, turning the tap on the prepared herrings, 'though I did not mean neurotic in an ugly sense. I meant no harm, but I'll say I'm sorry.' She dried her hands on her apron and tossed the first herrings on to a newspaper covered with flour. 'There is cooking sherry,' she said. 'That is all I can offer you down here.'

'Lovely.'

'Gallelty should take a drop too,' the other woman advised. 'Gallelty dear, sit down again and take a glass from Mrs Slape. It is not every day you meet the dead.'

'Have you had strong drink before?' Mrs Slape enquired, feeling Gallelty to be her moral responsibility. 'A girl we had here once went into a coma. She took a bottle when my back was turned and drank it all, thinking it was the thing she had a craving for: vinegar.'

'I have drunk all drinks in my time,' said Gallelty. 'Gins and tonics, wine, port, champagne.' She received the glass from Mrs Slape's hand and finished the sherry in a gulp. 'I am a Manx girl who has worked in Lipton's and then in the women's police. I have knocked about, I can tell you that. I was sent through my destiny to the boarding-house of Mr Bird, who was a father to me, as he was to all.'

'She knew him but a fortnight,' said Mrs Slape, and added: 'Destiny worked in Gallelty's bladder.' She laughed loudly, powdering the herrings with flour.

'What a nasty word,' one of the women protested. 'Mrs Slape, please.'

'Bladder,' the other said, for Mrs Slape looked puzzled.

'Gallelty was taken short. I opened the door and there she was with her haversack. "I am taken short," she shouted and rampaged into the house.'

The daily women looked at one another and then at Mrs Slape and then at Gallelty.

'I am in love with Mr Bird,' cried Gallelty. 'His fingers are running up and down my arm. I have known many a man, I can tell you that, but never a man like Mr Bird, who took me in and warned me of his premonition that I would meet my fate in Plymouth. He said it was a sailors' town. Well, I knew that.' Gallelty reached for the bottle of cooking sherry, and Mrs Slape said:

'What are you doing?'

'I am feeling faint, Mrs Slape. Mr Bird was a comfort, but now I am on edge.'

'A very coarse word,' said the woman who had objected to Mrs Slape's vocabulary. 'My hubby would not care to know that I heard that word today.'

'He is coming back,' cried Gallelty, staring at the door and pouring out the cooking sherry. 'Here comes William Bird.' But afterwards she admitted that Mr Bird had not come to the kitchen this second time. She agreed she had been having them on, trying on a pretence in order to distract attention from her hands on the sherry bottle.

'Let us get down to our chores,' Mrs Slape said then. 'We are paid to work.'

Later that day Gallelty told the residents that Mr Bird had appeared to her and to a daily woman in the kitchen, that he had worn a hat for the daily woman but had come uncovered to her. Nobody paid much attention.

18

'Mr Bird's will is being broken,' said Major Eele. 'An attempt is taking place to defeat the ends of justice.'

All the residents except Mr Obd, who could not be interested in the crisis at the boarding-house, having a crisis of his own, sat in Major Eele's room. He had convened them there to pass on his news, which he now did.

'I was informed by Mr Studdy that I should quit my room forthwith or on an agreed date. I was given my marching orders, and I protested at once; and later to Nurse Clock, thinking to find justice there.'

'Yes ?' said Rose Cave.

'They are in league, these two, apparently. Nurse Clock said all that Studdy said.'

'What were the grounds ?' asked Rose Cave. 'How could they request you to go, Major Eele ? The will says no one must go, unless voluntarily.'

'They said they were reading between the lines of the will. They said they had established its spirit.'

'Established its spirit ?' said Venables, holding back laughter.

Miss Clerricot sat silent, contained within herself, thinking, as she had for some time thought, that she was a woman who had suffered a little blow, and thinking too that it was she herself who had delivered it.

'They are up to no good,' said Major Eele.

'Did they give you no practical reasons ?' Rose Cave demanded. 'Did they just say go ?'

'No, it was not so simple. In fact, the more they spoke the more ominous it became. I stuck to my guns and in the end was offered the lordly sum of twenty guineas as compensation.'

Nurse Clock had said: 'We cannot have people carried into

the boarding-house by night. You must readily appreciate that.'

But he had replied that he did not so readily appreciate that and had added that he had a right to remain, under the will of Mr Bird. He would not win in a court of law, according to Nurse Clock; since the law would not look kindly on drunken rowdyism at midnight. She was frightened to have him in the house, she declared, and made the point that a magistrate would soon see that. 'I have friends at the police station,' she added. 'You would not stand a chance.'

'This is all preposterous,' said Rose Cave.

'Well, I thought I had better report the matter to all of you, since goodness knows who will be next on that list.'

'Quite right,' said Mr Scribbin. 'Quite right to tell us.'

'What can be done?' asked Rose Cave. She had feared this all along: she guessed there might be something in what the Major said, that they were all to go. The unexpected had happened apparently: Studdy and Nurse Clock had sunk their differences.

'Oh, they are selfish and ungrateful,' said Nurse Clock. 'The things they say can cut you to the core. They are quite irresponsible in most of what they say. They become dirty, cunning sometimes, and unpleasant. But I've said it once and I'll say it again: I'd rather nurse the aged than anyone else on earth. What is a bit of malice and unkindness when you can bring a spark of joy into their lives? Deep down they love you. I have an intuition that when they go to their Maker your name is first on their bloodless lips.'

Nurse Clock said these things many times and in many directions. It was a known fact in the neighbourhood that Nurse Clock loved the aged, especially when they had passed their ninetieth year. She said them now to Studdy, and he, stroking his nose, listened.

'The leaves are coming down,' Nurse Clock went on. 'We must be fixed up by the time the days draw in.'

'They are drawing in already. It is dark by half past eight. I have spoken to Mr Venables. It will cost us fifteen pounds if he is not to draw attention to the stipulations of that will. He wanted more, but for fifteen notes I think he will go quietly. I swore him to secrecy and said that others had already agreed. I put it to him, charitable work; he instantly understood.'

But Venables had afterwards taken the news badly, in the privacy of his room, where he cried for a while and then had gone out for a walk to think things over. Studdy, in fact, had offered him no money at all; Venables was frightened of Studdy and would do whatever Studdy suggested, though it made him feel sick to think that soon apparently, at the moment of Studdy's bidding, he must prepare to leave the boarding-house and seek a room elsewhere.

'I must take fifteen pounds out of the till to bribe Mr Venables.'

Nurse Clock shuffled her feet so as not to hear.

In Major Eele's room they came to no conclusion and were unable to formulate plans. They looked at the floor or at points on the wallpaper or at the window. It was a masculine room, a cheerless place, with a wardrobe and a table and a narrow bed. Major Eele's ties hung outside the wardrobe on a string attached by two large drawing-pins to one of its sides. In a small fireplace a fan of newspaper gathered specks of soot behind three curved bars.

The room was too small for the number it now held. Rose Cave and Miss Clerricot sat on the narrow bed. Mr Scribbin was in a chair. Major Eele and Venables stood, the former walking about. 'I am sorry I can offer you nothing,' he said, thinking he should have bought refreshments for the occasion, sherry perhaps, or beer.

They had never before talked in this close communal way. They had never felt that there was a single problem that affected them all. The boarding-house in Mr Bird's day had not presented such difficulties: there had never been a need to conspire together.

'I think we should take them to task, demand an explanation,' said Rose Cave. 'It could do no harm.' Her short grey hair shook as she spoke, as she moved her head to emphasize her serious attitude.

'Or wait perhaps until another of us is asked to go,' Miss Clerricot suggested, 'just to see what is in their minds.'

Rose Cave said: 'I would not have believed this of Nurse Clock,' and the others shook their heads. By silent consent they agreed that they would indeed have expected such conduct of Studdy.

'If we wait,' said Major Eele, 'what in the meanwhile becomes of me?'

'That is a point,' Miss Clerricot conceded.

'Go on refusing, at all costs, and no matter what happens, whatever the picture is,' Rose Cave advised. 'We will all back you up. I knew that trouble was on the way the moment Nurse Clock walked down that night and said that he had died.'

'He thought himself he would,' Mr Scribbin interjected. '"I am not long for this world," he said to me.'

'He should not have left that will,' said Rose Cave.

'Could it not be contested?' suggested Mr Scribbin. 'You hear of things like that.'

'We are wandering miles from the point,' said Major Eele. 'What on earth is the use of contesting the will?'

'I thought –' Mr Scribbin began.

'No use at all,' said Major Eele.

Major Eele had often shuddered in private since the night he had taken Mrs le Tor out to dinner. He was well out of those clutches, he assured himself. He saw Mrs le Tor as worse than Mrs Andrews.

'You cannot behave like that, bringing your fancy women here,' Nurse Clock had reprimanded him, as though she knew all there was to know, which probably she did. 'Disgraceful scenes in the Jasmine Café too.'

'Nothing happened in the Jasmine.' But Nurse Clock did not believe that. She said she had spoken to the Misses Gregory.

'You have upset Nurse Clock,' Studdy had said. 'Best that you pack your traps, you know.'

'I have done nothing wrong.'

'Nurse Clock is a most respectable woman. She says we are trying to keep a decent house.'

Major Eele felt far from safe. He knew that they had the

upper hand; he knew that they could say enough to turn the other residents against him; they could make out a good case for his dismissal. Rose Cave would not like to know that he had been to *Hot Hours*.

'You cannot believe all those two say,' he said now, experimentally.

'Oh?' said Rose Cave. 'Nurse Clock?'

'Mr Bird told me once that he did not believe all Nurse Clock said, and implied the same of Studdy. They have a way of blackening people's characters.'

That morning, in the lavatory at the office, Venables had found himself bent with a pain. He could not straighten up; when he tried to he felt the pain pulling inside him. He had been twenty minutes bent down, trying to fight it. Eventually it had gone and not returned. He felt quite well now.

There was a silence in the room for a while, that was broken in the end by a sound that seemed extraneous and odd.

'What was that?' someone asked.

'Scribbin,' said Major Eele. 'Scribbin here has begun his muttering.' But Scribbin denied that he had muttered or made any noise at all.

When Mr Bird had written his will and had read it over he became aware that he was laughing. He heard the sound for some time, a minute or a minute and a quarter, and then he recognized its source and wondered why he was laughing like that, such a quiet, slurping sound, like the lapping of water. It was something that occasionally had happened to Mr Bird, this abrupt awareness of some performance of his own. It had happened to him when he found himself peeping over the banisters to observe the return of a resident to the boarding-house, or when he discovered himself staring at Venables' navy-blue blazer or Nurse Clock's precisely cut finger-nails or the small eyes of Major Eele. Most of all, though, Mr Bird had found that when recording the idiosyncrasies of his residents he had been wont to do so with a ghost of a smile upon his lips. Invariably he came to, as it were, with a jolt, unable to explain to himself the presence of humour in his expression, and he made a point always of wiping away that ghost of a smile and murmuring a few words of apology. As he laid down the paper on which he had written his will and as he banished the soft ripple of his laughter, he recalled how recently he had lost himself in the study of a periodic and unconscious movement in Rose Cave's left set of fingers and how he had found himself, again, naughtily, smiling a little.

Venables could not bring himself to say that he, too, had been approached by Studdy and had in his weakness agreed to leave the boarding-house, although no offer of money had come his way. He tried to tell them, but when he opened his mouth, with the sentence already formed, he felt a dryness about his tongue that seemed to make speech difficult.

'I am making a list,' said Nurse Clock, 'of all that we need at first. It would surprise you, Mr Studdy, some of the articles that the elderly require.'

'You can't surprise Mr Studdy.' He wagged his head, a man of the world, a man who had been places, into many a house, a man who knew the elderly well and recognized all their foibles, who knew the middle-aged, too, and the young and the very young.

'I am going to an auction,' said Nurse Clock, 'after two commodes.'

'Definitely,' said Studdy.

In Major Eele's room Rose Cave said:

'There is that sound again.'

'It is Scribbin,' said Major Eele. 'Scribbin goes a-muttering on.'

Mr Scribbin repeated his denial and began to protest that he should continue to be accused. Venables opened the door and peered outside.

'It is only Mr Obd on the stairs,' he said, 'going up and down, talking and talking.'

In the kitchen Mrs Slape and Gallelty sat in silence, reading two magazines. Mrs Slape was in her big armchair, a chair that once had been upstairs, that Mr Bird one day had said she might have below to rest herself in, since it needed repairs to its upholstery and did not look right in a public part of the boarding-house. Gallelty had spread her magazine on the scrubbed deal of the table. She crouched over the print, her slight body shaped into a series of angles. She read in an absorbed way a story about an architect in love. By chance, Mrs Slape was reading, in a magazine given to her by Nurse Clock, the very article that Nurse Clock had been reading when Mr Bird had died.

'I would love to see Balmoral,' said Mrs Slape, sighing. But Gallelty, concerned with the fate of the architect in love, did not hear her. Mrs Slape sighed again and turned the pages to a story about an architect, a different one, but one who was also in love.

It was ten o'clock. The two read on, unaware that far above them the fate of the boarding-house was bouncing about like a tennis ball.

'We will not go,' they said, nodding their heads in agreement in Major Eele's room.

'They cannot,' said Rose Cave, 'they have no right.'

On the landing and on the stairs and in the hall, Mr Obd, allied neither with his fellow residents nor with the partnership of Studdy and Nurse Clock, was beyond them all and concerned with none of them.

Studdy and Nurse Clock continued to sit in Mr Bird's room, compromising, making the allowances on which their alliance was built.

'What was that?' asked Nurse Clock.

'Nothing,' said Studdy.

But Nurse Clock went to the door and opened it, and examined the gloom beyond. She saw Mr Obd moving about the landing, a dark figure in the greater darkness. He was speaking as he moved, for Mr Obd had imagined again that he had met Mr Bird in his wanderings and had said hello to him.

Nurse Clock shrugged her fattish shoulders and returned to the calculation they had been engaged upon. Studdy was sleepy. He rolled and lit a cigarette to keep him occupied and awake. Nurse Clock said:

'Multiply twenty-four by four.'

'Ninety-six,' said Studdy, doing the sum on the back of an envelope.

They gave no thought to Mr Bird, but Mr Bird lived on in the mind of Mr Obd, and in the mind of Mr Obd he laughed his soft laugh, like thickened water lapping.

19

It was reported in the newspapers that a girl would attempt to swim the English Channel under the influence of hypnosis. New insecticides in household paint caused a man in Cumberland to form a society for the preservation of the house-fly. Further cargoes of Australia butter were promised; a tiger sat on a child and caused no damage; a man in Tel-Aviv bit a dog.

The people of the boarding-house read such items day by day, as did others in London and beyond it, as did all those who recently had crossed the paths of the people in the boarding-house: Mrs Rush and Mrs le Tor, Mr Sellwood, the Misses Gregory and many another. Mrs Maylam no longer read a daily newspaper: her eyes, she said, could not steady themselves on the print.

In the boarding-house they were all worried by now, all except Nurse Clock and Studdy.

'I heard it at table,' Gallelty reported. 'They spoke in whispers: the house is up for sale.'

'Never,' said Mrs Slape.

But the atmosphere that obtained seeped through to Mrs Slape, and she in the end believed that all was hardly well. 'Are you selling out?' she put it directly to Nurse Clock, and Nurse Clock shrieked with laughter. They are selling out, thought Mrs Slape, and felt her stomach shiver, remembering the day she had come, remembering Slape and his ways.

'What is going on?' she asked Rose Cave.

'What do you mean?'

'What is going on? The house is up for sale, is it?'

Rose Cave told her what she knew, which was not much but seemed enough for Mrs Slape.

Rose Cave read about the man in Tel-Aviv who had turned

upon a dog, because, he said, the dog had chased his daughter. She was a keen reader of such details, on the bus that carried her to her work, and later in her lunch-hour. The owner of the dog, she learnt, planned legal action against the biting man. She did not find it amusing really, though she read with interest the news about the man in Cumberland who had formed a society for the preservation of the house-fly. She thought about that for a while, wondering if there was a reason good enough for taking trouble over house-flies. Privately she thought not, but reserved judgement because the report in the newspaper was brief.

Rose Cave was worried in two ways. She deplored the end of the boarding-house; as well, she felt that justice was at stake. Mr Bird had been clear in his wishes, as expressed through the will he had taken the trouble to leave behind: he had intended the boarding-house to continue in the same manner, with the same people living there. That much was clear to Rose Cave, as it was to all who were now affected. But no one knew that before he died, an hour or so before the end, Mr Bird had visualized the boarding-house as it would be after his time. He saw a well-run house safe in the care of his two chosen champions, with all its inmates intact and present, a monument to himself. He dozed awhile in peace, and then, awake, he imagined for a moment that he had died and that the boarding-house was dying too. He thought that someone asked him a question, seeking an explanation for his motives and his planning. He heard himself laughing in reply, the same soft sound, like water moving, and he said aloud: 'I built that I might destroy.' Nurse Clock had looked up from her magazine and told him to take it easy.

Rose Cave knew nothing of this. She reflected on people turned away from a home: Mr Obd, lonely and distressed, as increasingly he was nowadays, forced to flee to some other place to lay down his head. It was not, she knew, always easy for coloured people. She had read of cases in which Africans or West Indians had been glad to take rooms which were infested with mice or even worse. Mr Obd would suffer insults and rejections, he would feel the white world had turned against him. She thought of Major Eele, a man who was often absurd and cruel in his baiting of others, a man who now might be exposed to baiting and cruelty himself. There was a niche for him here: he had his place, his own chair in the television lounge. Some new abode, among people who were not prepared to honour his eccentricities, would not be the end of the world for Major Eele, but it would not be easy to accept either. The boarding-house was an ordinary enough establishment, but the devil one knew, reflected Rose Cave, was still preferable to the other one.

When she had thought about Mr Scribbin and Miss Clerricot and Venables, her mind turned to herself. But somehow she could not focus it on the future, perhaps because it simply did not wish to move in that direction. It strayed into the past, needling its way back to the bungalow in Ewell, throwing up scenes from childhood. 'Look, Mummy,' she had said when she was three. 'Look, I can touch the lavatory paper.' Her mother had come to see and had nodded absently over this new milestone, the child reaching up with the tips of her fingers, achieving something that delighted her.

Few people had ever come to the bungalow in Ewell. A clergyman used to call now and again, and an elderly woman who had a connexion with the sale of November poppies for the British Legion. Once, one Saturday afternoon, a man had called around, descending from the seat of a motor-cycle and walking up the short, red-tiled path to the front door with his goggles still covering his eyes. She had seen him from the sitting-room window. 'A man is coming,' she said, and her mother had looked up quickly from something she was reading by the fire. 'A man has got off a motor-bike,' Rose Cave had said, 'with goggles on his face.' 'My God!' remarked her mother, standing up and crossing the room quickly. 'Go and play in the kitchen, Rose.' The bell had sounded, and her mother, a hand to her hair, had gone to the door and allowed the goggled person to enter the hall and then the sitting-room.

'Not dead,' her mother often had explained about the man who had been her father. 'Not dead, Rose; it is just that he does not choose to live here with us.' And when she questioned that she was told that one day she would understand it better.

In the kitchen she took out baking-tins and strainers and played for a while, talking to a doll in the window-sill, arranging the cooking things on the kitchen table. She was six at the time; already she could hear herself saying one day soon at school: 'My father came in off his motor-bike and is not ever going away again, because he likes our house and wants to stay.' Someone, probably Elsie Troop, the girl who said she'd seen the King, would say at once: 'It's only a bungalow.' Elsie Troop said that invariably; she had said it so often that some of the others were beginning to say it too. But as she played with the baking-tins and the strainers she didn't mind at all what Elsie Troop might say. She tiptoed into the hall and peered through the coloured glass in the hall-door to see if she could catch a glimpse of the motor-cycle. She heard the subdued tones of her mother and the man as she tiptoed back to the kitchen.

Later her mother came out to make tea. She carried a tray back to the sitting-room, murmuring to herself in agitation, her face flushed, commenting that all there was was a pound of Lincoln Creams. 'May I have tea in there?' Rose Cave had asked, knowing through intuition that she would not be allowed this. Her mother did not reply, but poured milk into a mug and gave her a slice of bread and a Lincoln Cream, and told her to be good.

'Is that my dad?' she asked afterwards. 'Who?' said her mother. 'Was the man on the motor-bike?' But her mother shook her head, laughing a little. 'Do not say *dad*, Rose. Say *father* – if you have to say it at all. The gentleman is just a friend.' But Rose knew that this was not wholly true, because her mother did not go in for having friends. 'Is he going to come again, on his motor-bike?' Her mother said yes, she rather thought he was, and hurried away to wash and dry the tea things.

The following Saturday the motor-cycle had drawn up again and the man had walked up the red-tiled path with his goggles on. 'Go and play in the kitchen, Rose,' her mother said, but afterwards, after tea, Rose had been called into the sitting-room and had seen a tall, smiling man with a pipe in his mouth. His goggles were on the arm of a chair. 'I have a present for you,' the man said and took a bag of Fox's Glacier Mints from his pocket. Her mother said to thank him, calling him Mr Mattock. 'Thank you, Mr Mattock,' said Rose Cave, curtsying as she had been taught at school. 'Sweet,' said Mr Mattock.

When Mr Mattock had gone, strapping the goggles around his head and buttoning himself into an enormous coat, she had thought about him for a while. The smell of his pipe still lingered in the sitting-room and in the hall, which made it easier for her to carry the image of a man sitting down in her mother's arm-chair, his long legs stretched out on the hearth-rug, smoke enveloping his head, coming out of his mouth and, as far as she could see, his nose. 'What a funny man,' Rose Cave said, to see how her mother would reply. 'Funny, Rose?' She said she thought it funny to make so much smoke; she said he looked funny in his goggles. But her mother had not seemed to agree. 'I think Mr Mattock is a very nice man; a wonderful father for some lucky little girl.'

Her mother speaking in this vein reminded her of Elsie Troop. 'My dad put me on his shoulder so I could see all the better,' Elsie Troop would repeat; 'and when the King went by we heard him say: "Who is that pretty little thing on that gentleman's shoulder?" Rose Cave hasn't even got a dad.'

'Wonderful father?' she asked. 'Whatever do you mean, Mummy?' Her mother said nothing more, but the atmosphere was as thick with her mother's thoughts as it was with Mr Mattock's smoke, and in a rudimentary way Rose Cave was aware of the contents of her mother's mind. 'Shall Mr Mattock call again?' she asked. 'Next Saturday?' Her mother said he would, and added, laughing, that it was getting to be a Saturday thing with Mr Mattock. 'Yes, he shall come again,' she said; but in fact, and for a reason that had always remained mysterious, he hadn't.

'Poor Mother,' Rose Cave would say later in her life, throwing an arm about a pair of thin shoulders and thinking of Mr Mattock on his motor-cycle, Mr Mattock who had seemed so foreign in the feminine bungalow, with his goggles and his belching smoke.

As always, Rose Cave had not intended to become involved like this with her own past and with the past of her dead mother. She had wished to think of some practical course of action, some way of combating the machinations of Nurse Clock and Studdy or, failing that, the consideration of some provision for her own future living arrangements. 'We must go in a body and beard them,' she said to herself. 'The whole thing must be laid bare.' But she did not, even with this quite sound suggestion fresh in her mind, feel sanguine about the outcome. It seemed to Rose Cave that the die was already cast: the unlikely alliance was made of a stern fibre; indeed, it gathered its strength from its very unlikeliness. They, the residents, had been dilatory; the others were clearly well ahead, things were moving. The fabric of the boarding-house was under attack, she felt that in her bones. 'I could see a solicitor,' said Rose Cave on a bus, and opened her *Daily Express*.

'Miss Cave could be useful,' said Nurse Clock. 'I wonder would she take a small salary for full-time duties, or agree to her keep in lieu of wages? Pin money should see her through.'

'Miss Cave has no experience in the wide world.'

'What experience is needed,' Nurse Clock argued, 'for wheeling them around in a bath-chair, or putting a blanket on their poor old legs?'

Studdy shrugged, stating in this silent way that he agreed: he saw at once that no experience was necessary for wheeling about the aged or tucking them up with a blanket. 'I have a plasterer coming this morning,' he reported, 'to repair the ceiling in Mr Bird's attic. We can save that ceiling if we act pronto.'

'A stitch in time,' said Nurse Clock in a rumbustious way. 'But take care with Mrs Slape now. You upset her, you know, saying you wanted more fish served.'

For a moment Studdy wished for the days gone by, for the time when the hatred was ripe and uncomplicated between this woman and himself, when he had carried the small weapon in his lapel and had persuaded her patients to wear a potato. Then he remembered the vision he awoke with in the mornings: the old and the senile dying fast in his boarding-house. Studdy saw silver-backed hair-brushes brought in the boarding-house in a ninety-year-old's luggage, and brooches and ear-rings and small inlaid boxes filled to the brim with interesting letters. He saw himself in room after room, shaking his head over their little radios, saying that something was just a trifle wrong, that the radio would have to go in for a few days' repairs. He saw unhurried games of cards with old soldiers who had forgotten the title of their regiments, with clergymen and men who once had been men of business. He saw small sums of money thrown idly on the green baize, winking at him.

20

Mr Scribbin took off his shoes and placed them beside his bed. He clad his feet in slippers of fawn felt and found the change agreeable. It was gloomy in his room because he wished it to be so. In the dimness with his slippers on he was conscious of a certain peace, a peace that was complete for Mr Scribbin when the room was filled with the echo of wheels moving fast on rails, or the sounds of shunting and escaping steam.

He placed a record on his turn-table and sat in a wicker chair. It was dawn near Riccarton Junction; owls hooted far away, a light wind rustled the trees. Mr Scribbin shivered, feeling that light wind to be chill. He could hear the distant whistle of a V.2 with a freight as it approached the mouth of a tunnel. Then the rumble began, a harsh whisper at first, deadening the sounds of nature.

Mr Scribbin rose and increased the volume. The train crashed through the room, the sound bounced from wall to wall, the rhythmic roar of fast spinning wheels dominated his whole consciousness. Entranced, he returned to the wicker chair.

The train burst from the tunnel, gathered fresh momentum, and sped into the dawn. A curlew cried once in the remaining silence, and knuckles struck the panelled wood of Mr Scribbin's door.

'Mr Scribbin dear, we cannot have all this,' said Nurse Clock. 'We are all at the end of our tethers, losing sleep and peace of mind because of trains that rattle through our little boarding-house.'

'What?' asked Mr Scribbin.

'It is really better that you seek another place, with better insulation.'

'Insulation, Nurse Clock? I'm sorry, what are you talking about?'

The needle of the gramophone moved on to the next section of the record. A V.2 steamed placidly in Steele Road station.

'Please turn that off, Mr Scribbin. You and I must have a little chat.' Nurse Clock smiled and came further into the room. She sat on the edge of Mr Scribbin's bed. 'A little chat,' she repeated, smiling more broadly, trying to put him at his ease and make him see that what she said was for the best.

'What is the matter?'

'Nothing at all. Nothing is the matter except that there have been so many complaints about these trains. Our friends are kept awake at nights. There was a nice play on the television just now that you couldn't hear a word of.'

Mr Scribbin's ragged head sank on to his chest. 'I'm sorry about the noise,' he said. 'I get carried away. I am interested in trains.'

'Don't we all know that?' Her teeth were displayed generously. She was making a joke of it, softening the blow. 'So you see,' she said.

Mr Scribbin raised his head and shook it. His eyes looked larger and sadder in the gloom. His long fingers were clasped together.

'Let's have a little light on the subject,' said Nurse Clock, and rose and snapped on the electric light and then pulled over the curtains.

'Now I can see you.' She spoke almost flirtatiously, but Mr Scribbin did not notice.

'What is the matter apart from the noise? I am sorry I interfered with the television play. I did not realize.'

'I'm sorry to say, old boy, there have been complaints all along. People have come to me and to Mr Studdy and announced that they could not sleep at nights because trains were coursing through the house. That can be distracting, you know.'

'Oh, yes,' said Mr. Scribbin, and then he had an idea. 'Supposing I moved to Mr Bird's old room? It is way up at the very top, no one would hear a thing. That should solve the problem,

Nurse Clock.' He shot up his eyebrows, widening and rounding his eyes, presenting her with this questioning countenance. He was pleased that he had thought of the move himself and showed his pleasure by adding a smile to his face. He saw nothing wrong with Nurse Clock. It was funny, though, the way she had called him *old boy*: that was more a term between men. Was it, he wondered, some new fashion for women to use it, some expression of friendliness or endearment?

'No,' Nurse Clock snapped briskly. 'That would not do at all.'

'What?'

'We have other plans for Mr Bird's old room. We cannot switch you about, just because you have a whim for it. You must be reasonable now: if we did it for you we'd have to do it for everyone. The house would be a bedlam.'

'What are you saying to me then?'

'I have said it.' She was becoming a little impatient. She did not see why this miserable man should not accept his fate as fate was being accepted every day of the year by millions of others, the homeless, the refugees. What on earth was all the fuss about? London was full of houses with rooms to let.

'There are many nice places, a lot of them more convenient than here. There are places with huge big rooms where you can play your trains for weeks on end and nobody would ever know.'

'But Mr Bird –'

'He is dead.'

'In his will he laid it down that we should go only voluntarily –'

Nurse Clock laughed. 'That was far from legal. You cannot make stipulations like that in a will. Provisions like that aren't worth the paper they're written on.'

'I have my rights,' said Mr Scribbin, more to himself than to Nurse Clock. He revised his opinion of her; he recalled she had attempted to make off with his clothes in that casual manner, or at least had played some part in their thwarted conveyance to foreigners; he saw a glint in her eye as she spoke to him now, a glint that seemed like evidence of ruthlessness.

He did not know anything about her, except that apparently she and Mr Studdy had tried to send off Major Eele as well. He remembered what Major Eele had said.

'Compensation? What about that?'

'Now, now, my dear, you really do not understand. It is you who should be compensating us, the trouble you're causing these days. I assure you, I have had it on my mind, the way you carried on with Mrs Trine. Did it not occur to you that Mrs Trine must have been shocked out of her wits to have witnessed such scenes? How selfish, Mr Scribbin; whatever can Mrs Trine have thought of us? And then the everlasting puffing and rattling that comes out of this room. I must tell you now, though it hurts me to say it, Mrs Trine asked me quietly if you were in your right mind.'

Mr Scribbin looked alarmed, and then puzzled. 'Who is Mrs Trine?' he asked.

Nurse Clock jumped to her feet. 'You know full well who Mrs Trine is. You met Mrs Trine and argued with her and led her a long dance in the hall. Mrs Trine is important in the locality, Mr Scribbin, as most certainly you are aware.'

But he was not aware of this, though by now he had guessed that Mrs Trine must have been the woman who had come after his clothes.

'I could not let my things go like that,' he protested. 'I have not got so many that I can spare –'

'That's meanness,' cried Nurse Clock. 'That's downright meanness, Mr Scribbin: you should be ashamed of yourself. People are starving. People have no rags to their backs –'

'That is no excuse to thieve what I have. Three shirts and a suit, all in good condition, and ties, and things belonging to Venables –'

'We have been through it all,' Nurse Clock reminded him coldly. 'An error was responsible. Why are you grousing? Your property was returned to you.'

'That is not the point –'

'Change the subject, please, Mr Scribbin. Are we never to hear the end of that wretched occasion?'

'I am only attempting to explain.'

'Naturally, if you leave your clothes lying about they are liable to get picked up and confused with others. In a busy house like this one –'

'I did not leave my clothes lying about. Why do you say that to me? Nurse Clock, what is the matter? You come to my room trying to evict me, while previously your agents have attempted the purloining of my clothes. You are adding insult to injury. And now you say it was all my fault –'

'Oh, for heavens' sake, Mr Scribbin dear, give over about all that. You have had your moment of glory and your say as well. Let us try and forget the whole nasty business, though I doubt that Mrs Trine, poor woman, will forget it for many a day to come.' Nurse Clock smiled. 'I apologize for the inconvenience,' she added, thinking it wise to say that, since it cost her little and clearly would please Mr Scribbin. 'Now, as to this other matter, let us sort that one out as quietly as we may. We do not like scenes in the boarding-house. It would be nice if you went and left us all in peace. Both Mr Studdy and I are sorry to see you go.'

'But I am not going,' exclaimed Mr Scribbin, his face woebegone. 'Why should I go? Why cannot I go upstairs instead, to Mr Bird's old room?'

'Chatter! Chatter! You are like a little child. You would think this was the Regent Palace Hotel the way you are performing. I tell you, I am tired of listening to complaints. Complaints there were in Mr Bird's day too. Constantly, he spoke of them to me. Everyone has always gone on about the horrid noise; and how can we trust you not to create further scenes in front of strangers?'

'I do not understand.'

'Whose fault is that, Mr Scribbin? Is it the poor nurse's fault that you don't understand a single thing?'

'No one has made a complaint to me. I do not make scenes; only once when my belongings were being passed through the front door. What do you expect, that I should stand idly by?'

'What do *you* expect, Mr Scribbin? I have a duty to my residents, you know. Can I stand idly by and see them robbed of sleep and then embarrassed by violent scenes?'

Mr Scribbin again protested, denying the accusations that were being levelled at him and attempting to clarify his position and his point of view. But Nurse Clock appeared to have lost all interest in what he said. Her eyes moved about the walls of the room, along the ridge of the ceiling, into the corners.

'Let us fix a date,' she said finally, interrupting something Mr Scribbin was saying. She said she didn't wish to put him to any great trouble: one date was as good as another, provided they could agree on one that wasn't too far away. 'There's a desk sergeant's wife I know, in Peterloo Road; she'd take you in on a word from me. I saw her through pneumonia.'

'I shall see the other residents. I am being victimized.'

Greatly incensed, Nurse Clock rose and left Mr Scribbin to himself. Before the night was out he was visited by Studdy, who offered him eleven pounds.

'In the circumstances, you see,' said Studdy to Major Eele, 'it would save much embarrassment.'

'I have decided against a move, Mr Studdy. I regret that I cannot oblige you.'

'I think it would be better in the long run, Major.'

'I am nicely fixed here, thank you. No good can come of trapesing about like a gipsy. I have been in the boarding-house since my first days in London.'

'Well, I have put it to you, Major.'

'You have.'

'Only we have another lady coming. You understand what I mean. Mr Bird's old room is vacant. I only tried to save you a bit of embarrassment and offered you handsome compensation. Not to worry, Major.'

'I am not worried,' said Major Eele, who was anxious to be on his way to the West End. 'I am only sorry I cannot help you.'

'We couldn't keep that old room empty, not even to oblige a valued resident. You understand that?'

'Someone new is coming?'

'That's right, Major. A Mrs le Tor.'

'They are trying to get rid of me,' announced Mr Scribbin in the television lounge. 'I have been offered money.'

Rose Cave looked towards him, quizzical in her expression, seeking further information.

'That is Mrs Hammond,' said Venables, pointing at the television screen. 'That woman just come on is the Mrs Hammond that Major Eele talked of. She is going to do an act with birds.'

'Oh, yes,' said Mr Scribbin, interested, remembering Major Eele had said that the birds were trained to storm a castle. 'So that is the famous Mrs Hammond.'

'They have offered Mr Scribbin money,' said Rose Cave.

Miss Clerricot heard that and remarked on it inaudibly, deploring the development by pursing her lips.

'Money?' said Venables.

'Major Eele was perfectly right,' said Mr Scribbin. 'That thing in the background is the castle. In a moment we shall see the feathers fly.'

'This is most unpleasant,' protested Rose Cave, averting her eyes. Miss Clerricot nodded, crossing to the door and leaving the room.

'By George,' said Mr Scribbin.

'Why money?' repeated Venables. 'Who is offering him money?'

Rose Cave completed two rows of her grey knitting and then replied in a low voice:

'Nurse Clock and Mr Studdy have offered Mr Scribbin money to vacate his room. The same as with Major Eele.'

Venables felt awkward and wondered if it showed. He looked at the birds, hoping that Rose Cave hadn't noticed. He closed his eyes and saw the Flatrups: the snarling face of the father and the vast waddling mother, and Miss Flatrup herself with her hanging lower lip and sexual eyes.

'Eleven pounds,' explained Mr Scribbin. 'Heavens, did you see that?'

'You didn't accept?' cried Rose Cave, putting down her wool, suddenly struck by the thought that he might have. 'You didn't accept?' she repeated, since he seemed not to have heard.

'They said there had been complaints. Other people had come forward with angry complaints about the noise.'

There was a pause. Then Rose Cave said:

'In honesty, I am bound to confess that once I mentioned to Mr Bird that I found sleep difficult due to the thundering of railway trains. And Mr Bird – I admit, to my irritation – replied that we must learn to live with one another. I have never spoken of the matter to either Nurse Clock or the other, though if I may say so, Mr Scribbin, the noise is sometimes excessive.'

Applause broke out. Mrs Hammond bowed, festooned with birds.

'I asked for Mr Bird's old room. I was told that, too, was excessive. She said I was likening the house to the Regent Palace Hotel.'

'Ha, ha,' said Venables. For years he had pretended to himself that the Flatrups had returned to their native land, but one day in Oxford Street he saw the three of them, all walking abreast, scattering other pedestrians, shoving and hitting out like animals. The memory of that caused him to release the top button of his shirt, beneath his tie. He felt a churning motion in his stomach and the creeping warning of a pain.

'Compensation of eleven pounds,' said Mr Scribbin, and as he spoke he recalled that Major Eele had been offered twenty guineas. He saw that Rose Cave had remembered that too, though she did not remark upon it.

'We must approach them in a deputation,' said Rose Cave. 'We must get Major Eele and Miss Clerricot and on the first opportunity sort this matter out.'

Hearing this, Venables went away and Mr Scribbin agreed by nodding, though his thoughts still dwelt on the invidious fact that Major Eele had seemed to imply a greater sum than he.

'No trouble about Miss Clerricot,' said Studdy. 'Would you speak to her yourself? Say Mrs Sellwood has been on to us here.'

Nurse Clock was thinking that Mrs Maylam had been rude again but soon would be rude no more. There had been a day when Bishop Hode, a man in his time of education and power, had been incontinent in the airing cupboard and she had conveyed him to the bathroom. 'My love, my love,' she had cried when she saw him. 'My poor old love, you are safe with me.' And she gathered him up in her two strong arms and carried him to the bathroom and wiped away his tears of shame. She had whispered then that there was nothing to cry about, telling him the facts of life beyond the ninetieth year, and stripping him and sponging his worn old body. She would never be able to lift Mrs Maylam because Mrs Maylam weighted fourteen stone, but she could set Mrs Maylam to rights and could make it clear that the obedience she required grew out of love.

'Mrs Sellwood ? Who is Mrs Sellwood ?'

'I couldn't sully your hearing, Nurse. I'd never tell you the tale, not in a year. Not you nor any woman. Mention Mrs Sellwood just, and Miss Clerricot will make her tracks.'

Nurse Clock did not accept this. She said she could not simply repeat another woman's name and hope that Miss Clerricot would leave the boarding-house. But Studdy said :

'They must all be gone by the end of the month. There is no use them going in dribs and drabs. I think a fell swoop. A few weeks to set things to rights and we can fill the place up with the old.'

'I realize that, Mr Studdy. It is just a bit difficult about Miss Clerricot –'

'Say Mrs Sellwood has telephoned us. Put it to her that in the circumstances it would be better all round if she evacuated her room. Miss Clerricot'll understand.'

But in fact Nurse Clock never said those words to Miss Clerricot, because before she had an opportunity other things happened to occupy her mind.

21

Miss Annabel Tonks sat at her dressing table attending to the needs of her eyes. Before her lay tweezers and little brushes, mascara, eye-shadow and a preparation for lashes. It was a lengthy business, as Miss Tonks well knew, but perfection, she felt, paid in the end.

As she prodded and applied, Annabel Tonks was not thinking of Mr Obd. She was not, in fact, thinking of anything very much except that she was hungry, having eaten only a bar of pressed banana for lunch. So she felt herself empty inside and then began to think of things she would like to eat for dinner: avocado pears filled with prawns, *bécasses flambées, salsifis frits, cacciocavallo*, strawberries out of season. 'Darling, I'm starving for the most delicate things.' She could say that, looking beautiful, when she opened the door to him. And he would be delighted, she hoped, and would make some clever suggestion. He, of course, was not Tome Obd, but a rather different man, a man who belonged to the present and not to the past, a man with whom she had never played ping-pong and with whom she rather imagined she never would.

A mile or so away Mr Obd was purchasing flowers.

'Such a time of year!' said the assistant. 'In between everything. Why not these excellent asters, fresh today?'

'Ah, asters,' said Mr Obd. He looked at them and said they were beautiful. 'Have you ever seen the luku? No, you would not know. It only grows in Africa. Two dozen asters,' he said, and watched the assistant pick them out and then changed his mind, remembering that asters were what she had never really liked. 'No, no, something else. Not those, I have made a bad mistake.'

'But,' said the assistant, outraged.

'Anything else,' said Mr Obd. 'Carnations, chrysanthemums, sweet peas, lily of the valley –'

'Impossible,' exclaimed the assistant and offered him twelve rare roses at an exorbitant price.

In the boarding-house a deputation called on Nurse Clock and Studdy and found them in the room that had been Mr Bird's, inspecting the new plaster.

'He has made a good job of that,' said Studdy, examining the ceiling in an expert way.

'He may charge a lot,' Nurse Clock remarked. She was thinking that Studdy himself might have repaired the ceiling at no cost at all to the boarding-house finances. She had hoped to see Studdy aiding the man in the garden, wielding some heavy instrument with his coat off, but so far that had not come about. Studdy had spoken to the man, she had seen him at it, standing in the middle of the back garden, wagging his head. She had seen him roll a cigarette and offer it to the man. She had seen the man refuse it.

'It'll need a drop of paint,' Studdy now prescribed. 'The raw plaster is a bit rough without a coat of paint. What d'you say, Nurse?'

'Of course it must be painted. The whole room must be painted. All this wallpaper is coming adrift.' She pointed to a corner of the room where a length of paper was bulging away from the wall and was on the point of falling down altogether.

'That might be repaired,' suggested Studdy. 'That could be tacked back into place.'

'The walls need to be stripped and painted. That paper has been up for forty years. Isn't that a job you could do yourself, Mr Studdy?'

Studdy drew in a sharp breath. He shook his head.

'All hands to the wheel, you know,' Nurse Clock said snappishly.

'Oh, definitely,' said Studdy.

At that moment steps were heard mounting the stairs to the attic room. 'Listen to that,' said Studdy. 'Is that the Army?' He walked to the half-closed door and pulled it open.

Rose Cave entered the room, followed by Miss Clerricot and Venables and Mr Scribbin.

'We would like to have a word with you,' said Rose Cave.

'Well, I'll be on my way,' said Studdy. 'I'll see a man about that bit of painting.'

'Why are you going, Mr Studdy?' asked Rose Cave. 'We wish to speak to you.'

'I thought you said Nurse Clock.'

'We would like to speak to both of you.'

'What is the matter?' said Nurse Clock. She smiled. 'What have we done?'

'It is quite simple really –'

'Has Mrs Slape served something you do not care for? Mr Studdy, we must organize a complaints book, so that residents may write down anything that was not quite to their liking. You know what I mean?'

'Definitely.'

'It is not Mrs Slape,' said Rose Cave. 'It has nothing to do with food.'

'Well, then,' said Nurse Clock.

'We are all concerned with orders given to Major Eele and Mr Scribbin to vacate their rooms.'

'Heavens,' cried Nurse Clock, 'what orders?'

'Major Eele was offered twenty guineas to go and Mr Scribbin eleven pounds. That is against the wishes in Mr Bird's will.'

'We have interpreted the wishes in Mr Bird's will. This is all very embarrassing. Where is Major Eele? There is no need for anyone to take on so.'

'Why not? Why is there no need?'

'Complaints have come in about the noise in Mr Scribbin's room. We all know about Mr Scribbin's fancies. Well, we understand that, but it is hard on others. Mr Scribbin is not himself. We try to keep a happy house.'

'What do you mean, Mr Scribbin is not himself?'

'Yes,' said Mr Scribbin, 'what is meant by that?'

'Mr Scribbin dear, no harm in the world is meant. It is simply that we think you would be happier where the insulation is better. I told you I would look around on your behalf.'

'You are breaking the law,' said Rose Cave.

'No, no,' said Nurse Clock, sighing and leaving it at that.

They had asked Major Eele to join them in this approach to the authorities but he had shaken his head, saying that he no longer wished to argue, thinking of Mrs le Tor.

'Is everyone to go?' asked Miss Clerricot. 'You see, we do not know what is happening.'

'What is happening, my dear, is that Mr Bird has died and certain changes are vital if the boarding-house is to keep its head above water. Major Eele will tell you himself why I was obliged to ask him to leave.'

'No one should be asked to leave, though,' said Miss Clerricot. 'That is the point Miss Cave is making.'

Nurse Clock clicked her teeth. 'Someone telephoned for you, Miss Clerricot dear. Mr Studdy, what was that person's name?'

'Sellwood,' said Studdy, 'a Mrs Sellwood. She asked for Miss Clerricot and then said a thing or two to myself.'

'We are going off the point,' Rose Cave interjected. 'What has some friend of Miss Clerricot's –'

'Friend?' said Studdy.

Miss Clerricot's face had turned a deeper crimson. She did not speak. She wanted the floor to open. Studdy said:

'An agitated lady.'

Venables, thinking of himself, did not notice the blushing cheeks of Miss Clerricot or her general discomfiture. Any moment now, he thought, it would become clear that he had agreed to leave, even without the incentive of money. And then he thought that he could go back on his word because he had signed nothing; if anyone brought it up he would deny it, or say that Studdy had misunderstood him. He felt safe with the others around him. He cast a surreptitious glance at Studdy and saw that Studdy was watching him.

'Excuse me,' said Miss Clerricot and slipped from the room.

'She is taken ill,' said Studdy, as though she had said this and only he had heard it.

'We shall have to see a solicitor,' said Rose Cave.

Nurse Clock sighed, and then was soothing. 'My dear, none

of this affects you at all. Shall I guarantee you your room in writing? I was hoping to have a little chat in any case.'

'We are having a little chat now,' Rose Cave pointed out.

'Well, in private. I may have a little proposition for you –'

'I am concerned with Major Eele and Mr Scribbin. What is to happen to them? I am concerned with the wishes of a dead man, which are now being flouted.'

'Do not worry, my dear. Provision has been made for you.'

Rose Cave became angry. She shook her head. The fingers of her left hand moved of their own accord, as Mr Bird once noticed they were apt to. 'You are deliberately misunderstanding me,' she cried.

'Good night,' said Studdy, moving to go.

'Stay,' cried Rose Cave. 'You are in this too, Mr Studdy. You are the one who offered money.'

'I have a serious appointment,' said Studdy. 'I don't know what you're on about, Miss Cave.'

Studdy was behaving badly, Nurse Clock thought; he was trying to get out of everything.

'Stay if you can, Mr Studdy,' she ordered. 'We should hear Miss Cave's complaint together.' She looked at Mr Scribbin and Venables. 'Would the others like to go, perhaps?' Venables made a move.

'No,' said Rose Cave.

'This is the room I would like,' said Mr Scribbin. 'This room at the top of the house, far away from everyone, where the noise would not be disturbing –'

'The neighbours have been in,' cried Nurse Clock. 'The neighbours have said they cannot stand it. What can I do? You must see, all of you, how I am placed. Major Eele incapable in the hall at midnight, the roar of railways driving all in earshot mad. Be reasonable, Miss Cave.'

'In this room no one would hear a thing. I would play the records very low. Not a neighbour could hear. I would move in straight away. I don't need help –'

But Nurse Clock repeated that the boarding-house was not the Regent Palace Hotel, that the room was already assigned to other uses, that in any case it needed immediate redecoration.

Out on her rounds that afternoon Nurse Clock had run into Mrs le Tor. 'My dear, I'm sorry about all that fuss,' Mrs le Tor had said. 'It was the most unexpected thing: I did not know he was given over to drink.' Nurse Clock had shaken her head and said that she had not known that either. 'I'm only sorry you had to be woken up,' Mrs le Tor continued. 'A bad thing, a whole house roused for one man's selfishness.' The encounter had gone well between them, with both heads shaking and sympathy exchanged. 'Come and have a coffee in the Jasmine,' Mrs le Tor urged, and Nurse Clock propped her bicycle up and followed Mrs le Tor, resplendent in an orange suit and matching lipstick, into the Jasmine Café.

'You see how it is,' Nurse Clock insisted in Mr Bird's room. 'What on earth am I expected to do?'

'Nurse is in a fix,' said Studdy.

'I am trying to be fair to everyone.' She glanced quickly at Studdy, who was still standing at the door. He had a way of standing, she thought, with idleness in every bone and every muscle. Imagine saying she was in a fix: what did he mean by that?

Nurse Clock examined the present situation and kept the evidence of this labour out of her face. Major Eele, it seemed, was certainly going to move; and Venables; and now apparently Miss Clerricot. Mr Scribbin was being difficult, but she saw that as a temporary thing: Mr Scribbin would go in the end. Rose Cave was left, but Rose Cave was welcome to stay and help. Rose Cave was conscientious, there was no doubt about that. Nurse Clock could see her working till all hours, counting sheets and tidying up the day rooms.

'I arranged to see Major Eele,' Mrs le Tor had said, 'because of the letters I have been getting. Well, I got the first one about the donkey and I came post haste to see you all, to find an explanation. But then I received another that was downright libellous. I couldn't understand it, not a word. A most extraordinary letter. So round I came again and met Major Eele on his owney-oh and he engaged me in this amazing conversation.'

Mrs le Tor at this point had broken off to ask Nurse Clock's opinion of her orange suit. 'Such style!' said Nurse Clock. 'Wherever did you get it?' She was not much interested in clothes and was not always aware what the fashions were. In truth, she considered Mrs le Tor's orange suit rather hideous. 'Anyway,' Mrs le Tor continued, 'I ended up by taking it into my head that the brave Major was responsible for all. Well, you've heard of that kind of thing?' Nurse Clock shook her head, because she did not know what kind of thing Mrs le Tor meant. 'Filthy letters,' said Mrs le Tor; 'people who ring up on the telephone and say what they want to do. You must have had it?' Nurse Clock had smiled, without committing herself. 'Foolishly I did not retain that second letter. You know how it is, you are disgusted and must get rid of them. It was here, to the Jasmine, you know, he took me; he hired the whole place for after hours. The Misses Gregory worked like beavers.' 'How nice,' murmured Nurse Clock, thinking of something different. She knew that Major Eele had not written letters to Mrs le Tor. Major Eele was not the kind of man to write to a stranger and say that someone unknown to her had died and left her a donkey carved in bog-oak. 'Did the letters ask for money?' she asked. Mrs le Tor placed a cigarette in her cigarette-holder. 'Isn't that nice?' she said, drawing Nurse Clock's attention to the holder. 'I got it in that shop in Knightsbridge. The second one seemed to talk of money. I was to place a card in Dewar's window advertising for a basement flat. Of course, I never did. I'm only sorry I didn't go straight to the police. They're very good, I believe, in cases like this.' Nurse Clock knew then that this was the work of Studdy. Over the past few weeks she had seen evidence of Studdy's handiwork. She remembered his bleeding from the face, struck by the man from a Morris Minor. Clearly, he had been up to something similar with Mrs le Tor. And how did he know about this Mrs Sellwood in relation to Miss Clerricot? 'You should have gone to the police,' Nurse Clock said, a quick idea shaping in her kind. 'That kind of thing has got to be stamped down. Did you burn that second letter? It wouldn't be still in a w.p.b.?' As she saw it, Studdy's usefulness was fast coming to an end. What point would there be in having the man idling about, upsetting the elderly with his cigarettes and his quaint expressions? Studdy would never do a hand's turn. 'Oh, I threw the thing away,' said Mrs le Tor. 'Honestly, I can't remember.' In fact, the letter was still in a drawer of her bureau. It was a letter she liked to think about, but for some reason did not wish to show around.

'I must be going,' said Studdy, sniffing by the door. 'I have a serious engagement to attend to.'

'Off you go then,' said Nurse Clock. 'I will have a private word with Miss Cave.'

'What about me?' demanded Mr Scribbin. 'I don't feel like moving, you know.'

'It'll all pan out,' Nurse Clock assured him. 'Whatever happens will happen for the best. Take my word on that, Mr Scribbin dear.'

'No one must leave this boarding-house against their will,' Rose Cave pronounced. 'I really do insist upon that. Where would poor Mr Obd go?'

'Heavens above,' cried Nurse Clock. 'I had clean forgotten Mr Obd.'

Miss Annabel Tonks had completed the attentions to her eyes when the doorbell rang. She glanced at her watch and said to herself that he was early. He would just have to wait; she was still in her dressing-gown.

As she walked from her bedroom towards the hall-door she remembered that of course this was Mr Obd. For twelve years in this flat whenever the bell rang unexpectedly she thought of Mr Obd, and remained still and silent, so that Mr Obd would ring again, and then again, and eventually shuffle off. She had tried everything with Mr Obd; it was becoming difficult because quite often it was not Mr Obd at all who was ringing the bell but someone else whom she would have quite liked to see. She had explained to him a hundred times that she would prefer it if he did not call round without an invitation.

'Annabel,' said Mr Obd when she opened the door, holding out to her twelve red roses.

'Now, Tome,' she said, speaking crisply, ignoring the roses.

'Now, Tome, you know I do not like you to come here like this. I have repeatedly asked you –'

'Annabel, may I come in? For old times' sake?'

She shook her head, and then changed her mind.

'I am just going out. I am in the middle of getting ready. But come in for five minutes, because I have a few words to say to you.'

'Put these in water,' cried Mr Obd, shaking his roses in the air. 'It is indeed wonderful to see your precious flat again, Annabel.'

She led the way to her small sitting-room and told him to sit down.

'Take a pew,' she said. 'This will not take long.'

'You are looking sweet,' he began, but she held up her right hand for silence.

'I am tired of telling you, Tome, that you must not come here bothering me. You must try to understand that the years have passed by. For instance, I am engaged to be married.'

'Married?'

'Engaged to be married. Spoken for. Do you understand?'

'Annabel, you did not tell me this. You never told me. Why are you doing this? Whatever is happening?'

'Nothing is happening, Tome, except that I am telling you once again that it is my wish that you cease to bother me.'

'I do not understand. You say married, but I have been bringing you flowers for a long time, Annabel.'

'For twelve years.'

'I have written you letters. I have said what is in my heart. Tome Obd has hidden nothing. Who is ashamed? Annabel, this man before you now is not ashamed.'

'Of course not, Tome. Now, time is flying away. I simply wish to say to you that you must not come again –'

'You are surely ashamed, Annabel? Are you not ashamed to be talking of marriage in this way tonight? You are talking of marriage to me who has walked to see you, up the stone stairs, carrying you roses.'

'You must not bring me roses. I have asked you before –'

'Dear Annabel, I thought it was asters. I refused asters only today. This evening I said, "No, no, not asters, my Annabel does not care for asters." What is this about roses? I thought roses would please your heart.'

'You must not bring me any flowers at all. I have said that before; you cannot have forgotten.'

'When last I came another lady answered this door and told me you had gone far away. But in the hall I saw your coat and knew that the lady lied. Why did she do that? What is happening? Have you forgotten the days we played ping-pong? You were better than Tome Obd.'

'That was fourteen years ago.'

'What is time, Annabel?'

'I must tell you now, Tome, that I wish you to leave me alone. I wish you not to come here, with flowers and letters which I cannot read –'

'You cannot read?'

'I cannot read your handwriting.'

'So –'

'So it is useless to write long letters to me. There is no point to that at all. I am sorry to say it to one who has been a friend, but say it I must.'

'Do not say it, Annabel. Please –'

''Nonsense, of course I must say what I have to say.'

'You will break Tome Obd's heart. You will break an old African heart here in the lounge-room of your flat.'

'I have no alternative but to inform the police if you persist in coming here, Tome. I am sorry.'

Mr Obd rolled his eyes.

'What more can I say?' said Annabel Tonks, thinking of the time.

'You have said too much. Already too many words have passed. Oh, Virgin Mary.'

'Go now, Tome. Please go quietly.'

Mr Obd, his eyes rolling again, found them arrested by a mark that seemed to have appeared, like a spot of fog, high up in the room, on the ceiling. It was a shredded, lemon-coloured shape, with frayed ends that seemed to move about.

'Alas, Tome Obd,' said a voice in his mind, the voice of the dead Mr Bird.

'Alas,' said Mr Obd, 'how can I go?'

Annabel Tonks flung up her hands, annoyed, no longer prepared to be understanding. She tried to say something, to explain how he might go: by walking as he had come, across the room and into the hall and through the door. Words formed on her lips but did not materialize. She saw Mr Obd staring at the ceiling, opening and closing his mouth. Quickly she thought that she might be doing the same thing: opening and closing her lips, trying to issue words but failing for some reason. It was absurd, she saw, that she and he should be at the same moment in the same predicament.

'Why did we ever meet?' cried Annabel Tonks. 'What a lot of trouble it has been!'

She had not meant to say it quite like that. She had, in fact, not meant to release that sentiment at all. 'What a nuisance you have been' was a sentiment nearer to her, because that was true. But the way she said it made it sound as though the two of them had just indulged in some tragic love affair, which was far from the truth.

She lifted the flowers and picked up Mr Obd's *Evening Standard* and bundled all together and told him again to go. She pushed him towards the door, pressing his belongings upon him, rejecting the roses, and referring again to the police.

'The police?' said Mr Obd. 'What are policemen to me? I am a first-class citizen.'

He said no more. He heard the door clatter into place behind him and found himself on the stone landing, standing with rolling eyes, with roses and an *Evening Standard*, greatly shaken.

'I've been thinking,' said Nurse Clock into the telephone. 'It is your duty to report this. I know a desk sergeant.'

'A desk sergeant?' said Mrs le Tor.

'We would not have to go to the station. I know the house. Root out that letter and let us straightaway go round.'

'Oh, my dear, I have no idea where that old letter is. Maybe I burnt it.'

But Nurse Clock, who knew all about such matters, what one burnt in the way of correspondence and what one did not, paused judiciously, screwing her face into a grimace.

'Why are you phoning?' asked Mrs le Tor.

'Because I have discovered at last who is writing these ugly letters.'

'That old Major?'

'No, no. Major Eele would never be guilty of a thing like that. Major Eele's a gentleman.'

'Who then?' asked Mrs le Tor, disappointed. 'Who then, Nurse Clock?'

'Shall I call around? And we can go together with the letter?'

'Well, I will look for it,' said Mrs le Tor, weighing up the pros and cons and then deciding that a bit of excitement was more valuable than keeping the letter hidden.

'Ten minutes,' said Nurse Clock.

'Alas, Tome Obd,' Mr Bird had said almost every time the two had met on their own, in a passage or on the stairs. 'Alas, Tome Obd,' he would say again as he proceeded on his way, and often Mr Obd heard the words repeated softly a second or a third time. For Mr Bird had felt that the grey-black face of Mr Obd hid, or failed to hide, the most corroding sensitivity of all the boarding-house inmates.

'Alas, Tome Obd.'

He heard the words as he stepped down the stone stairs, feeling heavy in his body, as though he carried some new weight within him, as though emotional pain was made manifest in this physical way.

'Alas, Tome Obd.'

The words were there again, though the voice that spoke them was not the voice of Mr Bird, and it flashed into Mr Obd's mind, an absurd thing, that perhaps it was the voice of Mr Bird made clear and close through death. Maybe, he thought, Mr Bird had taken on the voice of an angel. And he saw again, as he had seen a moment ago on the ceiling of Miss Tonks' room, a floating form that was made, it seemed, of fog. 'That is Mr Bird,' he said to himself. For it seemed like Mr Bird with an angel's wings attached, trailing his leg and carrying a trumpet. Mr Bird soared nearer and caught his eye, and said again in the voice that was not his: 'Alas, Tome Obd.'

'Ho, ho,' remarked another man, going up the stairs.

'Yes?' cried Mr Obd, staring after him. 'I beg your pardon?'

The man looked down and laughed again, and Mr Obd heard himself saying: 'Alas, Tome Obd,' and realized that it was he who had been saying it all the time.

'Obd seems demented,' said the man when he reached Miss Tonks' flat. 'Whatever did you say to him?' He then embraced her, preventing an immediate answer.

'What could I do?' she asked when all that was over. 'I told him straight if he came again I'd have the police here.'

22

Rose Cave felt weary in the television lounge. She sat with her knitting, knowing what the matter was, feeling restless and fearful. She was aware of others in the room: Major Eele crouched by himself, reading something he had concealed in the *Radio Times*, Venables in pain, Mr Scribbin looking, she thought, a little cocky, as though some victory were newly his. It was she who had done the talking in the freshly plastered room upstairs: there was nothing for Mr Scribbin to seem so pleased about. In any case, Nurse Clock would winkle Mr Scribbin out sooner or later, employing ingenious methods.

She heard voices from the television set but did not examine the screen. Her fingers ceased to move; needles and wool fell motionless to her lap. 'I have sat too often in this room,' she murmured. She spoke to herself, keeping her words low so that they did not register beyond her. Music blotted them away; she murmured again but did not hear herself. She thought it might be a good thing that the boarding-house was coming to an end; in her despondency she saw it suddenly as a wretched place. 'The change of life,' she murmured – a thing she had always heard about and had of recent years prepared for.

Venables gritted his teeth, trying not to show them, trying to hold them behind his closed lips. The pain rose from the depths of his bowels and raced like fire through his stomach, spreading to his ribs. He thought he felt it in the bones themselves but thought again that that must be wrong, that pain of this nature could not invade the bone structure. A groan began at the back of his throat, silently, like a warning or an urge. He held it back, clamping his teeth together. He pressed his feet hard on the floor and tore at the flesh of his fingers with two sharp thumb-nails.

'For God's sake,' cried out Rose Cave, 'go to a doctor.'

Major Eele jerked his head, hearing these remote and unusual words. They rang in his ears, passionate like the cry of an animal in agony. They reflected all that was happening in Venables' stomach, but Major Eele did not understand that, because he had never known that Venables was in pain. He didn't know that Venables was dying on his feet because he feared the thought of hospitals.

'What?' said Major Eele.

There was silence except for a song on the television set.

'I am so sorry,' Rose Cave said quietly. 'Forgive me, Mr Venables.'

Venables swallowed, swallowing the groaning that was trying to break through. The pain lessened. He began to smile, breathing through his mouth. He was gasping but it was not noticeable. His feet still pressed the floor.

'I am so sorry,' Rose Cave repeated. 'I cannot think why I said that.'

'All right,' said Venables. 'That is quite all right.'

'I saw you were in pain.'

He shook his head. 'A touch of indigestion, nothing more. I forgot to take my Setlers.'

Major Eele glanced from one to the other, hardly comprehending. He grasped at least that Venables had indigestion and that Rose Cave had said to see a doctor.

'I am not myself,' explained Rose Cave, 'else I most certainly would not have shouted out like that.' She smiled, feeling silly and awkward. 'I hate to see people in pain.'

Venables began to move his body about, shifting the acids in his stomach, or so he thought.

Another silence fell. Everything hung in the air: all three were thinking of what had happened.

'The mint with the hole,' said a voice, and their three heads turned towards the television screen.

'Very good, that,' said Major Eele, laughing in a gamy kind of way, as if some esoteric jest had just been loosed upon them.

Rose Cave picked up her needles and shot them quickly across one another. She was aware of the speed of this motion and was glad that she could achieve the speed without going wrong, because the speed was a help. Her mother had spoken to her of the change of life, saying one felt different and sometimes irresponsible. Married women, faithful all their lives, left their families or did some silly thing, her mother said, when the change of life arrived. She said it was worse for women who had not been married, or rather who had had no children. It was the end of something, her mother said: the body withered. She knitted hard, wishing there was someone she could talk to at that moment. She wanted to tell all that had happened, how she had called out 'For God's sake' to the sick Venables, how she had invaded his greatest privacy and torn the shell off his lonely secret. She tried to imagine what he must be feeling, what now he must be thinking of her. He could not know about the change of life, probably he had never heard of such a thing.

'Is Venables ill?' said Mr Scribbin, who was sitting away from the other three and had been outside the incident. They had forgotten his presence, but some remark had registered with him, though he had been more intent on the television.

Rose Cave shook her head. 'My mistake, Mr Scribbin. Mr Venables had just a turn of indigestion.'

Mr Scribbin, an easy man to satisfy, said something quietly. He cleared his throat and settled down.

'Miss Cave.'

She looked behind her and saw Nurse Clock standing in the doorway.

Mr Obd realized that he was still carrying the twelve red roses and the *Evening Standard*. He stood on the pavement and felt rain on his face. 'I do not need these,' he said, and he threw them into the gutter. The bunch of roses fell apart and scattered on the wet surface. The soft white paper that had wrapped it turned grey before his eyes as it soaked up the grimy rain.

'Disgraceful,' shouted a man, pointing at Mr Obd, then at the flowers and the newspaper on the street. 'Disgraceful,' he repeated, coming closer. He held a black umbrella in his right hand, while with his left he gestured in a threatening way.

'What is the matter?' asked Mr Obd.

'Keep Britain tidy,' said the man. 'Pick up that mess, sir.'

Mr Obd made as if to pass by. 'You can be fined up to five pounds,' said the man. 'I intend to call a policeman.'

Mr Obd bent and collected the flowers and the sodden *Evening Standard* from the street. A couple passing stopped to watch.

'They come here,' said the man, 'and then they litter our streets.'

The couple took exception to this statement and said so. An argument broke out, and Mr Obd, with flowers and newspaper, went away.

He walked for a while in the rain, looking for a litter bin. Then he turned into a small café and asked for coffee. He did that because it was so wet and unpleasant, because he did not particularly want to return to the boarding-house. He stirred a cup of greyish coffee with the tea-spoon supplied but did not drink it. He left it there, with flecks of milk on the surface; and he left the roses and the *Evening Standard* on the floor near his chair. 'That black man forgot his flowers,' cried a waitress, and she ran into the rain to call him back. But Mr Obd was on his way back to the boarding-house and did not wish to be disturbed.

'You understand, my dear, the boarding-house must be organized on an economic basis.'

Nurse Clock thought about smiling in the pause after she had spoken, but she decided that a smile would be out of place, that the note of seriousness must be stressed. She sat in her own room, with the coloured photograph of the Queen glowing quietly on the mantelshelf and the little piece of the Garden of Gethsemane seeming ordinary beneath its glass.

Rose Cave had not ever been in this room before. She saw that it was tidy and businesslike: what she expected, more or less, of the room of a nurse. Her own, she thought, was cosier, with its pleasant curtains and new chintz bedspread.

'Otherwise,' said Nurse Clock, 'the whole place will fall into rack and ruin and there'll be no boarding-house at all. The state of Mr Bird's finances was not good.'

Nurse Clock was having a busy evening. Already she had seen Mrs le Tor and had read with interest the letter they had earlier discussed. Together they had taken it to the house of the desk sergeant. 'Nothing much about this,' the desk sergeant had remarked, irritated at being drawn away from a game of chance with his son. 'In any case, you know, I am not on duty.' But the man's wife had interrupted to say he must not stand on ceremony with Nurse Clock or be in any way stand-offish. 'I am making us all tea,' she said, and reminded her husband of Nurse Clock's past services in a medical way. 'Oh, not at all,' cried Nurse Clock, sitting down and feeling glad that this had come out in front of Mrs le Tor. 'Very well,' said the desk sergeant, and read the letter through again.

'That is libel,' Mrs le Tor had said.

'But how can we apprehend the miscreant?' demanded the desk sergeant, causing Mrs le Tor to think that that was a matter for him to work out on his own. 'There is no truth, I suppose, in any of this?' He examined her face for guilt. It was unlikely, he thought, that she had ever been apprehended herself: he would most surely have known about it. 'We can take it the insinuations are false?'

'My dear man,' said Nurse Clock quietly; and then to Mrs le Tor: 'A formal question. He is obliged to ask it.'

'How can we apprehend the miscreant,' repeated the desk sergeant, 'since we do not know who the miscreant is? You did not, I suppose, madam, write this note yourself?'

'Certainly she didn't,' cried Nurse Clock. 'Why ever should Mrs le Tor do that?' Nurse Clock was enjoying the occasion. Tea was brought in, which added to her pleasure.

'Of course not,' said Mrs le Tor. 'What a silly thing to say.'

'Archie, really,' said the desk sergeant's wife.

'It is far from unknown,' said the desk sergeant, rising to help himself to a macaroon and revealing to his guests that he was in his socks. His wife frowned at him, drawing his attention to his feet.

'What's the matter?' said the desk sergeant, and his wife laughed, pretending that nothing was.

'Well,' he continued, 'it is far from unknown.' he tapped

Mrs le Tor's letter with his finger. 'People are always drawing attention to themselves by composing works of this nature. We had a chap up the other day, an old Mr Pritchard –'

'I happen to know,' said Nurse Clock quickly, 'the hand responsible for this. A certain Mr Studdy.'

The desk sergeant mentioned proof, and Nurse Clock suggested a handwriting expert.

The desk sergeant laughed. 'Forget the whole thing,' he said. 'It is a storm in a tea-cup.'

The two women left the house shortly after that, having been told that they could make an official complaint if they wished, but advised against it.

'Mr Studdy will be moving on,' said Nurse Clock to Rose Cave, 'if that ever worries you.' It seemed to Nurse Clock that a person of Rose Cave's nature might well be affected by Studdy's coarseness. Nurse Clock had more than once heard Studdy use unpleasant-sounding words beneath his breath.

'Mr Studdy?' said Rose Cave. 'But how can that be?'

Nurse Clock coughed. 'I'm afraid Mr Studdy is in a spot of trouble. He may well wish to slip quietly off. Mr Studdy has been up to no good.'

'But the boarding-house? Mr Bird's will? What is happening, Nurse Clock? Really, this seems to be quite a case.'

'Well,' said Nurse Clock. 'I am going to tell you. Let's forget that old Studdy for a while. In a word, Miss Cave, the situation is this: to save the boarding-house it is necessary to transform it into a more profitable institution, an old people's home. That is it in a nutshell.'

'But in that case you would not be saving the boarding-house. The boarding-house would be gone.'

'That is true,' said Nurse Clock.

'I do not understand.' Rose Cave leant forward, as if it had occurred to her that she might be missing part of Nurse Clock's argument.

'I am saying this,' said Nurse Clock. 'I am saying this to you, Miss Cave: there is a place for you with the old folks.'

'But I am not old.' Rose Cave was certain now that Nurse Clock was engaged upon nefarious practice. Apparently she had turned upon her accomplice and had already come into the open with an admission that the boarding-house was to become a refuge for the elderly. Now, it appeared, Nurse Clock was regarding her as one of that number. 'I am not old,' she repeated, her forehead furrowed in bewilderment.

Nurse Clock gave a loud laugh.

'My dear, of course not. I meant it in another way.' She drew in a breath, and then explained that Rose Cave could be of value in the old persons' home, performing agreed chores and receiving a wage.

Mr Obd sat alone in his room and did not shave and did not report for work. After the third day a man telephoned the boarding-house and spoke to Mr Obd and said that as far as Mr Obd's employers were concerned Mr Obd need never report for work again. These tidings did not disturb him. He returned to his room and sat down with a piece of paper and a ball-point pen. He wrote down figures and made calculations. He worked out the accumulated cost of the flowers he had bought Miss Tonks over the years, the gentians and veronicas, the roses, dahlias, and asters in season. He delved into the past and calculated the cost of their cups of coffee, of bus fares paid, and then of such details as the evening newspapers he had had to purchase to while away the time while waiting for her in public places.

Mr Obd felt sick and could eat no food. 'I am surely deranged,' he said to himself, and he felt it a comfort, knowing that he was deranged, that that was the cause of his trouble and of all the calculations on the paper.

He no longer saw Mr Bird flashing through the skies in the guise of a Renaissance angel. Confused, he identified Mr Bird as the founder of heaven and hell and earth. He saw him now in his glory, glancing down on all of them, on Tome Obd and on Annabel, on the African leaders, on his late employers, on all of them here in the boarding-house. Mr Bird was smiling, and his bad leg was not noticeable, for he was neither standing nor moving about, but was sitting in majesty on a chair, wearing what to Mr Obd looked like golden raiment. Mr Bird was not saying 'Alas, Tome Obd'. He was not speaking at all, only resting there amongst laurels.

'You are surely not beautiful,' cried Mr Obd. 'You have done those terrible things.' He tried to strike at the image with his arms, but the image persisted, and in the end he lay down on his narrow bed and thought.

Mr Obd in his madness suspected that Mr Bird had been a man of infinitely subtle cruelty. He saw the gathering together of people in the boarding-house as a cruel action and he remembered that Mr Bird had said to him, the first day he arrived on the doorstep, that the solitary man is a bitter man and that bitterness begets cruelty. He saw the people in the boarding-house as reflections of Mr Bird, and then he lost track of logic and saw them as his creatures.

Mr Obd rose from his bed and again drew paper and ball-point pen to him. He made a fresh set of marks. He was hating Mr Bird now, hating him for ever saying 'Alas, Tome Obd'. He suspected now that the dead man had had some real reason for the repetition of that remark, that he knew about Tome Obd's fourteen-year courtship and had mocked it as often as they had met in the passages or on the stairs, raising his eyes and shaking his head and saying the inevitable words.

'You are the worst man of all, you are the worst man that ever lived,' cried Mr Obd. 'I shall kill you,' cried Mr Obd who had come to London to learn the secrets of the law. 'I shall kill you,' cried he again, and then remembered. He wrote on a fresh sheet of paper, creating his plan.

23

Once upon a time Major Eele had answered an advertisement worded thus:

> Required as a photographic model for a series of advertisements promoting a famous British product a gentleman of good appearance and bearing, of not more than fifty-five years. Write with details of education, background, and present availability at short notice.

He had written, and rather to his surprise had later been summoned for an interview. 'Who are you?' a man had enquired from behind an expanse of desk. 'Eele,' he had said. 'My appointment was for three.' The man behind the desk muttered something about an error and asked Major Eele to wait in another office. While he did so he heard the man's voice on the telephone. 'Eele. E-e-l-e. Like the fish. Well, take him away, will you?' A young woman had led him through passages to the entrance of the building. 'Thank you, Major Eele,' she had said, and vouchsafed no further explanation.

Now he looked through the advertisement columns again and wondered if in seeking a place of residence he would meet with such brusque conduct. He amused himself by imagining a series of landladies regarding him expertly as they opened their hall-doors. 'Oh dear me, no,' they would murmur, leaving him there as the young woman had. He had lied a bit about his age in replying to the advertisement for a man of bearing, but otherwise he thought they should have known what to expect. The whole episode had puzzled him greatly, and like the reported excursion of Bicey-Jones into the world of sex had remained in his consciousness as a source of wonderment ever since.

To Major Eele it seemed incredible that the inheritors of Mr

Bird's house were going to achieve their dire purposes through a series of tricks, subterfuges and small pecuniary inducements. There was something almost farcical about Nurse Clock and Studdy plotting together and sinking their differences towards a common end. Major Eele did not then know that Nurse Clock was moving in for the final kill, that she was even then preparing to be left triumphant and alone, like a beast that destroys the instrument of its past success.

Miss Clerricot took her small face between her hands and pushed the flesh about, a habit she had always had. Life was all right, she reflected, when it continued in a mechanical way, like the typing she had performed for Mr Sellwood and now performed for a Mr Morgan. Change, like the abrupt breach in her routine when Mr Sellwood had discovered she would listen and had started to take her to lunch and later to Leeds, was upsetting. She wanted to awake one morning and find herself in Kingston-upon-Thames, married to a man, and the mother of three children. She wanted to see in her bedroom mirror not the face of Miss Clerricot but the face of someone she did not know and did not care about, some face that she could take for ever for granted. She knew that none of that would ever be, not even the part of it that was possible. 'I am fit company for the typewriter keys in Mr Morgan's outer office,' she said to herself, and felt depressed because of all the topsy-turviness, because on top of everything else she would have to leave the boarding-house and Mr Morgan's outer office too. Mrs Sellwood, miraculously, had guessed what once had been in her mind and naturally had placed upon it the wrong construction.

'I do not know what to say,' said Rose Cave. 'I am quite unqualified, quite untrained. And I cannot at all reconcile myself to the break up of the boarding-house –'

'What good work it is,' murmured Nurse Clock. 'When they have passed their ninetieth year they rely on us for every little thing. It would be a happiness for the poor old souls to have kind Miss Cave dispensing this and that.'

'But Mr Bird –'

'My dear, give over about that old Mr Bird. Mr Bird, I assure you, does not care or matter in the least. Putrefaction has long since set in.'

'Oh, don't say that.' Rose Cave was shocked to hear the expression used about a man who not long ago had lived amongst them. But Nurse Clock, who was used, as she would explain, to death as well as to life, only laughed at the other's timidness and poured a cup of tea.

So it was that at the time when Mr Obd went mad the boarding-house was at sixes and sevens. Studdy did not yet know what was in Nurse Clock's mind. Venables had promised Studdy that he would seek accommodation elsewhere and had not yet confessed this to the other residents. Miss Clerricot expected Mrs Sellwood to come and create a scene which would disgrace her in the eyes of all. Major Eele awaited with apprehension the threatened arrival of Mrs le Tor and meanwhile scanned the advertisement columns. Rose Cave felt that a preposterous question had been put to her and yet was attracted by it. Gallelty and Mrs Slape prepared for their dismissal. 'When he comes again, I shall ask him what's best to do,' said Gallelty. 'As soon as he materializes in the kitchen I shall say at once: "Mr Bird, we are at sixes and sevens; we do not know what to do next." He will give us a lead, I am sure of that.' Mr Scribbin found three of his gramophone records broken.

'I was round at the desk sergeant's last evening,' Nurse Clock said, smiling, to Mr Scribbin, 'on a different matter altogether. She has a nice little room for you there. I said you'd be over to see it.'

'Who broke my records?'

But Nurse Clock said she didn't know who broke his records and repeated what she had already said.

Mr Bird, for his part, did not ever again seem to materialize in the kitchen. Mr Bird lived in the mind of Mr Obd and Mr Obd spoke to him, savaging him with his tongue. Sometimes he filled Mr Obd's small room with his murmuring and his sly grinning, and Mr Obd would jump up and down, extremely angry.

'I am busy, dear,' Nurse Clock told Mrs Maylam. 'No time for your chat today. Lift up your skirt now for our little jab. Have the bowels moved this morning?'

'My God, you're evil,' replied Mrs Maylam. Obediently, she exposed her flesh for the injection. 'You'll burn in hell, Nurse Clock.'

'Nonsense,' said Nurse Clock.

A year before his death Mr Bird had written:

Nurse Clock (50) has been with me now for fifteen years. She is quite an asset to the house, as on the occasion when Mr Venables caught his hand in a window and required instant medical attention. I met Nurse Clock distraught on the streets of this area, in the spring of '49. I was walking slowly and was approached by her with a request for a direction. She claimed to be lost, having been walking about for some time. She had a brusque manner and I saw that she was a woman who immediately interested me. I explained that the road she was seeking was quite some way away. 'Let me draw you a simple map,' I added, leading her to a seat by a bus-stop. We drifted into a casual conversation, during the course of which she inquired of me if I knew or had heard of Sir James and Lady Lord-Blood. I had, of course, the twain being notorious in the neighbourhood for the extraction of money from obese matrons. We talked further, in the course of which conversation I related to Nurse Clock the nature of my livelihood in Jubilee Road. Within a week she had called around at Number Two and requested to see me. Today she practises happily in SW17, riding about on a cycle. She is no longer brusque in her manner but has acquired quite an effecting sweetness. Nurse Clock has morbid interests. She is a woman I would fear were it not for my superior position.

'What do you want?' cried Mr Obd. 'Who is there? Is this the traitor Bird?'

Nurse Clock frowned on the other side of Mr Obd's door. Before replying she sought about in her mind for some reason for this second question of his: why should he imagine that Mr Bird could possibly be knocking on the door of his bedroom? She had heard of Africans drinking. 'Root beer,' she murmured to herself, having read about the stuff.

'Please go away,' cried Mr Obd. 'What do you want now? Tome Obd is a ruined man.'

'Root beer,' said Nurse Clock. 'Put it away, like a good chap. Mr Obd, you have been in there for two days.'

'It is surely Nurse Clock.'

'Only Nurse Clock,' said she, reminded of the times when she had spent an hour or so rapping on the door of Bishop Hode's airing cupboard. It must be a thing of the times, she thought, this creeping away behind locked doors. 'We are worried about you, Mr Obd. We have not seen you since Sunday.'

'Go away, Nurse Clock. Tome Obd is planning things out on paper.'

'I have a tray here for you, Mr Obd. Fish fingers and salad, a cup of strong tea –'

'Tome Obd will eat nothing till his people are freed.'

'Come on, Mr Obd.'

'No, no, I will not come on.'

'There is a good play on the television, Mr Obd.'

'Please to be on your way. It wearies this old African to talk.'

'You are not old, Mr Obd.' She thought immediately that this might be the trouble, that Mr Obd might feel that he was getting on too fast, that his youth was past and had been wasted. Women with the menopause often had this complaint. 'I have never thought of you as old, my dear. Somehow, you know, I always looked upon you – well, next to Miss Clerricot – as the baby of the boarding-house.'

'I am forty-four. Is it my skin that makes me look younger? How can a man of forty-four be a baby? Make sense, woman.'

'I only meant you were junior in years to others. To Mr Venables and Mr Scribbin and Major Eele and Mr Studdy.'

'It is still Nurse Clock surely? What age are you, Nurse Clock?'

'Now, now.'

'I cannot hear. I asked what age. I cannot hear your answer.'

'My age is my affair. In fact I am in my fifty-first year.'

'You will not get married now, Nurse Clock.'

'I would not wish to, Mr Obd.'

'Do you have a fellow?'

'No, Mr Obd, I do not have a fellow.'

'I would truly ask you to come out with me if it were not for the work I must do.'

'You're a scream, Mr Obd! Come on now, like a good man.'

'You would not come out with old Tome Obd? You would not be seen on a black arm?'

'Heavens above, I did not say that for a minute. I can tell you that in my profession –'

'Are you a professional man?'

'Well, woman. You know quite well who I am. I am a medical nurse, Mr Obd.'

'Ah.'

'I cannot stand here, you know.'

'It is surely a pity you do not have a fellow, Nurse Clock. Does it make you sad to remember that you do not have such. Do you not get sex, Nurse Clock?'

'That will do now. My advice to you is to open up this door and come out immediately.'

'I am on hunger strike. The badman Bird knows that. Ask him why Tome Obd is on hunger strike. Tome Obd must do his duty. Ask the man Bird.'

'Mr Obd, how can anyone do that? Don't you remember that Mr Bird died?'

'Mr Bird is in this room. I can see Mr Bird. Mr Bird is in golden raiment, smiling upon us. Talk to Mr Bird in your prayers. Surely you say a prayer?'

'You are light-headed for want of food. I have seen all this before. I know it, Mr Obd, you are going to make yourself ill.'

'I am going to die.'

'No, no. Not at all.'

'Was Mr Bird your fellow? Are you sorrowing now that he is in here with me in glory? I often wondered if you had sex with this man Bird. You must cleanse yourself –'

'Mr Obd, that is outrageous. I came up here to help you; all I get is dirty abuse. Take those words back now.'

'Mr Bird knew all the time. "Alas, Tome Obd," he said. Mr Bird saw to it as soon as he had the golden clothes wrapped round him –'

'Get it into your head, Mr Obd, that Mr Bird is dead. Put away the beer and have some wholesome food. You are doing your constitution no good. It's terrible to hear you talk so.'

'Mr Bird –'

'Mr Bird is dead and gone. We have put Mr Bird to bed with a shovel.'

'Please not to shout at me. I was here that night, sitting in the lounge-room downstairs. I turned the television off. I did not know that as soon as he entered heaven he would set about my private life –'

'Oh, nonsense.'

'My lady-friend said she would put the police on me. The big Alsatian dogs of your English policemen would gobble old Tome Obd up. Is that what you want, Nurse Clock?'

'Of course not.'

'Surely it is so? What better death for an old African? But it is not to be.'

'Of course it is not.'

'Why is it not?'

'Well, naturally, such a thing –'

'I must tell you why it is not. Tome Obd must tell you. His people await Tome Obd with the law, but he in the meanwhile, while the rain rains and the sun beats down on the heads of his people, must tell you now why Alsatian dogs shall surely not tear black flesh from the black bones of old Tome Obd.'

Nurse Clock was restive. 'Shall I come in?' she said. 'You can eat this up while you tell me the story.'

'Stay where you are! My lady-friend said the police were coming if again I brought her flowers. She handed me my letters, all unread. She had never read a letter Tome Obd wrote in all her life. She had not wished to, those were her words. And in any case she could not read his African handwriting. Do you know how many letters there were?'

'How could I, Mr Obd? How on earth could I know how many letters you have written to your lady-friend?'

'I have been writing letters to my lady-friend for twelve years. She has never read one of them. One thousand two hundred and forty-eight letters. She handed them all back to me, being unable to decipher a single one.'

'Heavens, Mr Obd!'

'Is that not sad indeed?'

'Extraordinary. Your lady-friend –'

'No longer. No longer the lady-friend of Tome Obd. She is a white lady, you understand, well-born. Babies she shall have by one other man. She said this to me. She said she did not care to receive flowers from the black hands of a faithful man. She did not care for the telephone calls I often made, much of them from this very house, from the coin-box in the back hall. No flowers, no calls, no letters any more. What must Tome Obd do? I asked my ex-lady-friend that and she said she could not know, how could she know, just as you said so a minute ago. Everyone is saying that to the faithful African. "Let us talk this through," I remarked to my ex-lady-friend and I made to sit myself down. "Find yourself an African girl," cries she. "Leave me alone, go with an African girl." Well, I do not like African girls; I do not like their hair. I began to say this, being patient in my explanation. "Go now," she said. "And if you come again I shall report the matter to the police authorities, citing you as a nuisance." Then I looked up at the ceiling and I saw Mr Bird with a trumpet, whispering down: "Alas, Tome Obd!"'

Nurse Clock said nothing. She placed the tray with the fish fingers and the salad and the cup of tea on the floor, and fixed her right eye to the keyhole. She could see nothing because the key was in the lock on the inside. She sighed, and drank the tea.

'Mr Bird is not like that now,' went on Mr Obd. 'He who made heaven and earth, He who sits in glory –'

'Shh. That's enough now. Put away the old beer, or measures will have to be taken about you, Mr Obd. We cannot have all this, you know. Go to sleep for a while, and when you wake up you will feel a better man. Open the door then and join us in the dining-room for breakfast. Nobody shall say a thing.'

'Nurse Clock, why do you keep talking about beer?'

She sighed. Once she had seen a man with delirium tremens; on television recently she had seen men and women who drank methylated spirits.

'You are not drinking methylated spirits?' she called through the door.

'Tome Obd is going to burn you all in your beds,' he replied.

24

Studdy left the boarding-house at eleven o'clock, banging the hall-door loudly behind him. He walked with a jaunty step, moving a little faster than usual because the tang of the air suggested it. A cigarette hung from the corner of his mouth and his face was newly shaven. 'That's a great day,' he remarked to a passing postman, and the postman agreeably acknowledged the observation.

He made his way from Jubilee Road to Peterloo Avenue, down to where the shops were, where all the local business was transacted. He passed the Jasmine Café and paused to watch the Misses Gregory placing trays of iced cakes in the window. He passed the corner public house where Mrs le Tor and Major Eele had repaired to that night, and later he approached and did not pass the public house he himself frequented.

'That's a great day,' said Studdy, sitting down at a small table and glancing about to see if there was a newspaper anywhere. 'A bottle of Guinness's stout,' he added.

On that morning, September 22nd, Studdy drank by himself and passed the time of day with the barman, and later complained to the landlord of the barman's insolence. He had intended to walk a little farther, to make arrangements with a decorator about the painting of the attic room, but the matter slipped his mind and when he returned to the boarding-house he had achieved only the exercising of his limbs and the purchase and consumption of a pint and a half of stout.

Later, in the dining-room of the boarding-house, Studdy sat down to a mutton stew and afterwards was served with stewed apple and pale baked custard. He called Gallelty to his table and spoke to her about the stewed apples, saying that there were stalks in them. 'Mr Studdy complains about the stalks,' she reported to Mrs Slape. 'Cloves,' said Mrs Slape. 'Tell him to leave them on the side of his plate.' But Studdy had consumed the cloves and sent an order to Mrs Slape that apples in future were to be presented without them.

'Stalks in the stewed apple,' said Studdy conversationally to Nurse Clock as he left the dining-room.

She smiled with sweetness at him, thinking what a scandalous man he was, noting the mark that had remained on her tablecloth because in passing he had leaned a knuckle on it. Nurse Clock drank an after-lunch cup of tea and felt, more or less, at peace with the world.

That morning, while Studdy had been drinking, while Nurse Clock had been apologizing to Mrs Maylam because of the bluntness of her hypodermic needle, Mr Obd had come out of his room. He had gone straight to the kitchen and had asked for an egg, which he had eaten at the kitchen table, whipped up in a cup of milk. Afterwards he had eaten mutton stew and stewed apple and had behaved quite normally, sitting quietly.

Late that afternoon Studdy was standing in the hall reading a notice that had recently been put through the letter-box. 'By dad, what's this?' he said, looking at the strange message: *The Rainbow Men are in your district!* 'Here's an invasion from Mars,' said Studdy to himself, and he chuckled loudly.

He was about to set out for his second walk, again intending to visit the decorator. 'The Rainbow Men,' he said to Mr Obd, who happened to be entering the house; and then, seeing a parcel in Mr Obd's arms, he asked: 'What have you got there?'

'Fire-lighters,' said Mr Obd.

'Sit down, Mr Studdy,' said Nurse Clock, pointing to the chair beneath the coloured portrait of the Queen.

'Her Majesty,' said Studdy, looking up at it.

'This is an awkward thing. I hardly know how to put it.'

Studdy took from a pocket the machine with which he rolled cigarettes and charged it with shreds of tobacco and a piece of paper. Nurse Clock watched him. When he had completed the operation and held in his hand a creased and untidy tube, she said:

'I'd rather you didn't smoke in here if you wouldn't mind.'

Studdy looked at the completed cigarette. He lifted it slowly through the air, towards his head, and placed it behind an ear.

'What can I do for you, missus?'

'I will put it plainly: you have been writing letters, Mr Studdy.'

'Letters home. Oh, definitely.'

'In particular to Mrs le Tor.'

'Mrs Tor.'

'You wrote a threatening letter to Mrs le Tor.'

'I know no one of that name. What's come over you, Nurse?'

'Did you ever know a Mrs Rush, then? A woman who used to bring Meals on Wheels to Mrs Maylam?'

'How's Mrs Maylam, Nurse?'

'It's Mrs Rush and Mrs le Tor I'm talking about. Mrs Maylam is as well as can be expected.'

'That poor old lady.'

'The letters are now in the hands of the police. A letter to Mrs le Tor, libellous in nature –'

'I know no Mrs Tor.'

'You wrote her letters, saying to come to the boarding-house, and later accusing her of intentions because she came. You are always writing letters to anyone who comes into your head. I have you taped, Mr Studdy.'

'We are partners, Nurse. We came to an agreement.'

Nurse Clock laughed. Studdy said:

'What are you laughing at?'

'You'd never do a hand's turn, Mr Studdy. You know that. You'd only be an encumbrance.'

'This house is mine, Nurse. I have a half share. You don't know what you're talking about. Are you trying to pick a quarrel with me?'

'I am giving you the facts, Studdy, so that you can hop it. Who wants a black maria drawn up outside the windows?'

'I think you've been drinking spirits.'

Studdy extended his head and sniffed the air around Nurse

Clock's face. 'That's disgraceful, Nurse, in a woman of your profession. I could report that, you know.'

'You are avoiding the subject. You know quite well I have not been drinking anything. What about these women now?'

'What women is it? Good night now, Nurse Clock.'

'Stay where you are.' She jumped to her feet and pointed a finger at him. 'Your salvation is in my hands. Leave this house this instant minute and never again shall you hear a single word about your evil ways and blackmailing past. Mrs Sellwood,' added Nurse Clock, guessing again.

'Mrs Sellwood? Who's she?'

'A victim, Studdy. The police have the files laid out before them. The net is closing in. I have it from a desk sergeant: you'll get fifteen years.'

'You have betrayed me, Nurse Clock.'

When she heard these words she felt a thrill of accomplishment. She knew then that she had triumphed, that the boarding-house was hers, that Studdy would go and would not ever return, that the aged would take their ease in the back garden, sunning themselves in the afternoon warmth.

'Betrayed you? Well, that's a funny thing to say.'

'You are sub-human.'

'Manners,' said Nurse Clock, and laughed.

For a moment there was silence in the little room. A clock ticked lightly by the bed and Studdy's eyes were drawn to it. They later fell upon the piece of stone on the mantelshelf, under its small glass dome. 'From the Garden of Gethsemane,' said Nurse Clock.

'Are you mad?' He asked the question seriously, wondering why she was talking in the midst of everything about the Garden of Gethsemane. 'I will speak to your superiors. You are unfit to be out.'

'There is nothing whatsoever the matter with me –'

'You are quarrelsome in drink. You are making terrible accusations, based on no facts at all. You are turning against your friends –'

'What friends?'

'Your partner and friend. You know who I mean. We have

a shared interest in this house. You are trying to do me out of my rights. Well, we'll see about that.'

'I am becoming impatient, Studdy. I have given you a chance and told you what I know so that you can do a midnight flit. Take it or leave it.'

Studdy reached for the cigarette he had placed on his ear. He lit it and blew smoke in her direction.

'I asked you –' She stopped, knowing that he no longer had a reason to be agreeable to her.

'You're a right bitch,' said Studdy.

'Mind that language, please –'

'I'll mind what I like, missus.'

'Let's talk this over sensibly. No need to get our rags out. Leave the boarding-house and you'll not hear another thing. I have certain influence with the police.'

'Is that so?' Studdy spoke scornfully. He began to roll another cigarette. 'Have a fag, missus?' he said, and Nurse Clock ignored the offer.

'I have influence with Mrs le Tor. Mrs le Tor might bring no action if I spoke to her in a certain way.

'Who is Mrs Tor?'

'It is useless talking to you. I see that things must take their course. Well, I am sorry it is so. A man cut down in his prime.'

'You are telling lies to the police and have a network of women to back you up. I'll deny it all.' But he knew that Nurse Clock held all the trump cards. He knew that what she required of him he must do. She looked like a great plump spider, he thought, and he wished he had a pin so that he could reach out and stick into her, all over her body, until in an hour or so she died.

'Have it your own way,' said Nurse Clock. 'It costs you nothing to think what you like, old boy. But I'll tell you this: there is justice still in England, and the extraction of money from helpless women is not the most popular of crimes.'

An idea, born of desperation, formed in Studdy's brain. The light was failing but he could see her still, looking like a spider whose legs have been forgotten, with the easy smile on her broad face and her hair neat upon her head and her shoulders thick and fat.

Studdy stubbed out his cigarette on the sole of his shoe. 'It's good of you to tell me,' he said. 'I wonder why you told me that now, and didn't let events take their course.'

'I am not an ungenerous woman.' He saw in the gloom her mouth producing these words, the flash of her even, artificial teeth, her lips settling into place. She smiled agreeably, as once she had taught herself.

'I think you are not,' said Studdy.

She was surprised to hear this. She said nothing for a moment, waiting to hear more. But Studdy did not speak either and after a minute she said:

'Well then?'

'To tell the truth,' said Studdy, 'I fancy you.'

Nurse Clock was unused to this form of words and did not at first understand it. Then, more by intuition than anything else, it came to her that Studdy was paying her court.

'I thought we got on together,' he said. 'I thought we were away for ourselves.'

'What are you saying?' cried Nurse Clock, as Studdy's meaning became clearer, and then perfectly clear. 'For goodness' sake, Mr Studdy.'

'I would have said it before, only I never had the nerve.'

'Said what, Mr Studdy? You've said nothing so far.'

'What about it, Nurse? You and me. Would you see yourself as Mrs Studdy?'

Nurse Clock contained herself no longer. She jerked her head upwards and to the left in a diagonal movement, and she snorted loudly with laughter. Peal after peal issued from the gaping mouth of Nurse Clock, and so great was the noise that they heard it in the television lounge through a comedy programme. The rise and fall of Nurse Clock's laughter was heard that night by passers-by in Jubilee Road and several remarked that here was someone in hysteria.

Studdy sat and watched the woman writhing and hooting opposite him. Her limbs contorted in her merriment, her head twitched and rolled. The tone of her laughter altered, like the sound of a vehicle changing gear: the notes were high and then dropped to a deep resonance. Nurse Clock was giving the performance of a prima donna, and she was well aware of it.

Studdy was thinking that the creature was an animal; he was saying to himself that it was surely in error that she had become a member of the human race.

'You are a goat, a fowl, a farmyard pest. You are a species of ape, a hard-backed rhino, a mad hyena. Yes, I think you are that: a mad hyena.'

Through her laughter Nurse Clock was aware of Studdy's invective, and of the animal names he was listing so effortlessly.

'You have the hide of an elephant and the heart of a toad. You are a snake in the grass. You are a treacherous possum. Do you know what a possum is, missus? Yes, I think you are a possum.'

'Mrs Studdy! 'cried Nurse Clock. 'Oh, God in glory, what a thing to think!'

Her laughter began again and Studdy sat without moving. If he had a garden shears, he thought, he would open them wide and fix the blades about her neck. He would tighten the handles slowly, bringing each handle towards the other. Blood would spatter the walls of this clinical room and a head with teeth still bared would pop like a cork and strike the ceiling.

'Wait till the others have heard that,' said Nurse Clock. She wiped her eyes with a handkerchief. She blew her nose. Her body heaved and she belched again with laughter.

Studdy saw the severed head strike the ceiling and drop to the ground, its spectacles caught about its ears, still poised on its nose. He looked and saw the trunk of Nurse Clock's body sagging in her chair, dark blood spurting as from a fountain. Blood flowed over her nurse's uniform and somehow touched his hands: he felt it between his fingers, warm and slippery.

'You are the ugliest, most repulsive thing in the whole range of God's creation.'

Nurse Clock shook her head, unable to reply, implying not a denial but a touch of scorn for Studdy's pronouncement.

'I think God did not make you at all. I think He said to Himself: "I cannot make the like of this," so He gave the job to some cheapjack conjurer who was passing outside.'

'You'll be the death of me,' cried Nurse Clock, and Studdy, who wished above all things to be that, opened his mouth and spat at her.

Mr Obd, alone in his room, heard the roaring laughter of Nurse Clock and leant an ear to it, for he associated it with Mr Bird. 'There is surely somebody else gone mad,' said Mr Obd to himself. 'The vile Bird is driving us all round the bend with his mockery.'

He rose and left his room, treading softly because he was anxious not to call undue attention to himself. He descended the stairs, slipping as he went a fire-lighter behind each of the three Watts reproductions. He put a couple in the drawer of the hallstand, beside three packets of seeds and the tennis balls that had been there since 1912.

In the television lounge Rose Cave was thinking that she could never accept a position from Nurse Clock, since Nurse Clock, it seemed, was guilty of something shady. She would not have minded looking after the needs of the elderly, helping to run a home, but she could not, ever, do that with Nurse Clock. 'But I could do it, or something like it, in a place that was established and run on proper lines,' she said to herself. 'I could look around and find a decent job, however menial – and perhaps it would be at first, for I have no training.' And she thought that it would all be more interesting than the work she had done for so long, which bored her so much. She would tell Nurse Clock that she would not be happy to work in the way that she had suggested; yet she did not feel as resentful as she had towards Nurse Clock, for it seemed that Nurse Clock in her shadiness had put a useful thought into her head.

By now Major Eele had become used to the idea of leaving the boarding-house. He would find, he knew, some other place in the same area, or at least not much farther out, so that he might make the journey to the West End on foot. The girl from the north of England had left the Ti-Ti Club and a buxom West Indian had taken her place. He felt happier about that.

Earlier that evening Venables had found a room. It was not a room in a boarding-house but one with a family who happened to have somewhere to spare and felt the need of the money. 'You will be quite snug here,' the woman had said to him. 'We will treat you as one of ourselves.' He said the room looked very nice, and in fact, in a way, it did, although it was smaller than his at the boarding-house. 'Weetabix for breakfast,' the woman had said. 'High tea in the evenings. Rent in advance, dear.'

In his room Mr Scribbin heard Class A4 Pacific 60014 hissing quietly in Grantham station, about to begin the famous climb to Stoke summit. When the record came to an end he had decided on a plan of action. He opened the door of his room. He could hear Nurse Clock laughing. He looked over the banisters and saw in the hall below Mr Obd distributing rectangular objects behind pictures and in drawers. Otherwise the boarding-house was quiet and without obvious activity. It took Mr Scribbin twenty minutes to move his belongings, including his gramophone, his mattress and his bedding, to the attic room that had once been Mr Bird's. Mr Scribbin thought of himself as a quiet man who had never in all his life given anyone any trouble, but he was not going to have his records broken and he did not intend to go and live with a desk sergeant just because Nurse Clock wished him to. He locked the door of Mr Bird's attic room and set the place to rights, stacking his remaining records in a cupboard.

Five or six years ago, one damp Saturday afternoon, Miss Clerricot had bought two bottles of aspirin tablets. She had read more than once that it was a simple thing to swallow too many aspirins: one fell into a sleep and did not wake up. Whenever she became tired of hoping that the ground would open beneath her, Miss Clerricot sat alone with her aspirins, looking at them, five hundred and six of them, and thinking about the embarrassment of life. She looked at them now, on the night that Nurse Clock laughed and Mr Scribbin moved his belongings, but she knew that she would never now do the simple thing she had once intended. The aspirins had become an ornament in her room, the reminder of a bad moment, and a source of small comfort. Because in her final analysis she was glad that they were there and she was glad that she was there to see them.

25

On the morning of September 23rd the members of the boarding-house went about their duties in a way that was now familiar to them.

Rose Cave left the house at eight thirty-two. She bought a newspaper on the way to the bus-stop and read it while she waited and again when she had taken her seat.

Mr Scribbin left later and locked the door of the attic room behind him and told nobody what he had done in the night. He resolved to replace the broken records in his lunch-hour, and as he walked down Jubilee Road he looked forward to that.

Little Miss Clerricot went to work for Mr Morgan and dreaded meeting Mr Sellwood. She would blush in an awkward way if she met Mr Sellwood, wondering how much he had told his wife about her behaviour in Leeds, wondering if he knew that his wife had been on to the boarding-house, wishing to speak to her. For a moment it seemed odd to her that Mrs Sellwood had not telephoned her at the office, where she must know she worked, but she dismissed this stray thought, assuming that Mrs Sellwood had her own reasons for what she did.

Venables arrived late at his place of work and found the punctuality man filing his finger-nails, waiting for him.

'You are late, Venables,' said the punctuality man. 'You realize, do you, you are consistently late in the a.m.?'

Venables stood by the door of the big general office where he worked, in his navy blue blazer and flannel trousers without a crease. He saw the punctuality man looking again at the dandruff on his shoulders. The man's glance shifted. The glance surveyed Venables' face, moving over his cheeks and nose, up to his pale forehead. Years ago this man had taken it into his head that Venables was a Jew and, disliking Jews, had made a point of taking Venables regularly to task. Another employee, later than Venables, entered the general office. 'Good morning,' said the punctuality man.

'The services are unreliable,' Venables began.

'Services?' said the punctuality man.

'I came in by bus and Tube.'

'How you come in, Venables, is not of interest to us here. Why should we worry how you travel? The fact is you are always late.'

'I'm sorry.'

'I suspect malingering. The management is watching you. I tell you that as a favour.'

Pursuit had featured grimly in Venables' life to date, and to Venables now, as he stood by the door of the general office, it seemed that pursuit would continue to feature in the future. His father, now safe with the Seventh Day Adventists in Wales, was no longer interested in pursuing his son, banging on the lavatory door and threatening attentions with a razor strop. But the Flatrups had said that they would never give up, that they would seek him until they found him, that some day somewhere they would run him to earth and wreak their vengeance, because the body of Miss Flatrup was ruined for ever by a bargain abortion.

'I am changing my residence,' said Venables. 'That may make things easier.'

'Who cares?' remarked the punctuality man, and he walked away, talking about Jews.

Studdy and Nurse Clock were not on speaking terms. Nurse Clock saw him in the dining-room holding his knife and fork in the air poised high above a plate of eggs. He had a habit which displeased her greatly: that of saluting people with his knife as they entered or left the room.

Studdy was thinking about a man who often came into the public house and was reputed to be a solicitor, or to have at least some connexion with the machinery of the law. He had resolved in the night to approach this person and to put his case to him, explaining the attack launched on him recently by

Nurse Clock. He assured himself that he was not the man to take such things lying down, yet he knew, after thinking about the matter, that his first reading of the situation had been correct: Nurse Clock held all the trumps. It was just that there might be some danger he could inflict before agreeing to move away, or some clever way in which he could extract money from her.

'Look at this,' said Gallelty in the kitchen. 'Here's a firelighter in with the laundry.'

Major Eele, avoiding the Jasmine Café, strolled along a back street. He was en route for the shop, run by a Mrs Rolfer, where he sold his back numbers of *Urge*. He passed down a street he had passed down before, a street in which children seemed always to be on the point of death, playing on the pavement and straying in their play on to the road. There were greengrocers' shops, and shops that sold hardware and selected groceries side by side. Men stood outside betting centres, reading the racing columns or discussing form.

'Well, dear?' said Mrs Rolfer, an occasional patient of Nurse Clock's, though Major Eele did not know it.

'Another half dozen,' he said, and drew the volumes from an inner pocket.

'One and six,' said Mrs Rolfer, stating the figure with firmness. She did not present it as an offer, as something he might decide he could not accept: people rarely bargained with Mrs Rolfer.

'Nice day,' said Major Eele. 'How's your back?'

'Sick,' said Mrs Rolfer, and Major Eele pulled a suitable face.

He walked on, wondering what to do. A child ran beneath his legs, a black and red ball struck him on the knee. He sighed, and thought suddenly that he might walk into London. There was a Lyons café on the way where he could obtain a midday meal by queuing up with a tray. 'Good idea,' said Major Eele, increasing his speed.

'Hullo there,' cried a voice, and he beheld on the other side of this difficult street the person of Mr Obd leaving a hardware store with a parcel held proudly in his arms.

'Narrow gauge on the Costa Brava,' said one assistant to another. 'God knows what that is.'

'A recording of trains,' said Mr Scribbin. 'I got it here before.'

'Oh, yes,' said the second assistant.

Miss Clerricot bought sandwiches for lunch and ate them in a park. She had not seen Mr Sellwood that morning. Mr Morgan had been brusque. She opened the early edition of the evening paper, looking at advertised accommodation.

'I know you people make a thing of food,' said the punctuality man. 'Remember the management is interested. Cut it short now.'

'What people?' asked Venables.

The punctuality man laughed, thinking that was typical.

Rose Cave ate shepherd's pie and apricots with cream. She wondered what she should do to further her plan of working in an institution for the elderly. 'Your mind is not with us today,' someone had earlier said, laughing over it, for Rose Cave's mind was nearly always where it should be. She thought she should go to a public library and look through advertisements for such positions. Hastily she paid her bill, excited by the idea of going at once to a public library.

'We must get this straight,' said Nurse Clock, meeting Studdy in the hall.

'What do you want?'

'We have a matter to discuss. We began a discussion and then you took it into your head to behave like an animal.'

Studdy sniffed. 'You have got it wrong. It was you –'

'You took it into your head to expectorate, Mr Studdy. Well, never mind. When may we expect to lose you?'

'Not at all,' said Studdy. 'I think I will stay on a bit. Don't try anything on now.'

'I will try nothing on. It is up to the police. Did I not make that clear?'

'I am seeing my solicitor tonight.'

'How amusing. In the meanwhile you will be arrested for libel and blackmail. You need to get your skates on, Studdy.'

'I will contact you first thing tomorrow morning, missus. Will we make that a bargain now?'

'As you wish, though I see no point in delay.'

'Good evening,' said Mr Obd, coming through the hall-door. 'I am getting on fine.'

'First thing tomorrow,' said Studdy.

Nurse Clock smiled and did not say anything. She watched Studdy at the open door, staring into Jubilee Road, examining the evening. She saw his hand reached out to close the door behind him and a moment later heard him blowing his nose and talking to himself on the front steps.

'There is a smell of petrol,' said Major Eele that night, for Mr Obd had worked hard all day, coming into the boarding-house with several gallons of lower grade petrol.

'The potatoes taste queer,' said Mr Scribbin, for Mr Obd in his keenness had poured petrol over the potatoes and later they roasted and exploded, those that were not already in the stomachs of the boarding-house residents.

In Miss Clerricot's room, Mr Obd, distributing fire-lighters, found two bottles of aspirin tablets in a drawer. It was an item he had forgotten to purchase himself that day, although he had written the word *aspirin* on a list. He took Miss Clerricot's, arguing that since he was leaving behind him fire-lighters without charge he had some right to her aspirins.

'We thought you had moved away,' cried Gallelty to Mr Scribbin. 'Your room vacated and your bed-clothes gone.'

'I have moved to the attic,' said Mr Scribbin, and made for that place in haste.

The solicitor who occasionally came into the public house did not come that night, and Studdy wagged his head as he sat alone, admitting defeat and thinking in terms of the midnight flit recommended by his adversary. He did not wish to see her face to face again, and he was suddenly frightened lest matters had already progressed too far. 'Three large Scotches,' said Studdy to the barman, who questioned the order, since Studdy was alone. 'Three,' repeated Studdy, and when the drinks arrived he tipped them, one after the other, quickly into his mouth. 'Twelve shillings,' said the barman, but Studdy claimed to have left his wallet elsewhere and arranged with the proprietor to pay the following morning.

'I will take a few hours' nap,' he said to himself as he entered the boarding-house. He sniffed, and added: 'Someone has spilt something.' He passed through the hall and mounted the stairs to his room. In the darkened television lounge Mr Obd was pouring petrol on the cushions.

High in the boarding-house, in the attic where Mr Bird had lived and died, the double-chimneyed *Lord Faringdon* burst from a tunnel with a mighty steel roar. Mr Scribbin, who had stretched on his bed to relax and savour the moment, dropped into a nap. The needle moved from the last spiral of the record, slithering on the smooth surface.

Rose Cave dreamed that she had given up her job and was tending an old woman in a wheel-chair. She tucked a red plaid rug about the old woman's knees and looked up to smile at her. But there was no face where a face should have been, only a tight line of a mouth bobbing in the air. 'Mother,' said Rose Cave, and the mouth turned to one side as though a head had turned away from her.

Major Eele sat back and watched the black breasts in the Ti-Ti Club. He heard himself shout, but he could not catch the words. The man who held the torch trained it on him for a moment, and Major Eele put his hand over his eyes. When he took it away he saw that Mrs le Tor was on the stage, taking off her brassière. 'She is black, she is black,' shouted Major Eele, and Mrs Andrews hit him on the head with a powder compact with roses on it.

Miss Clerricot slept and did not dream. Venables dreamed in unsatisfactory snatches: faces appeared and did not stay long; the punctuality man was threatening; there was a procession in the streets, and Venables knew that it was the Seventh Day Adventists, who had walked from Wales to London. He awoke and lay awake for a while, plump and white in his bed, not thinking of anything very much. When he returned to sleep he dreamed properly. Old Mr Flatrup chased him with a ham knife, round and round an enormous kitchen. 'You killed our beautiful girl,' cried a mountainous woman, the old man's wife. Mr Flatrup crept and Venables crept before him, and suddenly he saw that the kitchen had no door.

Studdy moved his heavy body about his bed, snoring, fast asleep. A suitcase was packed on the floor beside him. He did not dream.

Nurse Clock smelt burning and slipped her feet into her fuzzy slippers. Mrs Slape turned from her back to her side, awoke and saw at the foot of her bed a flame. Gallelty heard her cry and turned the light on. Smoke was everywhere.

26

The flames lit the sky, coming out of the windows, mingling with smoke. Clouds ran across the moon, and the moon gleamed like a thin coin suspended. A breeze blew, as though nothing had happened.

They stood in their night-clothes with overcoats and dressing-gowns pulled about them. Venables had seized his flannel trousers as he left his room; he had them now in one hand, with an electric razor in the other. They watched the firemen battle with the blaze, directing spurts of water and climbing on ladders. 'It is going up like a tinder-box,' one of the firemen said, and somebody repeated this and then somebody else.

'Sooner or later they'll pull down all of Jubilee Road,' a man from a neighbouring building remarked. He said it because he was reminded of the greater destruction by the evidence of destruction which he now beheld. He said it to comfort the people of the boarding-house, saying really: 'Soon we shall all be in the same boat.'

Major Eele stood in blue and red striped pyjamas, with a tattered dressing-gown on top of them. He had been watching Mrs le Tor and had been struck by Mrs Andrews, and then the holocaust had broken. People had hammered on his door. He remembered what Mrs Andrews had said when she discovered the match-ends in their bed: 'You could have burnt me alive.' She had not for a single moment understood his condition of distress that night.

'Where is Mr Obd?' Rose Cave asked.

They looked about them, looking at each other, checking the fact that one or another was alive. Miss Clerricot had cried at first. The smoke had stung her eyes and she had held the tears back and then released them. The redness of her face had deepened a little; there was a dark mark, a smudge or a bruise, on her left cheek. She wiped her eyes with a handkerchief given to her by a strange man.

'Where is Mr Obd?' Rose Cave asked again.

But Mr Obd, with two bottles of aspirin tablets in his stomach, was asleep and alight.

'There's a man inside,' shouted Major Eele, trying to attract the attention of the firemen. 'One other man, an African. You overlooked him in the darkness.'

The firemen looked into the rage of flames and shook their heads. 'Someone inside,' one of them called out, but the words were a formality, or sounded like one, as though a fact had to be registered and that was that.

Studdy wore his overcoat and a suit that he had swapped for one of Mr Bird's. By chance, he was better off than anyone else because he had lain down in the clothes he wore, thinking he would shortly be on his way. He had carried his suitcase from the burning house and placed it against a lamp-post.

In the attic room the flames caught Mr Scribbin's records in a cupboard; they blackened and then burnt the suits that Mr Scribbin had not so long ago defended in the hall. They tore at the wainscoting, leaping along it towards the pile of old magazines, causing pages to curl and crackle. Low in the pile, close to the floor, was Mr Bird's *Notes on Residents*. In time it burnt, as did almost everything else.

'He never took out an insurance policy,' said Studdy. 'Did Nurse Clock know that?'

She was standing a foot or so away from him. She said nothing. She did not look at him.

'Many's the time he told me that,' said Studdy. 'Mr Bird thought insurance a mug's game.'

Mr Bird had said that to others too; he had said it to Nurse Clock, but she had not thought of it until that moment.

'Mr Bird did not approve,' said Major Eele.

Miss Clerricot thought of Mr Sellwood and reflected how he would have been disappointed in this lack of faith in insurance, and how he would have held up as an example of his argument the predicament they found themselves in now. There was a little humour in that consideration of Mr Sellwood. Though her position was not enviable, Miss Clerricot was moved to smile.

'Funny,' said Studdy. 'Isn't that the funny thing, missus?'

Nurse Clock moved away, but Studdy picked up his suitcase and followed her.

'I was leaving like you told me. Well, there'll never be old folk in the garden now.'

'Mr Obd is dying and all you can say are unpleasant things. Have you not got feelings, Studdy?'

'Have you, missus? I think you have feelings OK. I think you're lost now, your evil ways have found you out. You tried everything on, Nurse. You're a terrible woman.'

'Go your way, Studdy. Leave us in peace now.'

'We're all going our ways, isn't that so?'

'You should be inside there. You should be fast asleep. Well, you'll soon see prison bars.'

'And you'll never see old folk in the –'

Nurse Clock turned and seemed as though she might raise her arm to strike him.

'Nurse Clock is quarrelling with Studdy,' said Major Eele.

'What a time for it,' said Mr Scribbin.

In Wimbledon Mrs Rush, who had been Janice Brownlow, slept and did not know, or ever know, about the fire in the boarding-house. Mrs Maylam knew because an hour or so later Studdy knocked on the door of her flat and asked for a couch to rest on. Mrs le Tor knew in time because she heard about it, and wondered until she was told to the contrary if Major Eele had perished. 'A black man died,' her informant said, and Mrs le Tor recalled that Major Eele had talked about African women but had not touched upon the African male.

'I will be on my way to Plymouth, as I was when first I called,' cried Gallelty in an excited way. 'I shall hitch a lift from a lorry and then take another one, and tomorrow or the next day I shall be in Plymouth, that sailors' town where I shall meet my fate.'

'Don't go,' said Mrs Slape, placing a hand on her arm. 'Stay behind and maybe we'll take on positions in another house.'

Gallelty shook her head. 'Where is the house like Mr Bird's house? We should have left when he died. We could not hope to carry on without him. 'Twas destiny sent me, 'twas destiny destroyed the beautiful boarding-house.'

'No, no,' said Mrs Slape. But Gallelty moved away, the first to leave the scene.

Studdy went near to Nurse Clock and lifted a pin out of the material of his overcoat and stuck it hard into her arm. Nurse Clock felt pain and shouted out. She turned on Studdy. 'He has tried to kill me,' she shouted out. 'He tried to knife me.'

Studdy laughed and held out his hands to show that he did not carry a knife.

'Please,' said Rose Cave. 'Please not now.'

'I am going on my way,' said Studdy. 'I was saying good-bye to this ugly woman.' He laughed again, feeling in his heart the heavy throb of hatred that for so many weeks he had kept in order. Nurse Clock felt it too, as she had felt it the night before, as she would feel it always for his memory.

'What a thing for Mr Bird to have done,' said Rose Cave, 'to have thrown those two together. What on earth was he thinking of?'

In the hallstand drawer the tennis balls of 1912 caught in the flames and were at once consumed. The Watts reproductions fell from the wall by the staircase, but the china geese at first did not. In the television lounge the antimacassars and the wedding photograph that Mr Bird had placed on a side table, and all that the room contained, went up in a ravaging gulp. The fire bit into the machinery of the television set; there were small explosions and the melting of metal parts.

The breeze increased. People shivered in Jubilee Road. Neighbours, informed that the fire was now under control and would spread no farther, spoke of cups of tea and offered hospitality to the people of the boarding-house. Water ran down the gutters of the road; something crashed in the dying inferno. 'It does not seem under control to me,' said Major Eele. 'Does the man know what he is talking about?'

A fireman said to be careful of falling wood that might be

hot and dangerous. He spoke hurriedly, telling everyone to stand well back. Pieces of glowing wood, like mammoth sparks, fell into the garden of the boarding-house.

'He is a criminal,' cried Nurse Clock. 'He writes letters to strangers. He extorts money from women. Mrs le Tor. Mrs Rush. Mrs Maylam. Mrs Sellwood.'

There was a silence for a moment after that. Miss Clerricot had heard the name of Mrs Sellwood on Nurse Clock's lips for the second time. She did not understand what Nurse Clock was talking about: had Studdy written to Mr Sellwood's wife, extorting money from her? How on earth, wondered Miss Clerricot, had Studdy ever come across Mrs Sellwood? Or was Nurse Clock confused or driven out of her mind by the calamity? Miss Clerricot did not know that her two bottles of aspirin were now in the stomach of Mr Obd. She herself lived to a great age; and though no man ever tried anything on, the years became easier as the years passed by.

'Mad as a hatter,' said Studdy.

'Did you take money off le Tor?' asked Major Eele.

'Don't worry,' said Nurse Clock. 'He's going behind bars.'

'Well, that's a good one,' said Major Eele.

Then Studdy went. 'Hell take the lot of you,' he said, and he walked away in a different direction from that taken by Gallelty. To the end of his days he carried a pin in his lapel to remind him of the night of the fire, of the moment when in front of everyone he had driven it deep into Nurse Clock's arm.

Nurse Clock wept for the first time since her life had changed. She had last been close to tears that morning in the Lord-Bloods' room when Sir James had been frank and his wife had agreed. Now, at a dispiriting hour and in awful circumstances, in her fuzzy slippers and dressing-gown, she wept unrestrainedly. What Studdy had said was true: the aged now would never achieve their greatest years in her house and in her care. Studdy, once and briefly her ally, had insulted her with a marriage proposal and had spat into her face and stuck a pin in her arm. Studdy walked away a free man, because she had no proof against him and in any case it no longer mattered. She thought of Mr Bird on his death-bed exhorting her to inform the newspapers of the manner of his passing; of how he had later appeared to her in the only dream of her life to admonish her for her failure; how Gallelty and a daily woman had said they had seen him in the kitchen when he was buried a month; how Mr Obd had talked of him and called him a traitor.

Far away, in her flat at the top of the flights of stone stairs, Annabel Tonks slept and knew nothing of the fire. She stretched in her sleep and was aware of the luxury of the movement.

Nurse Clock's tears abated. She sighed and looked at the window that had been the window of her room, and she thought of Mr Obd. Around her, the other people of the boarding-house thought at that moment of Mr Obd too. And had Mr Obd been with them then he would have glanced into the night sky and said that he saw there the floating form of William Wagner Bird, displayed in the darkness like a neon advertisement. But the others saw nothing: not Mr Bird in golden raiment, playing a trumpet or seated on a chair in glory. They thought of Mr Obd, and Mr Obd died in the moment they thought of him, and did not feel a thing. And William Bird, called Wagner after a character in a book, died again as his boarding-house roared and spat, and his people watched in Jubilee Road. They stood alone and did not say much more, as the morning light came on to make the scene seem different, and the sun rose over London.

MORE ABOUT PENGUINS AND PELICANS